It's Hotter in
Hawaii

It's Hotter in Hawaii

HelenKay Dimon

B

BRAVA

KENSINGTON PUBLISHING CORP.

www.kensingtonbooks.com

BRAVA BOOKS are published by

Kensington Publishing Corp.
850 Third Avenue
New York, NY 10022

All Kensington titles, imprints, and distributed lines are available at special quantity discounts for bulk purchases for sales promotion, premiums, fundraising, educational, or institutional use.

Special book excerpts or customized printings can also be created to fit specific needs. For details, write or phone the office of the Kensington Special Sales Manager: Kensington Publishing Corp., 850 Third Avenue, New York, NY 10022. Attn. Special Sales Department. Phone: 1-800-221-2647.

Brava and the B logo are Reg. U.S. Pat. & TM Off.

ISBN-13: 978-0-7582-2227-5
ISBN-10: 0-7582-2227-0

First Kensington Trade Paperback Printing: April 2009

10 9 8 7 6 5 4 3 2 1

Printed in the United States of America

To my husband, James,
the ultimate Hawaiian hero

Chapter One

"**M**ove one inch in any direction and you'll be sipping your food through a straw."

Caleb Wilson jerked back at the sound of the outraged feminine voice and smacked his head on the frame of the jimmied window. He cut loose a stream of profanity inventive enough to make even his old Air Force buddies proud.

He had come to an empty house in the middle of nowhere Kauai, Hawaii, just after midnight, looking for information about a missing friend he now feared dead. Instead of explanations, Cal got a welcoming committee of the angry female variety. His least favorite type of woman.

As plans went, so far this one sucked.

Since the element of surprise no longer rested on his side, Cal decided to try a new tact. Until he figured out who the unidentified woman with the big mouth was and what she was doing in this small house, he would stay right where he was.

He cleared his throat in an attempt to sound as reasonable as a guy curled in a ball on a windowsill could sound. "Maybe I could—"

"No."

So much for the reasonable route.

He twisted his six-foot frame around in the small opening. Finding a tolerable position grew more impossible by the second. His muscles hardened and his patience started a countdown to zero.

"Ma'am, I'm stuck." He attempted to laugh, but being doubled over the sound came out more like a wheeze.

"What you are is trespassing."

Okay, that too. "You have me at a disadvantage here."

"And?"

He moved to his next plan. Charm.

"I'm sitting in a window," he explained, throwing in an endearing chuckle to see if that could win over the woman with the voice so throaty it should be illegal.

"I didn't put you there."

Also immune to charm. *Check.*

But she did have a point. "Admittedly I got into this position without your help, but if you could—"

"Don't move."

Then he heard it. An unmistakable metal clicking sound. The noise chased away all thoughts about the long legs that might complete the matching set to that husky voice.

The woman held a gun. He survived for thirty-six years on the planet without having a female threaten to shoot him. Looked like he could consider that streak broken.

With the door locked, slipping through the window seemed like a good idea a few minutes earlier. Now he was sorry he skipped his initial plan to pick the lock and use the door like a normal person.

"I'm not a thief." He played many roles in his life. Not that one.

"Then why are you breaking in?"

Tough talk, but he heard it. A subtle and unmistakable hitch in her voice. One that meant she was not as in control or calm as her words suggested. One that made that gun of hers even more dangerous.

Cal went with an abbreviated version of the truth. "This

house belongs to an old friend of mine. He invited me. Now I'm here."

A beat of silence filled the room as his arm fell asleep. The whole idea of Hawaii being the perfect beachside paradise was lost on him at the moment. So far, it had been an obstacle course. No sign of Dan. A round of apologetic glances and mumbled comments about being "sorry" when Cal asked after Dan at the private hangar where Dan kept his helicopter.

Top all that with a near-black night and a tire-rutted dirt road leading to a cabin in a wooded area in the middle of Kokee State Park. The same cabin not being anywhere near the beach.

Yeah, not exactly what Cal expected to find when he got on the plane that morning. Neither was the non-welcome from a female with questionable emotional stability.

Cal toyed with the idea of launching the still-awake parts of his body at his perfumed attacker. Without seeing her, he guessed he outweighed her by at least fifty pounds. That made the chance of knocking her down pretty damn good.

But the gun posed a problem. A big one. If the lady with the deadly weapon and deep voice was a novice, he might leave Kauai in a zipper bag. An amateur would shoot first. Probably fire straight into his forehead. On the other hand, a skilled markswoman *definitely* would hit him in the forehead. Fifty-fifty and both options ended with his death. Not the best odds.

Then there was the problem with the tremor moving through her voice. Now that he was listening for it he didn't hear anything else. She was afraid. Probably smart under the circumstances. Still, there was another emotion mixed in with the fear. He was just clueless enough about the inner workings of the female mind to not be able to define it.

He inhaled, drawing in the strong floral scent on the warm Hawaii night air. "I'm here to see Dan Rutledge."

"Wh-what?"

The stumble in her voice was more obvious that time. It gave her away. Stern words wrapped around a mushy inside.

Now Cal was getting somewhere in analyzing his opponent. He decided to test her. "What part of the comment didn't you understand?"

"How do you know Dan?"

The woman's tone softened. Cal guessed she was one in a long line of his friend's spirited bedroom conquests. Being a commercial pilot in an island paradise apparently had not cut into Dan's ability to score with the ladies.

Cal just hoped this woman didn't fall into the ex-girlfriend-of-Dan category. Calming scorned women was not one of Cal's skills. Especially another guy's scorned women. He had enough trouble keeping his own sex life straight without taking on someone else's.

"Look, can I step down or not? I'm losing feeling in my legs and my neck is getting stiff." Not to mention the spasm in his back and the fact his defenseless position made him wary.

She—whoever *she* was—treated him to a sigh. "Fine. Go ahead and stand up."

"You're too kind," Cal said in his most sarcastic tone.

"I can still change my mind, you know."

"Well, I do now."

Thanks to years of military training, his body functioned at high level. He could outrun and outshoot men much younger. But the combination of the long plane ride from Florida, the break-in and trying to decipher both Dan's cryptic message, and the odd reaction to his name by everyone on the island took a toll. Cal feared the worst and so far he had not been wrong in his low expectations.

"My initial threat still stands," she said in what Cal took to be her shoot-first-say-hello-later hint.

"Understood."

He unfolded his cramped legs and stretched, working out the kinks in his muscles one at a time. Feet hitting hard floor had never felt so good.

When his nerve endings started firing again, he glanced over at his gun-toting greeter. Now that she backed up, a halo of yellow from the weak night light in the kitchen cast her in shadows in the dark room.

Cal blinked, straining to see the owner of that raspy voice but could not make out her face. Did see the glint from the barrel of the gun, however. That was enough to keep him from moving closer.

"Put your hands on your head." She did not so much ask as she ordered.

"You can't be serious."

"Just do it."

Seemed she was serious. "What if I like my hands right where they are?"

"I have the gun, so I decide."

He wondered what she'd say when she realized he possessed a weapon or two. Hell, she wasn't the only one in the room who knew how to wave a gun around and make threats.

"Why don't we turn on the light so we can see each other?" He shifted until he felt the secure press of his gun against his lower back.

The silhouetted woman reached to her left. Cal heard a scratch as she grazed the wall for the switch. After a click, a soft white glow poured through the small room and over the furniture.

Not just any furniture. Broken furniture. Torn overstuffed chairs with ripped fabric. Crushed glass and documents littered the floor. Someone had tossed the place.

He mentally inventoried the damage before settling his

gaze on her. When he did, his blood froze. Hiding a face like hers in shadows should be a sin. Long blondish-brown hair and amber eyes.

And the way her snug white T-shirt pulled across her chest highlighted her high, round breasts. Hell, if she were more blond she'd be a living, breathing Barbie doll. Also made him think the doll's measurements were not quite as unrealistic as his sister insisted.

He tried not to gawk as he visually toured her lean legs from the bottom of her cut-off blue jeans shorts down to her painted pink toenails.

Tried and failed.

"Is there a problem?" she asked as she buried the shaky voice under the growl of a drunken sailor.

"About a dozen of them," he mumbled.

Her eyes narrowed until only slits of gold were visible. "Who are you?"

Under those impressive looks she carried a gun. Since he did not know if she intended to use it, he fell back on his plan of appeasement. "Tell me what happened in here."

"I guess you weren't the only person who tried to break in here tonight." Her gaze moved from his chest to his shoulders. "Wearing black from head to toe. Subtle, by the way."

He glanced down to his dark sneakers. Maybe the monotone outfit amounted to overkill. He chalked it up to another choice that made sense at one point but now seemed a bit over-the-top.

"Despite how it looks, I'm not here to burglarize the house," he said even though he knew it sounded lame.

"You just *really* like black?"

The time had come to shift attention away from his wardrobe choices. He moved around discarded pens and miscellaneous papers with the tip of his shoe.

Her frown slipped, showing the much more vulnerable face of the woman behind that, at times, unsure voice. "Tell me who you are."

"We're not going to play the game this way."

"Oh?" She waved her weapon from side to side as if to emphasize her point. All that did was convince him of her novice status.

That shot to the forehead looked more and more inevitable.

"We're going to share information. Give and take." He rested his hands on his hips, close to his weapon.

"You've got the gun. I got time. We can stand here all night for all I care." He figured a smile would work right about now, so he shot her one. "But you might want to remember something else."

"What's that?"

"You think I'm a criminal."

"That's where the evidence points, yeah."

"If I'm such a bad guy, chances are you'll blink long before I do, sweetheart."

Chapter Two

Forget about later. Cassie Montgomery fought off the urge to blink right then. If she swallowed any harder her tongue would end up in her stomach.

She had yelled and ordered this guy around while panic flooded her insides. She was not the type to take on complete strangers with little more than a bad attitude. Unlike her mysterious guest, she did have something to lose—like what was left of her life.

The wide-shouldered stranger with the dark brown hair and piercing hazel eyes kept breaking her concentration. In the safety of the darkness she had not been able to see Mr. Tall, Dark, and Deadly.

Well, she saw all of him now. Criminals were not supposed to look like him. Hell, no one should look like him. Slim black jeans and a sleek black shirt that hugged his body, molding to his muscles like a second skin. Not exactly an outfit meant for late-night hiking.

Sun-kissed hands peeked out from underneath the covert clothing, suggesting that whoever he was, he liked to be outside. With her luck, he was probably an escaped convict who worked on the road crew during the day. The fact the man knew her brother's name kept her from engaging in a bit of uncontrolled screaming and gunplay.

That and the fact the guy looked vaguely familiar. Cassie could not place him, which was odd since this guy wasn't exactly the forgettable type. Still, something about that face tickled at her memory.

She'd spent weeks trying not to remember anything. Now that she needed to call something up, her mind stuttered to a halt.

Grief sucked.

Anger she could handle, so she went that route. "I'm waiting for a formal introduction. And if I have to ask again, I might just go ahead and try talking with the gun."

A sly smile crossed full lips as Cal nodded toward the overturned chair. "May I?"

Muscles strained against the fabric of his pants as he hitched one of his thighs on the arm of the chair. He picked the only piece of furniture not smashed to pieces. That left her to stand, but hovering above this guy felt better than the reverse.

"You can actually sit down," she said so she would have the advantage if he decided to strike. Despite his athletic look, she'd bet he could not outrun a bullet.

His smile only grew. "I'm good here on the edge."

That made one of them. "Are you ready to talk?"

"Didn't exactly come here to chat."

A good reminder. She knew staying at Dan's house carried a few risks. She expected a flood of tears and regret. She had not counted on a six-foot-something walking risk with broad shoulders and an intelligent flash behind his eyes.

Time to act like a woman being hunted. "Talk or I'll call the police."

He shot her one of those all-too-knowing smiles that all men seemed to have mastered. "I'm not going anywhere."

"Option B it is." She flipped open her cell phone and pretended to dial.

"You won't."

True. She didn't really have anyone to call, but how could he know? "That's wishful thinking on your part."

"More like a calculated guess. One I'm willing to play out."

"This isn't a game."

"Sure feels like it."

Before she could maneuver him to the door, he sprang from the chair and knocked the gun and phone from her hands, sending them skittering across the smooth hardwood floor. Losing her balance, Cassie crashed to the ground on her stomach and smacked her forehead against the chair leg.

In a panic, her heart raced and her head spun. She had been numb for weeks, like the walking dead, but nerve endings snapped to life at the unexpected assault.

She kicked out aiming for any weakness she could find on her visitor's trim, lean body. He blocked her attack and launched one of his own. The breath whooshed out of her lungs as he squeezed her upper body in a fierce bear hug against the floor.

Being surrounded and crushed by about a hundred and ninety pounds of furious male made her adrenaline pump. Finding strength she didn't know she had, she flailed and tried to punch. Nothing worked. When he flipped her onto her back and pinned her hands above her head, a squeal escaped her tight throat.

Heavy breaths beat against her chest as he straddled her. Long-distance running and hours at the gym had not prepared her for this fight. Not now. Not after all that had happened. No, with the weight of everything crushing in on her she lost ground almost from the start.

"Now you don't have the weapon," he said, more as a fact than a threat.

She calculated the distance from her knee to his groin and waited for the right time to attack. "Get off of me."

"Tell me who you are first."

His face did not look quite so handsome now that it loomed over her. And that bored look he wore before, yeah, that disappeared as fast as her balance.

"Go to hell." She wiggled her shoulders, trying to break his stranglehold, but his weight held her down.

The vulnerability of her position set her heart pounding until it formed a steady drumbeat in her ears. She bucked her hips and went rock still when her midsection met with his lower body.

Big mistake. No reason to encourage anything down there.

"Don't look so horrified." A rough edge tinged his voice. "I'm not going to hurt you."

Easy for him to say since he was on top and in control. "Like I trust you after that tackle and roll move."

"You're fine."

The pounding in her head suggested otherwise. For the first time in weeks Cassie felt something other than frustration and sadness. But she wasn't sure terror-filled minutes were any better than those that came before.

"Let me up," she said in the strongest voice she could muster.

He loosened the grip on her wrists but kept her pinned. "Stop moving around and tell me who you are and how you know Dan."

She glared but stayed quiet.

"Okay then. We'll skip the introductions and get to the point. Where is Dan?"

The question showed this guy lived somewhere else. Either that or the story about being Dan's friend was just that, a story. "I thought you and Dan were supposed to be so close."

"What does that have to do with your name?"

"If you really were friends, you'd know." And she would not have to say the words. She could keep the pain and hurt locked in the back of her mind as she searched for the truth.

"You're talking in riddles."

She searched the guy's face one last time trying to figure out where she had seen him before. Something about his tone or affect . . . something kept her from pulling that trigger before and from kneeing him now.

"You gonna say anything anytime soon?" he asked.

The dizzying sense of loss, all that gnawing disbelief, exhausted her until she gave in and provided the answer he wanted.

"Dan's dead." Saying the horrible words sliced her to the bone.

Her attacker did not take them any better. He loosened his grip as his tan face blanched chalk white. She'd seen that horrified look before. Every single time she glanced in the mirror.

"That can't be right." Distress filled the man's voice. His words came out choppy and low, almost like a growl.

She nodded, unable to say the truth about Dan a second time.

"Oh shit." The stranger landed on his backside on the floor beside her with a thump.

Stunned surprise. The flash of pain behind his eyes. The tightening of his skin around his mouth. Cassie recognized the signs. The man was trying to hold back the emotions that had his hands flexing and his shoulders slumping in defeat.

"They tried to tell me at the hangar," he said in a faraway voice. "But I . . . it didn't make any sense."

None of it made any sense to her, either. No matter how many times she tried to take apart the pieces and make the facts fit, the story fell apart. Most days, her fight for the truth about Dan was the only thing that got her out of bed.

"How?" The mysterious man sat back on his haunches, head hung low, body slack. "I mean, when?"

She knew what he was asking. She swallowed the mountain of tears clogging her throat. Telling the horrible news rubbed her raw. She expected it always would. "Helicopter crash. Close to four weeks ago. We had a private memorial service for him shortly after that."

"But he contacted me—" A deep frown marred the attacker's face. "Who the hell are you?"

"Cassie Montgomery."

"Dan's half sister?"

"I don't make the half distinction." And she hated when other people pointed it out. "But, yes."

"Damn."

She sat up straight as he jumped to his feet. "And now it's your turn to fess up."

From the small shake of his head to the sad echo in his voice, she knew the surprise news had the guy reeling. Shock, confusion, and anger all raced across his face.

"Are you okay?" she asked.

He paced around at a near stumble. "No."

"How about you tell me who you are and what you're doing here."

"Caleb Wilson. People call me Cal."

Even though he mumbled it, she heard him. The name triggered the flood of memories she had been searching her mind to find. She had seen a few of Dan's group photos over the years. Cal always stood near Dan with a stupid grin on his face. That was years ago, in uniform. The cockiness and command still remained, but the clothes differed.

"You were in the Air Force with Dan. Worked together as pararescuemen, right?"

"PJs, yeah," he said with a hint of pride.

She had heard the horror stories. Not from Dan, but on

the news and in her various internet searches for information on her brother's elusive career.

Search and rescue. Extractions out of hostile territory. Water rescues. She knew the danger Dan and Cal thrived on and what it did to them. Dan had retired but his adrenaline-seeking ways never abated.

Oh yeah. She knew all about one Caleb Wilson.

Dan shared the stories. Cal had years of survivalist training. Controlled his environment with deadly precision and left behind a string of heartbroken sweeties as he moved from one military town to the next across the country.

The guy's reputation with the ladies bordered on infamous. Dan bragged about his carefree, no-ties, always-looking-for-a-bigger-thrill buddy all the time. Then one day, Dan stopped talking about Cal completely.

"Why are you really here?" she asked.

Cal's legs carried him back and forth in front of the door. "Tell me about the crash."

"Dan was on a routine run, scouting out potential places to take tourists for helicopter rides along Waimea Canyon. He crashed."

Cal wore the same sort of skeptical grimace she imagined she possessed when she first got the news.

"Any reports of trouble with the engine, plane, instruments, or anything like that?" he asked.

"No."

"Bad weather? Wind shear?"

"No."

He studied her. "What aren't you telling me?"

The part that filled her with a killing rage. "The police think Dan got sloppy, wasn't paying attention. That's the official line."

"And you think there's another line."

She sat down on the seat Cal abandoned for his football-tackling imitation. "Foul play."

Cal stared at her for a second before resuming his agitated pacing. He rubbed the stubble on his chin.

"Dan was the type to take care of his plane," she said, repeating the argument she had used over and over with the crash site investigators.

"He liked to goof off. Made some mistakes in the past. Big ones."

"Excuse me?"

"But not like this."

Cal's muttering set a red light flashing inside her brain. "What mistakes?"

He waved off the question. "Not important. Continue with your story."

She decided to get it all out, analyze his reaction, then go from there. "Dan flew in and around Kauai ever since he left the service. This is his life. He knows the area. Knows the people. Depends on tourist traffic for his livelihood. He would not have done something stupid."

Cal stopped shifting around. "You're not buying the accident theory."

"Absolutely not."

The haze of sadness cleared from Cal's deep, hazel eyes. "Got any proof or just going by blood ties?"

"I know Dan better than anyone." That was far from true, but she wanted to believe it so she said it. "The police version is wrong. The deputy chief handled the case. A guy named Ted Greene. He concluded this was Dan's fault and called in the National Transportation Safety Board investigators to make a final determination."

"Isn't that a good thing?"

"Their report could take years. In the meantime, Dan is seen as a screw-up and the people who killed him go free." The sting of that reality refused to fade from her memory.

"And you're conducting a private investigation." Cal wiped a hand over his face.

"Dan did not cause the wreck."

"Uh-huh." If Cal was listening, he managed to do it while scanning the floor.

She hated when people ignored her. With everything she'd been through, she did not need another boneheaded male doubting her brother's skills or dedication. Nothing made her change faster from feeling useless to feeling furious.

"I guess you agree with Greene."

Cal's head shot up. "What?"

"You better understand that I won't tolerate one more person speaking ill of my brother."

"I said 'uh-huh.' " Cal stood in the middle of the floor with papers he picked up from the floor wadded in each fist. "So?"

"That means I agree with you. There's nothing negative about an 'uh-huh' response."

"It sounded more like a grunt than an actual word." The way he stared at her, as if she were insane, put her on the defensive. "Guess I need a male-to-English dictionary to follow along on your side of the conversation."

"You're a tough woman to please."

"I am—"

"Then we agree."

"I didn't finish my sentence."

"I mean that we both agree there is something in this story about Dan worth looking into."

Committing to the idea that they held a united front on anything seemed premature since she still did not understand half of what the guy said. "Why are you here?"

"Dan wrote me."

Her heart jumped at his straightforward answer. "When? About what?"

"About a month ago."

"Why after all this time?"

"He said he has a problem with—"

"What kind?"

The corner of Cal's mouth kicked up. "If you let me finish a sentence, this will go faster."

Cassie doubted that. Nothing about Cal had been easy so far, including that skid across the floor. Her shoulder still thumped from the acrobatic move.

"Sorry to interrupt your long-winded version of the story, Your Royal Highness. But, as you might imagine, I'm interested in figuring out what happened to my brother as soon as possible."

She could tell the news of Dan's death had not been easy on Cal. His skin tone still looked more off white than fleshy. A tug of sympathy pulled in the area near her heart for him but she knew she could not afford to let her guard down.

She had been chased, shot at, and lost her brother under mysterious circumstances. Trust was not something she had in great supply.

Cal shrugged off her concerns. "Dan's message didn't make a whole lot of sense. He referenced a problem, an operation that smelled funny. He asked for my help. It took awhile for the message to get to me—"

"Why?"

Cal's eyebrows lifted. "As soon as I got it, I came."

"You expect me to believe that you just jumped on a plane and flew here."

He smoothed crumpled pieces of paper and piled them in a stack. "It's a hell of a long walk to Hawaii from Florida. Those last two thousand miles underwater would be a bitch."

"My point is that it's a long trip to make based on a few messages." Dan's SOS to this guy made no sense. The fact her brother called a virtual stranger rather than her hurt in ways she refused to think about. "Tell me what really happened between you and Dan a few years back."

"It's an old story." Cal stopped picking up the paper around her feet and leaned in until only a few inches separated their faces. "And none of your business."

"I got time."

"And I have no intention of filling it. Believe it or not, Cassie, I didn't come here to be cross-examined by you."

"I asked a simple question."

"And I gave a simple answer. No."

Chapter Three

The man made Cassie want to strangle something. Mostly him. "So, I'm just supposed to trust you? You could be anyone, for all I know."

Cal sighed, then reached into his back pocket and took out his wallet. Flipping the worn leather open, he showed her his driver's license. "Better?"

"Not really."

"The bottom line is that Dan knew if he had trouble, I'd help."

She had seen the haunted look in Dan's eyes when he walked away from the service for good. He refused to talk about what had happened. Code of silence and all that. But that did not explain Cal's cryptic remarks now.

"Is this rush-to-help thing some kind of military code?"

"That Others May Live. That's the only code I've lived by for years."

She recognized the PJs' motto. "Seems to me whatever friendship you had with Dan was over."

"So, do you live here?"

Interesting time for a topic change. "On a neighboring island. This one is Kauai. I live on Oahu."

"I'm aware of Hawaii's geography. I was stationed here at one point."

He was? "When was—"

"Now that we know everyone's address, what's your story?" Cal asked as he continued to pay more attention to the room than to her.

She sensed the air of relaxation that stole over him was one he practiced and learned. Being in that many treacherous situations would make a man develop a façade. Still, she preferred asking the questions to answering them. From the way he kept circling her questions and asking his own, she guessed he felt the same way.

"I'm Dan's sister. With our parents being gone and Dan being single, the job of cleaning out the house fell to me."

"And your husband or boyfriend doesn't mind you running over here?"

Sounded like fishing to her. She refused to take the bait. "Let's stick to Dan."

Cal stared at her for an extra beat before switching directions again. "Was the house in this condition when you got here?"

"Yeah." She looked around the disheveled room. "This isn't exactly my idea of decorating. Dan could be sloppy, but this is something else."

"Why do I think you're not telling me the whole story of how and why you're here?"

Because she wasn't. Not even half of it. "I don't know what—"

A crack split through the quiet night and glass from the window shattered with a bang and showered the hardwood floor with small pellets.

"Get down!" Cal leaped across the room, dragging Cassie to the floor with him.

She landed on the wood with a thump and a hard slam. Her face hit the floor as his stomach covered her back. After a bounce, strong arms surrounded her, wedging her under his firm body. This time she didn't struggle to get away from him. If one of them was going to get shot, she voted for him.

"What's happening?" She started squirming to get a better view.

"Gunshot"

"Again?" she squeaked out.

"*Again?* You're telling me this sort of thing happens often in your world?" Shock shook his deep voice.

"Just twice." She bit her lip.

"Oh, that's better." He leaned up and whipped out a small gun from his waistband.

"Where did you get that?"

"My pants."

She refused to think about what else he kept in his pants. "Since when did you—"

He motioned for her to stay quiet.

Which she ignored. "What are you planning to do with that thing?"

"I'm a second away from shooting you to keep you from talking." He eased off of her and crouched down in a squat.

"Where are you going?"

"Do you not know what *quiet* means?" His whisper hit her with the force of a yell.

Cal balanced his athletic body on his elbows and muscled forearms. Gliding with the stealth of a predator, he traveled to the other side of the room, then sat up with his back to the wall, under the broken window. Seconds of silence ticked by, broken only by the sound of a slamming car door.

Cal jumped to his feet and peeked out into the dark night. "Damn."

"What's going on?"

"Other than you disobeying direct orders?"

She rolled her eyes even though she doubted he could see her. "I'm not in the military."

"Which is a good thing."

She sprinted across the floor, pressed the front of her body against his back, and peeked around his shoulder. As far as she could tell, in the bleak darkness of the night nothing moved. "I can't see anything."

"Because whoever it was is gone. The car took off."

A wave of disappointment moved through her. Just as her blood started pumping, it now needed to cool. "That's not good."

He stared down at her. "Let's talk about how this wasn't your first shooting."

An unexpected spark of electricity shot through the room at the sound of his deep voice. "We already did."

"I'm thinking I need a bit more information."

"Then you should have stopped the bad guys before they jumped in the car."

"Uh-huh." He turned around until little more than an inch separated their bodies. "Explain why people keep taking shots at you."

"No idea."

His inviting mouth loomed just inches above hers. "I knew you were going to be trouble."

Chapter Four

Cassie's head snapped back. "What are you doing?"

The woman asked a *very* good question. "Standing here."

"You were going to kiss me."

For a second there he toyed with the idea, yeah. "Think a lot of yourself, don't you?"

"I know when a man wants to kiss me."

She didn't have to sound so appalled by the possibility. "So, that's a 'yes' on the arrogance thing?"

"Come off it. I saw you."

"Then you need glasses." And a drink. Maybe that would help.

"You're two inches away and swooping in."

"Swooping?" Cal stepped back and well out of swooping range.

Mauling complete strangers was not his style. Neither was making a move on an estranged friend's grieving sister. Make that grieving baby sister. She was somewhere around thirty and hot as hell. Dan probably hadn't slept through the night since Cassie turned fourteen. No sane man who wanted to protect her would.

Cal chalked up the moment of stupidity to the long flight and the shocking news about Dan his brain still refused to compute. Just a heap of pent-up energy with nowhere to go.

Yep. Nothing more than a near-miss brought on by low blood sugar . . . or something.

"Reaction." One he insisted had more to do with the heat of the situation than the length of her legs.

"To what?" Those amber eyes narrowed.

"This," he waved his hand back and forth. "Between us. That and the by-product of the gunfire. It's not real."

Her lips twisted into a look of disgust. "Did your head slam against the floor or something?"

Now she was ticking him off. "Give me a break. Are you trying to tell me this only goes one way?"

"Define *this*." She mimicked his hand gesture by waving her hand back and forth between them.

"Interest."

"In you?"

Now she sounded horrified. A guy could get a complex. "Do you see someone else here?"

"No, but I'm not the one who's lost his mind. That seems to be you at the moment."

"You're trying to tell me—"

"Yes."

"You felt nothing when—"

"Exactly."

"At all?"

"Not even a twinge." She topped the response with a smug smile.

Well, hell. Here he thought they both were fighting back a heavy-duty case of adrenaline-fueled lust. Looked like he stood alone on that score.

"You're not my type. Sorry." The smirk suggested she felt the exact opposite of apologetic.

"Right back at ya, sweetheart."

Cassie's mood sobered. "And then there's the fact we're standing in the middle of my dead brother's house."

At her reminder, the mental door Cal had slammed shut on that news burst open. He could not wrap his head around Dan dying in a crash. The idea he arrived on the island too late to help his old friend rumbled around in Cal's gut. If he hoped to understand what happened and check out Cassie's claims, he had no choice but to tuck the loss and need for revenge back behind that door. Grief would come later.

"Are you listening to me?" Cassie pinched his upper arm. Whether she meant to get his attention or tick him off, she managed both.

"Damn, woman. What are you doing?"

"Trying to get you back to the subject at hand."

"Which is?" He rubbed the spot where she twisted his skin.

"Dan. His burglarized house. Your break-in. The gunshots. Pick any of those."

"You ever heard of trying to get a guy's attention without giving him a puncture wound?"

"You don't have any fat on your arm." Her gaze moved over his biceps with increasing interest.

The woman clearly had lost her mind. "So you pinched me?"

"I pinched you to get your mind back on helping me. The remark on your lack of body fat was just that. A comment."

To the extent he needed proof that women, as a sex, were nuts, he just got it. "Anyone ever talk to you about the concept of sending mixed signals?"

"Don't be ridiculous." She tugged on the hem of her shirt to cover the thin line of skin open to his view. "I was only making an observation."

"Which was?"

A pink blush stained her cheeks as her voice dropped. "You're muscular."

She was embarrassed. That worked for him a hell of a lot better than sad Cassie or fuming Cassie. He could work with embarrassed.

"Uh-huh." He squatted on the floor, looking for evidence from the shooting.

"What are you doing now?"

"Taking a nap."

"Are you always this much of a jackass? Let me know now because there's a gun or two around here somewhere and I wouldn't mind using them."

When she started looking around the room Cal figured it was time to end the verbal sparring. "Cassie."

"What?" The word was sharp.

"Let's call a truce."

She went still. "Can I shoot you as part of this deal?"

He sighed. "Look, I'm at a disadvantage here."

"No kidding."

"You know the turf. You know the facts. Right now, that makes you necessary."

"Please, all this flattery will go to my head."

"I'm serious."

"We're even then because I'm annoyed."

That much was obvious. Her voice had risen to a near roar. All traces of the weepiness she showed when talking about Dan's death had disappeared. And Cal could not be more grateful.

"I think we should join forces, share resources." At least until he had the background he needed. After that he'd get her to a safe place. One a good distance away from flying bullets.

"Fine."

"That was too easy." Even knowing her for only about an hour, he expected more of a fight.

"I have two conditions to this truce of yours."

The woman would make a monk turn violent. "No conditions."

"Well, then. Good luck gathering that background on your own." Cassie spun around and headed for the door, her head held high. "Remember that the police turned this over to the feds and aren't talking. You won't get any help in that direction."

Cal swore, but relented. "Man, you're prickly. What are your conditions?"

She leaned a shoulder against the doorway. "First, and this one is the most important condition, I'm in charge."

Yeah, now they had a problem. "The rest of the sentence better be, 'of getting lunch.' "

"Oh, so you're a sexist pig."

He had wanted her attention and he got it. Better to keep her feisty than let her mind wander. "Some women find me charming."

"I doubt that. And I'm not waiting on you." She lifted her eyebrows. "Ever."

"You're not bossing me around, either."

"Right, then. You have a nice flight back to Florida." She treated him to a little wave before reaching for the doorknob. "Sorry you had to come all this way for nothing."

This is why some men preferred dumb women. "Wait."

She turned around and shot him a superior smile. "That's the deal."

"Fine," Cal said through clenched teeth. "You want to be in charge, you got it."

"Why do I think you don't mean that, flyboy?"

Because he didn't. There was no way in hell he was going to let her lead, but better to pretend than get a proverbial kick in the balls. "You asked to be the leader. Lead."

"That was only the first condition."

"The second is?"

"A deal-breaker."

"I can hardly wait to hear it." He wondered if he should sit down.

"Simple. You aim that attraction thing of yours at someone else."

Chapter Five

Cal still had not said a word a half hour later when he pulled the rental Jeep into a parking space behind the beige one-story police station.

Cassie noticed how he found the building without any directions from her. The concrete office in the middle of a paved parking lot was not the usual tourist destination. Not a lot of green or any surfing here. Just a slight ramp that led to glass doors at the back of a nondescript building.

"You've been here before?" She put a shaky hand on the dashboard as she tried to stop her body from swaying now that the car had stopped.

"It's on the map I checked out at the airport."

The guy had an answer for everything. "Do you always drive like that?"

He slammed the car into park. "Nothing wrong with the way I drive."

"Not if you're on a racetrack."

"I wanted to get here at a decent hour."

"It's six in the morning." Which explained the lack of people and cars in downtown Lihue.

The area did not resemble Oahu's Honolulu with its high-rise buildings and varied restaurant choices. The island of Kauai tended to the tourist trade like the rest of the

Hawaiian Islands, but at heart, it remained an agricultural center and surfing haven.

Plush and green, with wide-open spaces, low-slung buildings, and a slower way of life, Kauai appealed to people looking for the Hawaii immortalized in postcards. Sun, surf, flowers, and land.

From the sweet scent in the air to the sweeping waterfalls of the Na Pali Coast that could only be seen by helicopter, boat, or on foot, Dan had loved this land. He retired from the military and returned to Hawaii, their home since their teens.

Whatever plagued Dan followed him here. Cassie vowed to figure it out and clear his name. To the extent Cal was the key, she'd drag him along for the ride.

"The way I see it," the key in question said, "there's no reason to wait to get our day started."

Cassie disagreed. A shower, change of clothes, and a big cup of coffee sounded better than an early-morning drive around the island at a speed that defied nature. The sun just started coming up. A few more minutes in the car, and so would her granola bar.

"Kauai might not be Miami, but there are traffic laws here. I'm pretty sure the speed limit isn't ninety." Even though the car had stopped, her stomach continued to flop around.

"Panama City." Cal turned off the engine, letting his keys dangle in the ignition.

"Are we throwing out the names of cities now? If so, I pick Minneapolis."

He finally looked in her general direction. Or Cassie thought that was true. His dark sunglasses hid his eyes and any expression.

"I live in Panama City. Not Miami," he said.

Probably a question she should have asked earlier. Not

knowing anything about this guy except that he was the only person to ever take a good driver's license photo lacked a certain level of safety.

"Mind telling me what you do back in Panama City?"

He flashed her a killer smile, showing off rows of perfectly aligned white teeth and an irresistible dimple in his left cheek. "Finally figured out you don't know anything about me, huh?"

"Just answer the question." Before she wised up and got nervous about being in a car with a perfect stranger.

"Yes, ma'am." Cal pretended to snap to attention. Even shot her a half-salute. "Until a few months ago I was a lieutenant colonel in the Air Force with the Sixteenth Special Operations Wing out of Hulbert."

"Hulbert?"

"Hulbert Field. Most recently, I've been training PJ recruits at the Combat Dive Course, which is why I'm in Panama City."

She tapped her fingers on the console between their seats. "What did you do a few months ago that caused the switch?"

A warm, rich laugh escaped him. "You assuming I did something wrong?"

"Actually, yes."

Cal rested his hand over the steering wheel, letting his long lean fingers hang down through the opening. "You sure know how to kick a man's ego."

A tiny spark of guilt flared at the edge of her mind. He had not given her any reason to expect the best in him except the fact he hadn't shoved her in a closet and left her there after she turned the gun on him earlier.

Still . . . "Feel free to answer."

"For the record, I didn't do anything bad. I retired from active duty. Now I'm a consultant."

"Military life not exciting enough for you?" She stopped tapping and wrapped her hand around the gearshift instead.

"Don't touch that."

"The car is off."

"And your gun wasn't loaded." That dimple grew more prominent. "Yeah, I checked."

She peeked in the side of his glasses and watched him track two officers as they walked out of the station and slid into a patrol car.

Not much action at this time of the morning. No horns honking. Just a few cars passing by and the light rustle of the warm breeze through the palm trees. Must not be much crime, either, if no one bothered to notice a car sitting just outside the back door of the building.

"So, you're not going to tell me the real reason you're a *former* military guy?" she asked.

"Let's just say I was ready to move on to another, more exciting, challenge."

Now there was a mentality she despised. Always seeking something faster, a thrill more dangerous, a better-looking woman. Typical.

"Once a flyboy, always a flyboy," she mumbled in the direction of the window.

"I sense you're not big on pilots."

"I prefer grown-up men to little boys who dream of owning the skies."

"Ahhh." He drew out the sound to four syllables.

"Having a problem talking in complete sentences?"

"Nuh-uh."

The guy should do a comedy show. "Any chance of you elaborating for those of us who prefer English?"

"I get the problem here."

Since he was her main problem at the moment, she decided to ask. "Do tell."

"It's obvious." He waited a beat. "A pilot dumped you."

"You're an idiot." And far too clever for her taste.

Cassie had not only been dumped. She had been cheated on, humiliated, put down, and *then* dumped. Dating Han Rodman, pilot extraordinaire, had been the worst three months of her life. Escaping him with a piece of her self-esteem intact qualified as her best day ever.

Instead of taking the hint, Cal droned on, annoying her with every word. "Not every woman can handle a military man. Don't be hard on yourself."

Now he was being cocky. Part of the breed. An annoying part.

"So, why did we drive all over the island before I'm even awake?" she asked.

"Technically, you haven't slept yet."

"Believe me, I know." A few more minutes and she'd be eating the steering wheel then curling up on top of it for a nap. "Are you ever going to tell me what we're doing?"

"Just trying to follow your directions, *boss*."

Funny how she forgot the part where she ordered him to drive in circles until she threw up. "My plan would have included coffee and probably a doughnut or two."

"We need to report last night's incident to the police."

"You mean your break-in?" She chuckled, proud of her joke.

But nothing in his frown suggested he found the situation funny. "I'm serious, Cassie. Getting shot at is nothing to play with. The police need to know what happened at Dan's house."

That killed her brief good mood. "This is a waste of time. The acting police chief—"

"Acting?"

"The real one is Kane Travers. Good reputation, well-liked, and all that. He's also on some sort of extended honeymoon and hasn't been around for weeks."

"That's helpful."

"Either way. The police moved on. They think I'm . . ."

Cal's eyebrow lifted over the frame of his glasses. "Yeah?"

If only she could back out of this conversation. "Hysterical."

"I assume you don't mean really funny."

"More like crazy. Insane. Whatever word you want to use. The police think I'm too stricken with grief to be rational and accept Dan's accident for what it was."

Cal took off his glasses. "I can think of a lot of ways to describe you. Hysterical isn't one of them."

"That sounded suspiciously like a compliment."

"You sure seemed in control of your emotions when you aimed that gun at my head."

"Ah, yes. That. Where is my gun, by the way?"

His sunglasses slipped right back into place. "I'll hold it for you."

"I thought I was the boss."

"One incident of assault with a deadly weapon is enough for today. Thanks."

Chapter Six

Cal pushed open the glass door to the police station with Cassie close at his heels. He took the minute of quiet to glance around and get a feel for the place.

The small building consisted of two distinct areas. The first was an informal common room with a few fake leather chairs and racks of pamphlets about various issues and government services. A long wooden counter separated the welcome area from the closed portion of the office. Except for a small window, there was no way to see into the back.

Cal pressed the buzzer on the counter to get someone's attention. When a woman in her late fifties and a brightly colored Hawaiian dress popped up from out of nowhere, he nearly shit.

"Damn," he said under his breath, along with a few more curses. "Didn't see you there."

The woman treated him to a broad smile. "What can I do for you?"

"We need to talk with Ted Greene."

The woman glanced at Cassie and her smile faded. "You're back."

Cassie reacted to the woman's flat tone with one of her own. "Yes."

Cal tried to remember when he'd ever heard two women less happy about running into each other. Couldn't think of one. "I take it you two know each other."

"We thought you went back to Oahu," the woman said.

Whatever welcoming aloha spirit the older woman felt earlier had disappeared. Cal was beginning to think Cassie had that effect on most people.

Cassie drummed her fingers on the countertop loud enough to give him a headache. "I brought a friend this time."

Is that what he was?

The woman's gaze traveled between Cal and Cassie before landing on Cal. "Do you have an appointment?"

"No." Cassie jumped in before he could answer.

Cal ignored her. Even angled his body so that he half stood in front of her. "Could you check, please?"

The woman shook her head. "Then I don't think—"

He tried again. "It's important."

"Fine," she said with a sigh. "I'll see if he's here."

And she sure did take her time about it. She straightened up the paperwork in the metal bin in front of her. Moved the phone from one side of the desk to the other. Even plumped up her hair in the back. It took another two minutes before she slipped out of sight.

Once they were alone, Cal leaned against the counter. "You could use some work on your how-to-win-friends-and-influence-people skills."

Cassie did not seem the least bit impressed with his suggestion. She plopped down in one of the chairs and crossed those long, lean legs. "Did you see her being friendly to me?"

Well, Cassie wasn't exactly wrong about that assessment. "I take it you've caused the police trouble."

"Let's just say I've spent some time here. More time than

they wanted me to spend here." She moved the magazines around on the table.

"Talk about your non-denial denial."

Her tough demeanor faltered. "I was doing what I had to do to get some answers about Dan's death."

The same answers they still didn't have. "Why do I think you being with me is going to make our job harder?"

"I'd get used to it if I were you."

A man in his thirties stepped out of the back. No uniform. No badge. Just a navy blue polo shirt and khakis. The guy was part Asian. So far he was smiling, which Cal took to mean the guy hadn't noticed Cassie yet.

Cal rushed to introduce himself before Cassie spoke up and did more damage. "I'm Cal Wilson."

"What can I help you with, Mr. Wilson?"

Cassie picked that moment to stand next to him. She wasn't quiet about it, either. She came over and grabbed the car keys, jingling them and banging them against the counter.

Cal closed his hand over hers and talked to the officer. "I wondered if I could have a moment of your time."

Cassie snorted. "He means 'we.' "

A wary look washed over the officer's face. "Ms. Montgomery. I thought you had headed back to Oahu."

"That's a popular sentiment around here." The way Cal figured it, the officer would have paid for Cassie's plane ticket if that got her out of his way.

"Yeah, well, he's not that lucky."

Cal raised an eyebrow at Cassie's curt response. "Maybe I should do the talking."

The officer held out his hand. "Ted Greene, the deputy chief."

"Deputy?" Cal asked.

"The chief's away on a family matter," Ted said.

"Yeah, about that." Cal slipped his keys into his pocket

before Cassie could grab them again. "Where does a guy go for his honeymoon when he already lives in a place like Hawaii?"

"Seattle."

Cal decided to try to get on the investigator's good side since Cassie seemed to be spending most of her time on the opposite. "Really? I would have bet on something like Tahiti."

Ted shrugged. "Go figure."

Cassie knocked on the counter until both men stared at her. "Uh, hello?"

Cal fought the urge to shake her. If she noticed Ted taking in and analyzing every word and action, she sure hid it well. The woman was determined to be as difficult as possible and make sure no one on the island wanted to help them.

"What's up with you?" Cal asked in a low voice he hoped would have some impact on Cassie.

"You're wasting time," Cassie shot back.

Not one ounce of impact. Cal decided right then that tact was not one of Cassie's strong points.

Ted smiled. "If it helps, I don't have anywhere else to be."

Cal ignored Ted's amusement and concentrated on telegraphing a silent message to Cassie. "Deputy Greene and I are talking."

"We're here for a reason. You guys can bond over football another time."

"Did someone mention football?" Ted asked in a voice that suggested he was not taking the conversation very seriously.

"Let me cut through all of this." Cassie exhaled loud enough to wake most of the neighborhood and then pointed at Ted. "He's the one who decided Dan caused the crash."

With a scowl plastered on her face, she looked more unapproachable now than when she was holding the gun. Cal knew from the flat line of her lips she wanted to unload on Ted. A whole lot of cursing and shouting was trapped in there.

And that was just about the last thing he wanted to hear at the moment. "Cassie—"

"Actually, Ms. Montgomery, the coroner's report and the evidence pointed to an accident," Ted said right over Cal.

"But it was your call."

"It's the NTSB's call. They'll do the formal crash investigation and let us know." Ted glanced in Cal's direction. "Are you here about the accident?"

"It wasn't an accident," Cassie mumbled.

Cal talked right over her. "I'm an old friend."

"You're not from here." It was a statement, not a question.

Cal wondered if all of the locals could spot a non-local. Certainly seemed that way. "I came to see Dan and found out about the crash when I got here."

Sympathy flashed across Ted's face. "Sorry for your loss."

"He's good at saying that," Cassie said.

"The accident took all of us by surprise." Ted balanced his hands against the counter. "Despite what Ms. Montgomery thinks, I liked Dan. He was a good man who cared about Kauai and was invested in its future. His death was a tragedy."

Cal nodded. "Agreed."

Cassie's eyes closed for a second, but when they opened again that painful look was gone. "But it wasn't an accident."

"Cassie, we're just here to ask some questions and tell the deputy chief about what just happened."

"What are you talking about?" Ted asked.

Cassie rolled her eyes. "Here we go."

"Give the man a second." Cal clenched his teeth hard enough to make the blood in his temples pound.

"I'm not the enemy, Ms. Montgomery."

Cassie ignored Ted and spoke only to Cal. "He's not going to care about this."

Ted shifted his weight to get into her line of sight. "Why don't you let me decide that?"

"Someone shot at us in Dan's house last night," Cal said, and then waited for a reaction.

"A real gunshot?" Ted asked after an extra second of silence.

Cassie threw her hands up. "Told you. This is where he starts telling you how crazy I am."

Cal felt his control slipping. Next time, he'd leave her in the car. "Yeah, I wonder why the good officer would jump to that conclusion."

"He doesn't care if I get shot at, or stabbed, or anything else so long as I leave him alone."

Ted rubbed his forehead. "Wait a minute. Someone actually shot at you this time?"

"Someone shot at me last time, too." Cassie glared at the officer. "It was not a car backfire, or whatever other ridiculous excuse you gave."

Cal decided it was time to jump in and steer the conversation back on track. "I can't comment on whatever previous incident you're talking about, but I've been shot at before so I recognized the experience. Someone definitely took a crack at us."

Ted nodded in Cal's direction. "You police?"

"Retired Air Force."

"Figured it was something like that. Retired Navy."

"For heaven's sake." Cassie engaged in her now familiar huffing and puffing. "Do you guys have some kind of secret signal or something? Maybe you'd like me to leave the room while you thump your chests."

Ted ignored the outburst. "What happened?"

Cal skipped over the more interesting parts like the legal technicality of breaking and entering. Ted already thought Cassie was a bit off balance. One of them had to look stable or they'd never get any help.

"Sounds like a pretty bad evening."

Cassie jumped at the rumbling sound of a new male voice

coming from the office entrance behind them. On instinct, Cal stepped forward, shielding her from potential danger by placing his body in front of hers. She showed her appreciation for his efforts by shoving him in the side.

Ted did not even flinch. "This is Josh Windsor. He's with the Drug Enforcement Agency."

Josh lounged in the doorway. Blond-haired, blue-eyed, this guy stood out. And the way his gaze traveled over Cassie, smiling with approval at every inch of his visual journey, spread fire through Cal's insides.

"Good morning, folks." Josh flipped a pen between his fingers.

"DEA in Hawaii?" Cal asked.

"We have drugs here." Josh focused on Cassie. "Ma'am, I'm sorry about your brother."

"Josh helped out at the initial crash site," Ted said.

The way Cal figured it, Ted was leaving out the most interesting part of the explanation. "And what does the DEA have to do with a helicopter accident?"

Josh shrugged. "Just happened to be in the area and rushed to the scene."

"Then maybe you could answer some questions about the crash," Cal said.

Josh shook his head. "Happy to try, but there's not much to tell. Looked like Dan lost control in the canyon. His helicopter whacked into the side of the mountain and then dropped like a stone."

Cassie crossed her arms over her stomach. "Thanks for that image."

Cal winced at the harsh words but asked the questions he needed answered. "Fuel line, everything else was in working order?"

"Yes," Ted said. "Tox screen was clean. No health issues. No drugs or alcohol."

Cassie spun around and stared at the officer. "Of course

not. And Dan flew up and down that canyon for years. He was not a novice to be taken in by sudden wind."

Josh stepped farther into the room and joined Ted behind the counter. "Actually, accidents like this happen more frequently than you know."

"I live in Hawaii," Cassie said.

"Then you know that the islands are famous for freak occurrences of this type. We lose several helicopters each year. We tend not to advertise them because it would kill the tourist trade."

Too little action and far too much talking. Cal had just about had it with the empty words. "Seems to me, unless these tourists who crash into the side of the canyon also get shot at, we have a different situation here."

Ted and Josh exchanged glances before Ted spoke again. "Any chance you brought an enemy with you on your trip to our fine state?"

Cal felt the power base shift in the room. He finally had their attention. "Doubtful."

"Could just be someone trying to take advantage of Dan's death to rob the place," Josh suggested.

"We'll look into it and let you know." Cassie delivered her implied threat with a smile.

"Whoa." Ted held up his hands. "Let the police handle the detective work."

"We tried that," Cassie said.

Ted braced his arms on the counter, looking far more serious and deadly than he had a second earlier. "If I find myself tripping over you two while we investigate, we're going to have a problem. You think the locals are going to open up to you? All you can do is cause trouble."

A chill moved through the air. The warm and sunny island welcome was over. They had moved to the posturing portion of the program. Cal also noticed no one had bothered to explain why the police were talking about an investigation when they insisted Dan's case was closed.

But he had their attention, and that's what he wanted. "Fair enough."

"I mean it." Ted's dark eyes gazed at Cassie. "Both of you."

Cal decided to agree for both of them. "We'll go ahead and get out of your way."

He grabbed Cassie's elbow and dragged her toward the door. She frowned at him but took the hint and kept her mouth shut . . . until they were out of earshot.

"I told you that would be a waste of time," she grumbled under her breath.

"On the contrary. The conversation was pretty revealing." He matched her volume by keeping his voice low and even. "Those two are hiding something. Something big."

Life sparked behind Cassie's eyes. The hurt lingering there gave way to budding excitement. "I told you so."

Cal could not help but smile. "I thought you might say that."

Chapter Seven

Josh watched Cal hustle Cassie out of the building. "Now there goes a bunch of trouble."

"Like we needed more." Ted sighed. "She was tough to deal with on her own. Adding on this guy is bad news."

Josh leaned down on his elbows. "She can't let it go."

"Would you?"

"Hell, no." Josh broke eye contact with Cassie's butt for a second and glanced up. "It's the never-ending questions and amateur sleuthing that's the problem."

"She's desperate for answers. Can't say that I blame her."

The phone started ringing, but Ted didn't move. After three rings, someone in the back office picked it up.

"You're in charge now, so you don't answer phones?" Josh asked.

"Not unless I have to."

Josh appreciated Ted's comfort with his new title. The guy was solid. Dependable.

"Either way, she's not the same teary-eyed woman who first came to your office right after the crash. She's gotten harder." And the part Josh could see of her looked just fine.

Ignoring the lady's impressive backside, it was her potential for problems that worried him. Cassie Montgomery had a killer bod and a deep loyalty to her dead brother. The second she heard the news about the crash, she dropped everything and flew between the islands to be there for Dan. She had not gone back to her life since.

Her mouth was the problem. It never stayed closed. She had spent a good portion of the past three weeks or so bad-mouthing the police and raising questions about Dan's accident in the press. She morphed from shocked and crying to an angry vigilante in a matter of days.

But Josh could handle all of that. The threat to his informal investigation was the problem.

Ted stepped into Josh's line of sight. "Hello?"

"What are you doing?"

"Focus."

Josh watched Cassie disappear from sight. "I was. Trust me."

"Seriously. What are we going to do?"

We. Josh liked the sound of that. Kane was both the police chief and his best friend, but with him out of town Ted was a good temporary substitute. Kane could travel around with his new wife Annie. Josh and Ted had to concentrate on the mess swirling around them.

"Josh?"

"I'm thinking." The sound of a ringing phone wasn't helping with that. "I'm balancing a lot here."

Bucking his boss's orders, conducting an undercover drug operation, and spearheading an informal and totally un-sanctioned investigation into Dan's death. Yeah, a guy could get a bit pissed off with an agenda like that to worry about.

"What about the shots," Ted asked over the ringing phone.

"A last-minute thing. Cassie walked right into the middle of my setup. Bobby Polk was within seconds of getting to the house."

Ted opened the door to the back office. "And Cal?"

"Didn't even know he was there. I was trying to get Cassie

out of there before she ran into Polk. What was I supposed to do?"

"Ever think of handling the situation without bullets?"

"Uh, no." Hadn't even crossed his mind, actually.

"Just a sec." Ted shouted into the opened doorway. "Anyone going to get off their ass and answer the phone, or do we not care if someone needs our help?"

The door fell shut on a few mumbled apologies, but Ted kept muttering under his breath.

Josh could not help but be impressed. "That should win over your staff."

"Let's focus on your problem. This Cal character brings the game to a whole new level. He's smart enough to know something's wrong. If nothing else, the shoot-out clued him in."

Josh tapped his pen against his lip. "It seemed like a good idea at the time."

"Can't imagine that being the case." Ted laughed. "I'm starting to think you wouldn't know a good idea if it bit you in the ass."

"The goal was to protect Cassie."

"You gonna stick with that when this whole thing goes down and she decides to sue you?"

That wasn't Josh's biggest concern. His boss told him to stay quiet about Dan and let the NTSB handle the investigation without providing any information. Josh balked and nearly got fired. Now he had to handle the situation on his own, without DEA resources or help.

"Cassie will get the truth eventually. That's all that will matter to her," Josh said.

"I'll remember that when I lose my badge for helping you." Ted shook his head. "I can't believe I went along with this."

"Didn't exactly give you a choice."

"No wonder Kane took a six-week vacation."

Ted was a decent man and damn good at his job, but Josh wanted Kane back at his desk. "I think that has more to do with Annie."

"She still hate you?"

"She never hated me." Josh smiled at the memory of his past sparring with Annie. "I saved her husband's ass once or twice. She owes me."

"In the meantime, we have a mess on our hands. Drug-running. A dead pilot. And now an amateur detective team determined to blow the whole thing to hell."

"Yeah, this one isn't exactly going according to plan." Josh dragged his notepad out of his pocket and jotted down Cal's name for a background check.

"Any closer to figuring out your boss's reluctance to talk with the NTSB?"

Josh had shared the barest of details of that problem with Ted. Better he not know the entire story. As far as Ted was concerned, the folks at DEA didn't want Josh talking to anyone about what he'd seen at the crash site that day. No one was even to know Josh had been there.

But there was more. A lot more. Josh knew his boss, Brad Nohea, was covering up a much bigger disaster. One that he did not want reported back to the home office, the Los Angeles division of the DEA. And one that could cost Nohea his job and take out Josh as collateral damage.

Josh kept those problems to himself. No need to implicate Ted or condemn Kane's office and the decent officers who worked there. This was a DEA mistake, not a Kauai police mistake. Unfortunately, Dan was the one who paid.

"Officially, I'm on loan to the police, to you, on this one. I answer to you, not Nohea, as part of this operation," Josh said.

"Since when?"

"Since right this second."

"So, we're pretending you're working on some kind of special drug case?"

"Yep."

Ted managed to roll his eyes and let out a loud exhale at the same time. "The same case that doesn't actually exist?"

"Something like that."

"Sounds like a lot of unnecessary paperwork to me."

Josh shrugged. "Kane used to do it for me."

"Shame we can't wait until Kane gets back and let his butt be the one that gets in trouble." Ted grabbed a piece of paper from under the counter and wrote down a few notes.

"Is that a no?"

"You see me writing, don't you?" Ted shook his head while he did. "So, what are you going to do to bring this to a close?"

"Whatever it takes."

"Getting Cassie and Cal to back off will be tough."

Josh flashed his cockiest smile. "I'm up to the task."

"Sounds like I should start looking for another job, because chances are you're going to get me fired with this stunt."

"I'd say that's likely. Yes."

Chapter Eight

Cal kept trying to pull Cassie back to the car, but she dragged her feet and slowed him down. His dark burglar outfit had helped him blend into the night, but it would soon be a hindrance. In a few hours the warm Hawaii sunshine would roast him like a pork chop.

Cassie smiled at the thought.

Then she focused on Cal's broad back. His muscular arms moved in a controlled rhythm. Every line in sync, every movement calculated. A silent strength radiated off him in waves. How a man could look this good and be this insufferable at the same time was a mystery.

If she didn't have such a desperate need for help to clear Dan's name, she would have run screaming in the opposite direction from this guy. She had been around enough military men to know that Cal Wilson was one of those you stared at, maybe even worked into your nightly fantasies, but then ran from like hell when he started looking back in your direction.

He never came home with Dan for a visit. Dan gave cryptic excuses about Cal not being a home-and-hearth type of guy. About how he didn't understand or enjoy family time. Something about a newspaper headline–making divorce years ago that put Cal and his sister in the middle of a horrible fight.

The bottom line: when it came to women, Cal was dangerous.

And obnoxious.

"For a military man, you're not very good at obeying the chain of command," she said to his back.

Cal scowled at Cassie over his shoulder. "You pulling rank?"

That sounded good, so she decided to try that. "Absolutely."

He reached out and opened the car door. "Let's go."

So much for being in charge. "Do we have an actual destination in mind or is the idea to drive around in circles until I vomit?"

He ignored her and walked around to the driver's side of the car without answering.

Not so fast. "Ummm, hello?"

Cal stopped, then marched back to her. Judging from the harsh lines etched on his handsome face, he was ticked off.

Well, join the freaking club. She wrestled with her emotions on a nearly hourly basis, rocking back and forth between wanting to cry over Dan and wanting to scream in rage. The horrible events of the past few weeks twisted her nerves, making her less tolerant of his Neanderthal act than she might otherwise have been.

"You don't scare me." She said it and actually meant it.

"Oh really?"

"Not even close."

The tension on his face eased a bit. "The plane is in the hangar."

Cassie wondered how she had lost the thread of the conversation. And it was happening almost every time she talked with Cal. "When exactly did we decide to visit a plane?"

"Cassie." The tone was a warning.

"Don't pull that macho crap. What's going on?"

He held up his hands. "Oh, I forgot. You're in charge."

She wasn't about to back down now. With her knees locked and her legs braced apart, she stared him down. Unfortunately, she had to look up to do it. "That's right."

"Okay, boss lady, what's your suggestion?" He dropped his hands along with the mocking tone.

"First, lose the attitude."

A smile flickered at the corner of his hard mouth. "Fair enough. After that?"

She would have kicked him in the shins if he weren't a wall of pure muscle. There was no reason to injure her foot or scuff a perfectly good pair of sneakers. "You clearly have a plan in mind."

"Yeah, I do." That intriguing dimple appeared in the corner of his cheek again.

"Never let it be said that I can't delegate. Let me hear it."

He crossed his arms across his broad chest. "You sure? I wouldn't want to disrespect the chain of command or make you think I'm planning a coup."

He threw out that suggestion a tad too easily for her liking. "You have ten seconds to talk or I call a taxi."

"Are you always this difficult?"

"Yes."

Cal chuckled. "At least you're honest. Okay, my plan is simple. We visit the crash site and look into whatever investigation has been done and get access to Dan's offices, files, and records."

Crash site. The words flipped her heart inside out. The shocking smell of torched trees and burning fuel was seared in her memory. She could still taste the horrible mixture.

"The police took his computer and most of his records. You're not going to find much at his office," she said rather than deal with the worst of his suggestion.

"And the plane?"

She shook her head. "The parts, everything that's left, are here somewhere, with the police or the NTSB."

"Yeah, well, something tells me that Deputy Ted and Agent Blondie aren't going to be too helpful on that score."

Angry tears pushed against the back of her eyes. "Nothing new there."

Something in Cal's dark eyes cleared. He stepped forward and rubbed his calloused palm up and down her arm. His movements were awkward and stilted, but Cassie found the gesture oddly comforting.

She leaned into his touch, seeking his warmth. "I'm being stupid."

"Give yourself a break. This is rough."

"I still can't believe Dan's gone."

"If you'd rather—"

She peeked up. "You're not going there without me, so don't even ask."

The edge of Cal's mouth kicked up. "Yes, ma'am."

"As far as I'm concerned your loyalty track record isn't great."

That half smile of his disappeared again. "I came to Hawaii, didn't I?"

"And I'm still not sure why."

Cal opened his mouth, but then closed it again. After a few seconds of silence he started talking. "Let's get back to the subject."

He was hiding something. Something that went very wrong in his friendship with Dan. Whatever it was, she would find out. No way would she let that subject go away.

But for now she moved on to another subject.

"I was there. After the police told me, I hiked into the canyon and saw the wreckage." She swallowed hard to get the words out over whatever had lodged in her throat. "The forensic crew was working, so I couldn't get too close, but I could see the rock slide where the plane hit."

"You're not so tough, you know." He gave her upper arm a gentle squeeze.

"I'm tough enough to be your leader."

His mouth broke into a wide grin. "True enough. Lead on."

Now he had her. "To where?"

"The hangar."

She dreaded the idea. Since learning about the plane crash, she could not ride in or even think about one. To get to Kauai from Oahu she took a boat, preferring to keep her feet as close to the ground as possible. If the worst happened, she could swim. She'd have a chance. If something awful happened in the air, she'd die just like Dan.

"Cassie? You up for this?"

It looked as if the time had come to conquer that fear. "I don't have a choice."

Chapter Nine

About a half hour later, after a round of badge flashing by Cassie to prove they belonged in this area of Lihue Airport, they stood about fifty feet from the hangar where Dan ran his charter business. Cal conducted a visual tour of the area. Even though it was early in the day, the establishment served a steady stream of vacation travelers who wanted to explore the wonders of the garden isle by air.

According to Cassie's nonstop explanation in the car ride over, Dan had subsidized the tourist side of his operation with private rides between the islands for locals. Businessmen depended on him for basic transportation, and a few of them wandered around now.

"Tell me why you have a security badge for this area again," he said.

"It worked, didn't it?"

"You're saying I should just be happy you have it?"

"That and that you should walk faster." She picked up her pace as if to prove her point.

Cal compromised and took longer strides. He'd gawk at the planes later.

Helicopter blades thrummed in the distance as small groups of travelers bustled back and forth across the tarmac in their wild print shirts. Cal felt at home in the heated atmosphere, with planes lined up ready for flight.

He stole a quick glance at Cassie as they walked in silence toward the hangar. She was classy, tough, and beautiful. Dan rarely spoke about her. The eight-year age difference
and not sharing the same father put their lives on different
paths. Still, Cal couldn't help but wonder if Cassie was as close
to Dan as she professed or if this was a case of hero worship
mixed with guilt.

The guilt part he understood. He had a heaping share of
that where Dan was concerned. Cal knew he could not fix
what he had done, but he could do something. He could solve
the mystery surrounding Dan's death. Later, in private, he
would mourn the man lost. Right now, he had other priori-
ties.

"What are you hoping to learn here?" she asked.

The sadness that clouded her stunning amber eyes had
begun to clear. Cal was grateful for that. Weepy women
were not his strong suit. They cried. He ran for the bar . . .
where he stayed until the waterworks stopped.

Seeing Cassie upset, knowing Dan's loss was the cause,
made walking away impossible. Cal tried to block out the
reality of Dan's death so he could focus on figuring out
what really happened. Still, seeing Cassie's anguish tore
through him.

"I need to talk with the people at the airport who knew
him," he said.

"Dan was more or less a one-man operation, but he depended on mechanics, bookkeepers, and so forth to handle
the non-flying duties." Cassie yelled the last part to be heard
over an incoming helicopter.

"We'll start with them."

They slowed down to watch the flight land. Saw a tourist
family pour out of their sightseeing venture with cameras
around their necks and matching faux Hawaiian shirts. The
kids talked and ran around, and the parents were just as an-
imated.

Cassie stopped and reached out for Cal's arm, forcing him to join her. "What exactly did my brother tell you when he contacted you?"

"Not much."

She dropped her hand. "Try again."

"Are you tapping your foot?" he asked as he watched her sneaker bounce up and down.

"I can stand here all day and wait for an answer."

"That makes one of us." He inhaled the jet fuel. "I came to Hawaii for fresh air, not this."

"You came here to help my brother." She scraped the toe of her shoe against the tarmac. "Or was that a lie?"

"You can be a pretty unpleasant chick."

"Chick?" She sounded appalled at the term.

He didn't blame her. He'd used the term on purpose to take her off task. And it worked. "Do you prefer 'lady'?"

"Whatever nickname will get you talking is fine with me."

She deserved that much. She might be mouthy, but mouthy for the right reason. Whatever the reason for the loyalty, it existed. In his experience, finding allegiance in the civilian community was tough. It thrived in the military but very little elsewhere.

Cal knew most people searched a lifetime for that type of devotion on a romantic scale. Not him. His pull-up-stakes-every-few-years lifestyle did not lend itself to long-term commitment. Knowing his job did not suit a forever world, and knowing that forever usually only meant for now, he never longed for it.

"Dan said he'd seen a lot of truck movement in and out of an abandoned government site on the main road leading up to tourist look-out sites around the rim of Waimea Canyon," Cal said.

"So?"

"He thought it looked suspicious." And since Dan was dead, Cal figured Dan was right to be skeptical.

"Let me guess. Your brilliant plan includes storming up the mountain and into the building."

Uh, yeah. "I thought we could drive, but if you tell me what's involved in 'storming' we'll give that a shot."

She started walking again. Didn't even look back to see if he was following.

"You need to spend a little more time coming up with these ideas of yours," she said over her shoulder.

He caught up in two steps. "You have no faith in my sense of subtlety?"

"Absolutely none."

He chose to ignore that. "How's this for a plan? We'll figure out as much as we can about Dan's operation and his last days."

"Unexpectedly rational."

"We'll get to the building eventually, but we need background first."

"And here I thought you didn't know how to make a plan." Cassie stepped up to the building's entrance.

"How much do you know about your brother's business?"

Her hand hesitated over the doorknob. "Almost nothing."

"Then we'll need to talk with someone who does."

She turned and stared at Cal. "You think complete strangers will just open up to you, flyboy?"

"Why not?"

He had never met anyone with less faith in him. He was accustomed to having people trust him, follow him, and listen to him. This exact opposite reaction sort of pissed him off.

Actually, not *sort of*. Totally pissed him off.

"You're not Hawaii homegrown," she explained. "Folks around here don't take strongly to outsiders poking around."

"They'll talk to me." He reached around her and pushed open the door to the business office and marched inside.

"This should be good," she mumbled under her breath.

Cal was prepared to drag out the information he wanted. What Cassie didn't know was that he had an edge. The pilot community was a small one where people tended to respect the flying credentials of others even before deciding on the quality of the person.

The deeply tanned man lounging behind the desk did not disappoint. He was in his late fifties, his dark hair streaked with gray and his flower print shirt loose and open, revealing a white, ribbed tank top.

"Ed."

Cal could hear the smile in Cassie's voice as she walked around the desk to the grizzled older man.

"Cassie darling. What brings you back here?" Beefy arms wrapped her in a firm bear hug.

When she squealed with delight, raw fury shot through Cal. The other man was old enough to be her father, but the sight of his hands on Cassie's slim body filled him with a fighting rage. He refused to analyze why or examine his motives except to say her brother was gone. Someone had to look out for her. That job fell to him.

Yeah, that was all this was. A case of unwanted brotherly-like protectiveness.

"Are you going to introduce us?" Cal asked over their whispering and laughing.

"What's this?" The man's head popped up from Cassie's shoulder. "Who's the young man, Cassie darling?"

Young? He was thirty-eight. Not old but hardly young.

Cassie snuggled into the other man's arms as if she had

no inkling of the tension pumping through the room. "Ed Golden, this is Caleb Wilson, an old friend of Dan's."

"Cal?" The man's smile wiped out the confusion playing around his eyes. "Why, of course."

"Do we know each other?" Cal asked, knowing he absolutely did not know this guy.

"Sure. You and Dan served together. He told me all about your stunts." Ed managed to keep his protective hold on Cassie and step forward to shake hands at the same time.

Cal hoped to hell that wasn't true. He stayed quiet but gripped the older man's hand in a strong handshake.

"Yep." Ed squeezed Cassie even tighter. "Dan told me about you."

The idea that he couldn't reciprocate with some personal information on this guy made Cal edgy. There were certain things he wanted to keep private. There were things about him, about Dan, that even Cassie did not know. Somehow he sensed that Ed might have an idea.

"Then tell me," she said. "He's barely shared any information so far."

"Cassie darling, Cal and I understand each other."

"How?"

"We both sailed the skies for our country with a chunk of metal strapped to our backs. Those of us who fly for a living know."

Cassie twisted her lips in an appalled frown. "What?"

Cal had to smile. He could tell she was not impressed with their show of silent male bonding. He took pity on her. "We know what it's like to be up there when everyone else is down here."

"What the hell does that have to do with anything?" Cassie stepped out of Ed's embrace and propped her thigh on the edge of Ed's desk.

Ed barked out a laugh. "Everything, darling."

If the pounding headache behind his eyes was any indication, Cal figured his brain might explode if Ed called Cassie "darling" one more time. The other man's age didn't matter. For some dumbass reason, he didn't want any man touching Cassie unless that man was him.

So much for the idea of brotherly protection.

Ed fell back into his big chair and looped his arms behind his neck. "So, what brings you two out here?"

"I just found out about the accident," Cal explained.

Cassie started shaking her head before he even finished his thought. "It wasn't an accident."

Saying Dan was dead over and over was not an option Cal wanted to consider. "It's just a word, Cassie."

"The wrong one."

His headache was not getting better. The loud thumping drowned out most other sounds around him. "Can I just answer the man's question?"

Cassie glanced at Ed. "He broke into Dan's house."

Ed raised an eyebrow. "Interesting."

Cal exhaled, letting his exasperation show. "For the last time, I did not break in."

"Because I stopped you."

This small woman could not actually believe she had the physical strength to best him. "You've got to be shitting me."

"You're lucky I didn't shoot you."

Ed lowered his arms an inch at a time. "What are you doing with a gun?"

Cal pointed to the older man. "He asks a good question."

"He wasn't there. He didn't see you come through that window. I should have hit you over the head with a chair right then." Her foot bounced around even faster.

"Give me a break," Cal said.

"I seem to remember you hitting the floor when the bullets started flying." Cassie smiled in smug satisfaction at the reminder.

"I was trying to keep you from getting shot. Some women would call that chivalrous." His shouting was less so, but Cal thought he needed to make the point.

"Whoa." Ed held up his hands again. "You shot at him?"

Cassie's face fell. "Of course not."

"Then what bullets?" Ed practically yelled his question. The grandfatherly bear was gone. In its place was a ticked-off man who wasn't getting his questions answered.

Cal sympathized.

Cassie had a more basic reaction. Her cheeks flushed as if she had just been scolded. "Someone shot at us."

"Again?" Ed's voice shot up an octave.

The woman was making him crazy. Cal started to wonder if he would survive this little island vacation. "You really need to explain why people keep shooting at you."

"If I knew that . . ." Her voice faded away.

Ed's scowl hit with the force of a hammer. "Last time she was outside Dan's house right after the funeral. A shot whizzed by her head. She heard the crack and fell to the ground."

Cassie touched her hand against Ed's arm. "Don't—"

"Cassie, the man is with you now." Ed pounded his finger against the desk while he made his point. "He has a right to know."

Cal wasn't sure he liked the way that sounded, but he let it go. He needed to hear what the man had to say. God knew Cassie didn't plan on sharing the bad parts about the story.

"The police never found the bullet, so they didn't believe her. Thought she was too busy crying over Dan to think straight."

"Ed, stop."

"Let the man talk." Cal realized he finally found a person who could tell him something worth knowing.

Ed's eyebrow crept up a notch. "Nothing more to tell. Not from me anyway. I do find this interesting, though."

Cassie's eyes narrowed. "What?"

"You." Ed cleared his throat. "With him."

Oh, no. Time to stop that line of thinking. "Wait a second."

Ed's attention stayed on Cassie. "I've only seen two things get you this riled up—the investigation and . . ."

Cal noticed everyone started looking at him. "What?"

Ed smiled. "You."

Cal had no idea what to say to that. He didn't get a chance to come up with a zinging response because Cassie jumped in.

"Spend a few minutes with Cal and you'll be screaming, too," she muttered.

Cal ignored the slight. "You're trying to tell me she's not usually like this?"

Ed patted the corner of the desk near Cassie. "She's quite calm and lovely."

"Really?"

"You're no prize, either," she said.

Cal's headache kicked up to Big Band levels. It didn't help that the older man's face broke into a wide grin. Cal swore he heard Ed whistle a strange melody.

Cassie tapped her fingers against the desk. "We're getting off track here."

"I'd say," Cal mumbled in agreement.

"We'll deal with all that later." Ed leveled a knowing look in Cal's direction.

For the first time since he was thirteen, Cal thought about running for cover. "I don't think so."

"What are you talking about?" Cassie asked.

"Never you mind, Cassie darling. Cal, here, has some questions about Dan's work. Let's get them answered."

"I need to see Dan's flight logs and take a look at his books. It would be helpful if you had a map around that sets out the crash area."

Ed nodded. "Have plenty of maps, and you're welcome to whatever the police left behind."

"Can you tell me anything about Deputy Chief Greene and that DEA agent he's hanging out with?"

Ed's mouth screwed up in a frown as he thought about the question. "Ted? He's solid. From Kauai. Straightforward."

The assessment mirrored Cal's impression as well. "And Windsor?"

"Well, now, he's a different story. He's been in the papers a lot lately. Usually does joint drug cases with Travers. Seems inoffensive enough but his discipline is a question."

"The timing is interesting," Cassie pointed out.

"Meaning?" Cal asked.

"The chief goes away, Dan dies, and the police part of the investigation is rushed through before the chief can get back and look into anything."

Finding the truth would take forever if Cassie kept finding conspiracies in every corner. "Could be a coincidence."

"You know what?" She tapped that foot again. "I'm sick of everyone using chance as an excuse for everything."

"Are you pouting?" The opportunity to provoke her was too appealing for Cal to pass up.

A rosy hue burned in her cheeks almost immediately. "When I find that gun, you're a dead man."

"I'll take that as a yes." Cal turned the conversation back to Ed. "Anyone around here know about Dan's business?"

"Normally I'd say no but there's been some talk about a silent partner and some business dealings other than flying."

Cassie jumped off the desk and glared at the older man in a way that would make most men hide. "You never told me that."

"Because I can't imagine Dan getting hooked up with that character."

"Who?" Cal asked.

Ed hesitated as if wondering how much to tell. "Man named Bobby Polk. The kind of guy who has his fingers in everything, pretending he's the boss when he's really the problem."

"Dan didn't need a partner," Cassie insisted.

Cal admired Cassie's defense of Dan, but from the way Ed's eyes narrowed Cal guessed the older man believed the rumors. Cal had his own concerns. He knew the real reason Dan left the Air Force. Nothing voluntary about that choice.

Cassie didn't know, and Cal didn't want to be the one to disillusion her. He also didn't want her to know the part he played in Dan's removal from the service.

Ed slipped his hand into Cassie's. "All I know is that Polk started showing up around the office and dragging his pretty young girlfriend with him. Louisa something."

"How young?" Cal tried to assimilate the information.

"Early twenties, maybe. Polk's more than twice her age and not in her league, if you know what I mean."

Cal did.

"Anyway," Ed continued, "Dan was pretty secretive about the deal. I figured he was transporting something for Polk."

"Something illegal?" Cal asked since someone had to.

Cassie's eyes grew wide. "That makes sense. If Dan knew someone was using his business to carry out illegal operations, he would do something about it. That might be the motive for killing him."

Cal put the brakes on that line of thinking before Cassie

tried to make a citizen's arrest. "Let's not get ahead of ourselves."

"Why not?" she asked.

Cal ignored the question and went back to Ed's story. "Is this Polk character still around?"

"He does business here on Kauai. No idea what kind. That's one of the mysteries surrounding the guy. There's a storefront but not much activity there."

Cassie nibbled on her bottom lip. "You don't believe Dan was—"

Ed tightened his hand around Cassie's. "It's all rumors, Cassie darling. Don't concern yourself."

Cal filed the information away for later. "I want to take a look at the crash site and maybe scout out a few other areas."

Ed's solid form seemed to shrink. He shot a sheepish glance in Cassie's direction. "Maybe you and I could go down into the canyon."

Cal appreciated Ed's protective streak. "Sounds good."

But Cassie was having none of it. She stepped between the men, making them focus on her. "I'm going."

The older man's dark eyes grew soft. "This isn't necessary."

Cal decided that coddling her was the exact wrong approach. It made her weepy. He needed her strong. "You still think you're so tough?"

She turned on him in an instant. Just as he wanted her to do.

"I'm the one who's been down there."

Ed frowned. "You hiked eight miles through rough terrain to the site by yourself?"

Cal wondered if he would survive this brotherly protectiveness thing. "You weigh almost nothing and walk around like you're invincible."

She stepped right up until she stood less than a foot away from him. "I can take you any day, flyboy."

"That sounds like a challenge."

Her chin lifted a notch. "I guess it is."

He flicked a finger under that pretty round chin. "You're on."

Chapter Ten

Cassie counted to ten in an attempt to simultaneously stop her body from shaking and fight off a wave of nausea. Didn't work. She was going to be sick right there all over the shiny control panel of Ed's borrowed helicopter.

Ed was going to kill her when she messed up his aircraft, but her stomach wouldn't obey her command to settle down. This was her worst nightmare, strapped helpless and terrified to a tiny seat in a flying death trap no larger than a can of tuna.

Getting in this thing was hard enough. Her newfound fear of planes battled with her distaste for being left behind. Cal handled the whole scene by pretending it was no big deal. He got into the helicopter without a fuss. She didn't have a choice but to follow or a minute to worry. She just hopped on the airsickness generator and off they went.

Which would have been fine, sort of sweet even, if Cal weren't sitting there with that stupid grin enjoying every minute of her discomfort.

Bastard.

"How ya doing?" Cal shouted into the small microphone attached to his headset.

Even with him being loud, hearing him over the roaring noise of the aircraft fighting against the wind proved tough.

And the wild sway of the ground beneath her and the deafening thrum of the blades prevented her from doing what she wanted to do—reach out and slap his smug face. She was too busy digging her nails into the faux leather armrests and trying to remember the prayers she had learned as a kid in catechism class.

"Soak your head," she mumbled back.

"What?"

"I said 'fabulous.' This is fabulous." She screamed to be heard.

When he turned a wicked grin in her direction, her stomach flipped, but this time not from airsickness. No, it was something very different. Something that started with a shot of warmth spiraling up her spine and ended with her skin prickling with extreme heat.

Something absolutely inappropriate.

Cassie had grown up with a man obsessed with flying and the military. She knew from experience the control it took to fly through a hail of fire. Knew the type of man who jumped out of a plane to rescue others. Saw the toll all of that pressure took on her brother's emotions.

Then in a complete act of masochism, she had dated one of the breed. Han Rodman. Yeah, she still had the scars inside and out from that nine-month nightmare. She had no plans to travel down that road either permanently or for a night or two.

Which brought her mind right back to the flyboy beside her. Mothers warned their baby girls about men like Cal Wilson. She planned to proceed with caution.

"Where are we going?" she asked in an attempt to drag her attention away from the barfing, the noise, and the man.

"Ed gave me the coordinates."

Cal was definitely a man of few words, and most of the

ones he managed to spit out annoyed her. She decided to focus on the only benefit of the ride—the view.

When she found the strength to lift her head through the waves of nausea, she gazed out across the blue horizon. Fluffy white clouds whipped across the sky, moved by the strong winds racing up the canyon. Below her, a deep grove cut through the island. Where the rest of Kauai was lush with garden tropics, this area resembled the American Southwest with its brown landscape and scattering of trees, many bent back and down from the force of the wind whipping through the cavern.

"We'll set down on the ledge over there." Cal pointed to a large outcropping of rocks and a small flat surface the size of a postage stamp.

"I think that's called a cliff."

He smiled. "Not quite."

"Oh, I'm pretty sure I'm right about this. You're supposed to admire the landscape from afar, maybe slide down it hooked to a safety harness, but not try to land a two-ton aircraft on it."

"Don't be nervous."

Maybe the man was deaf. She decided to talk even louder. Maybe a little slower. "There's a difference between being nervous and being completely crazy."

"There's a landing spot there." He pointed toward nothing. "Trust me."

Yeah, ten minutes after never. She clenched the armrests with all her might. "I thought I was in charge."

"You want to fly?"

Heaving up yesterday's lunch was more likely. "Being superpilot is a job I'm happy to leave to you. Thanks."

"We're close to the crash site."

She concentrated on the thump of the helicopter blades as she pressed her forehead against the side window. The move knocked her headset back a bit, but she could see just fine. How was she supposed to distinguish one brown rock from another? How was he?

"Nothing looks familiar." She whispered the thought but he heard her over the noise bouncing around the inside of the small cockpit.

"It will when we're down there."

At least one of them had a positive feeling about this. The only thing she was sure of at the moment dealt with never getting in anything with wings or a propeller ever again.

His forearm muscles flexed. "We'll set down and then hike the rest of the way."

She was dressed for grocery shopping, not mountain climbing.

He was dressed for prison.

With her head still balanced against the window, she pivoted to stare at him. "You do know Waimea Canyon is considered the Grand Canyon of the Pacific, right?"

"So said Mark Twain."

Just what she needed, a well-educated flyboy who could spout historic quotations. "At least he was smart enough not to try to land a helicopter on the side of a rock face."

"Only because he didn't have a pilot's license."

She decided to try one more time to talk some sense into Cal before he managed to get them both killed. "This is not a leisurely hike through the countryside or on the streets of Miami."

"Panama City."

"Whatever. The point is neither one of us has the proper clothing or equipment. I don't even have a bottle of water. This is serious, Cal, we could get hurt."

Without moving his hands, he nodded over his shoulder. "We have supplies."

Cassie spied the green backpack sitting behind his seat.

Where the hell had that come from? "Any chance you have a pair of hiking boots in there? My slip-on sneakers are not the best for this terrain."

"We'll be fine. Watch and learn."

Before she could scream or grab the controls, Cal rolled the helicopter to the left and circled around a tourist lookout high on top of the canyon. Her stomach lining crept up her throat when the aircraft started to dive. She braced one hand against the seat and the other against the wall of floor-to-ceiling windows next to her.

"There's no need to hold on like that," he said.

She thought about using his head to steady herself. "From now on, we're going to discuss your plans and agree on them before we start."

If they lived.

And if the past ten minutes were any indication, that was a big question.

"It's as easy as riding a bike."

"I assume you've flown a lot of helicopters in your time. That this was all part of the Wing thing you were in."

His attention stayed focused on whatever was happening outside the front window as his hands tightened on the controls. "The Sixteenth Special Operations Wing."

As if she cared. "Yeah, that."

"Could we talk about this later?"

That would be wise since she needed him to concentrate, but she also needed to know how much she should panic. "Cal, you have flown a helicopter before, right?"

"Of course." He glanced out the window to his side, then out the front. Everywhere but at her. "Just never in a situation like this."

"How about in any situation that was close to this?" She squealed the question.

"No."

"*What?*"

The wind whipped up, whistling through the seams of the helicopter and rattling its sides. As the ground grew closer, Cal held on tighter. "I'll make a deal with you. I get us down safely and you lead us to the crash site."

"So, if I survive the landing, I still have to survive the hike. There's a great deal."

"I thought so."

"For you, maybe."

The brown patches below inched closer. The outlines of scattered trees and shrubs became more defined. She could make out the landscape and see that there was no visible landing site.

The question she was about to ask blended with a scream lodged in her throat. Both escaped in a rush when the helicopter started to drop from the sky like a stone.

Cal shot Cassie one more know-it-all smile. "Time to land."

Dirt kicked up and small rocks pelted the side of the helicopter as it hovered over a small patch of solid ground. The thundering inside the aircraft vibrated in her ears as it swayed from side to side.

She could see from the tension in Cal's arms that he fought with the air rushing up beneath them. Nothing comforting there. Her heart raced and perspiration dripped down her back.

Cal stayed perfectly composed. His long fingers danced across the instruments with surprising precision. With steady hands and spare movements, he lowered the craft to the ground.

He even had the nerve to whistle.

"Still doing okay?" He shouted again.

She would be better in two minutes when her feet touched Mother Earth and she dropped to her knees in thanks. "Just great."

"Some people don't like helicopters."

She wished he would stop the chitchat and just land, but he continued his steady stream of conversation.

"Not you, though. You're tough and in charge," he said.

And too nauseated to speak. Cassie tightened her death grip on the door frame and mumbled a little prayer. "Feel free to concentrate on flying."

"It's fine now. I can talk and fly at the same time." He shot her a quizzical look. "You sure you're okay?"

"Eyes forward and land this thing."

He nodded. "Yes, ma'am."

The aircraft hesitated, floating right above the surface. One last plume of dirt and leaves kicked up before the helicopter bounced against the ground. After the third rebound it settled.

Cassie almost bolted out of the small door before the helicopter came to a full stop. She figured Cal would enjoy her distress in some weird macho way, so she forced her body to stay still.

"Here we are. That wasn't too bad," he shouted over the whapping of the copter blades.

Cassie thought about poking his dimple but stuck her tongue out at him instead.

He smiled back at her. "Very mature."

"It was either that or throw up on your lap."

"Good choice then." He hopped out and stretched his muscular frame. He moved with the grace of a primitive jungle cat. His limbs were long and every inch of him firm and chiseled. If the Air Force put him on a poster, the ranks would be bursting with eager female recruits.

Typical flyboy. Handsome and cocky as sin . . . and nothing but trouble.

Chapter Eleven

Cal stood by Cassie's door and watched her fumble with the seat belt. Her hands shook too hard to dislodge the buckle. To do anything, really.

He flipped her door open before she lost her cool, something he didn't want to see. As frustrating as the fiery Cassie could be, he preferred her to the sad Cassie he glimpsed when she thought he wasn't looking.

"Here you go," he said as he reached in. "Those belts can be a bit tricky."

He knew he had terrified her. Hell, she had not been the only one. The canyon acted like a wind tunnel, sending dangerous gusts ricocheting through the helicopter. The wind rocked the aircraft until he thought the metal would fly apart.

He should have insisted Cassie stay in the safety of the airport office. Hell, he should have stayed in Florida.

"That was fun." A small, almost imperceptible tremor moved through her usually husky voice.

"Now, why do I think you're not being honest?"

"Because my stomach is still stuck about two hundred feet in the air."

He nodded. "It was a bumpy ride."

"There's an understatement."

She jumped out of her seat before he could caution her. As expected, her legs buckled the minute her feet hit the dirt. To keep her from slipping to the ground in a heap, he balanced his hands on her slim waist and pulled her close.

"You okay?"

"Been better."

"When?"

"Almost always."

Cal paid a price for his chivalry. The small touch, inhaling that fruity feminine fragrance that wove around her, shot a beam of electricity up his arms, through his body, and directly to his groin. His gaze skimmed down her tanned legs to her flimsy white sneakers. Her legs were firm and lean, and the perfect length to wrap around his waist. The T-shirt was just thin enough to scratch at his imagination.

His attraction to her was primitive and raw as it gnawed at his control. Rather than give in, he trampled it down. "Time to go."

"Can I try to walk first?"

"By all means." He moved his arm in a sweeping gesture, hoping she would take the hint and step back. He needed a minute or two of breathing room.

No such luck. She stood there shaking out one leg then the other. When he turned back to the aircraft to gather their provisions, she was right there with him.

"I still say we are dangerously low on supplies to try this walk," Cassie said as she peeked over his shoulder.

"So noted."

Her arms shot up behind her head and her fingers went to work on curling her hair into a complicated design. The move highlighted her firm breasts.

Cal watched, fascinated at this private female ritual. He

preferred Cassie's hair down, all soft and bouncy around her shoulders, but the ponytail had its charms, too.

"Is that your macho way of telling me to be quiet?" She smoothed a palm over her hair, taming the delicate waves.

"No." Watching her do something so utterly feminine and mundane made his blood run white hot. "When I want quiet, I'll say so. That was my way of saying I heard the whining."

She stopped moving around long enough to glare at him. "I do not whine."

"Are you kidding?"

"No."

"Complain. Argue. Boss. Call it whatever you want, but the result is the same. Annoying."

The color rushed back to her cheeks. "We'll see how you're doing after the hike."

That lack of faith thing again. "I was in the military. Had to pass physical exams. I'll be fine."

"Yeah, right. We'll see how long it takes you to melt into a puddle in your commando outfit."

The pretty woman had a point. But in keeping with his training, he worked in a contingency plan. He peeled his long-sleeve T-shirt over his head and dropped it on the ground. Down on one knee, he rummaged through the backpack in search of a lighter shirt.

"You act like I'm an Army man or something." He chuckled at the inside military joke. When she didn't join him, he glanced up.

Her pale face struck him. *Damn.* Maybe she was sicker than he thought. "What's wrong with you?"

"Nothing," she mumbled.

Cal grabbed the closest shirt, which happened to be the

only other shirt in the bag, and stood up. "You look like you've seen a ghost."

The haze clouding her eyes cleared but it took a few seconds. He followed her gaze to his bare chest, then satisfaction roared through him like wildfire. Little Miss Not Interested liked the view.

He could live with that. He could certainly torture her about it. "Enjoy what you see?"

She snorted. "Don't flatter yourself."

But Cal noticed she did not turn away or stop stealing quick peeks at his pecs. "I could keep my shirt off if you prefer."

"Or I could strangle you with it."

Since she suddenly looked like she was toying with the idea, he dropped the subject. Cal shrugged into the white undershirt. The fit was snug but the material would breathe better than his other shirt as the heat built throughout the day.

"Ready?" he asked.

"After you."

He cleared his throat. "I thought you were in charge."

"I'm delegating again."

"Fair enough, but you're the one who's been here before and knows the way."

"You saw the site from above. Besides, I can guide you just fine by letting you clear the path. If you get injured, I'll know not to step there."

"Very nice of you." He pointed toward a semi-clear path. "This way."

They had walked for about a mile, their bodies dragging in the stifling humidity, when Cal realized they were no longer alone. He grabbed Cassie's elbow and pulled her off the rough trail he had been forging.

She squealed in surprise. "What are you doing?"

"Shhh." He motioned for her to duck down as they squatted behind a pile of brush.

"What do you hear?" She lowered her voice that time, but only a little.

"What is it with you and the confusion over the word *quiet*?"

Twigs crunched in the distance. The wind rustled, but Cal could make out the distinct sound of footsteps. Carefully placed footsteps.

"Stay here." He glared at her until she nodded. He could only hope the woman would listen this time. This job of protecting someone who didn't want to be protected got old.

In a crouch, Cal dodged past a clump of bushes and stopped behind a large rock formation until he retraced their path a short distance back up the canyon wall. His muscles clenched as he took his position and prepared to pounce.

The approaching steps grew louder but were still guarded. When the unwanted visitor stepped into the small clearing, Cal prepared to make his move. Land one punch and then ask questions. That was the plan.

He stopped in mid-flight. It was either that or knock down a DEA agent. Tempting, but not going to happen until he had a better handle on Josh Windsor's real reason for being there.

But since Cal figured the visit was not a coincidence, he decided to have some fun. "Good morning, agent."

Josh jumped a foot at the unexpected greeting. His hand flew to his gun. The telltale reaction of a man accustomed to danger and drawing a weapon.

"I thought I was alone out here." Josh patted his chest in what could have been a check for a pen or a check of his heart. "And it's afternoon."

"I guess I lost track of time." Cal looked around for a second plane. "And how did you get here?"

"Hiked."

Cal didn't believe that for a second. "Uh-huh."

Josh squinted into the sun. "You've been a busy man today. First the police station, now here."

"The little woman and I are doing some hiking."

"Little woman?"

"I hate to answer to that introduction, but I'm tired of standing in a bush." Cassie stepped up beside Cal. "You're a child."

In reality Cal enjoyed making her feisty. "Yet you can't resist me."

"Really? Watch me."

Josh did just that. He smiled in appreciation as his eyes conducted a quick tour of her body. "Ms. Montgomery."

Cal reconsidered knocking the guy's head into the ground. He could understand the agent's reaction. When Cassie turned her wide smile on a man, he lost all common sense. Hell, her frown wasn't half bad either.

"The DEA has business inside the canyon?" Cal asked.

"Just checking out the area."

Like hell. "For lost drug addicts?"

"If so, you're going to be disappointed since we seem to be the only ones here." Cassie scooted closer.

Cal took that as a good sign. If she was silently taking sides, he was damn glad she chose his.

"And since we aren't drug dealers or users, we'll get out of your way," Cal said.

They went about two steps before Josh started talking again. "You're off the established hiking trails."

Cassie stopped walking and forced Cal to do so, too, with a tug on his pants leg. "We prefer a tougher hike. The brochures say we're free to explore at will."

Josh glanced down at her sneakers. "So this doesn't have anything to do with Dan's accident and the site that's right around here?"

"A simple hike." Cal said the words in as harsh a voice as possible. It was a dare to see if the other man would pursue his questions.

Instead, Josh gave Cassie's sneakers a second look. "Be careful. Storms move in here without warning and the wind gets dangerous."

"I live on Oahu. I'm familiar with the weather issues in Hawaii," Cassie said.

Cal could not help but smile. Nothing like a turf war to piss off the locals.

The agent's frown suggested he was not impressed with the outburst. "Then you know you should think about leaving the park soon. Otherwise, you'll get stuck sitting in here until the storm blows over."

"Thanks for the advice," Cassie said with a smile Cal now knew to be fake.

"You need anything, I'll be here." Josh walked around them and took a sharp turn to the right. After a few steps, the greenery closed in around him.

Something about the agent's actions and demeanor made Cal's neck itch. Something unrelated to his drooling over Cassie. The guy had a habit of being where he shouldn't be. He popped up at the police station. Now he was out running around an isolated part of the canyon. None of it made sense.

Cassie tore her gaze away from Josh's retreating figure. "He acts like he's on the Kauai welcoming committee."

"I'd prefer to read that brochure you were talking about."

Her head snapped around at his tone. "And what's

wrong with you? Besides the obvious lack of social skills, I mean."

"I don't like that guy." Certainly didn't like the way Josh looked at Cassie. Her looking back pissed him off, too.

"He has an agenda—"

"No kidding."

"—but he seems harmless enough."

Women. "You think a guy who looks like him can't be a bad guy?"

She gave him a you-need-meds look. "I think our rough flight knocked some wiring loose in your brain."

Definitely. That was the only explanation for the surge of anger that hit him when he saw Cassie smile at the agent. He had no reason or right to be jealous. She could flirt with any man.

He would let the conversation drop . . .

But then something inside him wound even tighter and his mouth began spewing before his mind could catch up. "See, that's the problem with women."

Cassie's eyebrow inched up. "Do tell."

"You never know how to distinguish the good guys from the bad. Then when a guy you thought was worth something turns out to be a complete ass, you blame all men. You tag us all as abusive losers." He shook his head in disgust. "It's predictable."

She leaned back against a large boulder and crossed her arms over her waist. "Any other observations you'd like to make?"

"Oh, I have more."

"I had so hoped," she said with an equal load of sarcasm.

"Maybe if women spent a little less time flirting . . ." Cal realized where that conversation would lead and stopped. "Never mind."

He stalked back to his abandoned backpack and scooped it off the ground. The conversation had gone so far off track that he did not even know where it had started anymore.

He looked back over his shoulder at her. "You coming?"

"Depends. Are you done dispensing your misguided, macho crap advice?"

"It's not—"

She did that toe-tapping thing again. He hated the toe-tapping thing.

She stared him down. "Look, I know you're used to giving orders, Lieutenant Colonel Caleb Wilson. I'm cutting you some slack for that, but I have my limits."

What the hell was he supposed to say to that? "Uh, okay."

"But the me-Tarzan-you-my-property act needs to end."

He could pretend not to understand her point, but he did. She wasn't the first woman to comment on this part of his personality. He had a tendency to take charge. It came with the career. The nature of rescue required quick thinking and total command.

But he learned the importance of structure long before joining the Air Force. He grew up in a house out of control. He took over the parenting roles as to his sister when his parents were too busy waging war to do it. Once his life went in that direction, it never wavered, and that was fine with him.

"So we're just going to stand here?" he asked.

"Depends. Are you going to continue to piss me off?"

"Probably."

She sighed as she pushed away from the rocks. "Then we might as well go."

"You sound so excited about the idea."

"I can barely contain my glee."

"Did you just use the word *glee*?"

She matched her pace to his. "Forget that. Tell me about this problem you have with Josh."

"Didn't we just go over this?"

"I have no idea what we just talked about."

She had a point. The past few minutes were more about him wrestling with his attraction for her than about anything she did. "Josh didn't ask any questions."

"Meaning?"

"We're in the middle of the canyon without a guide or any equipment, and he doesn't ask how we got here? If we have water? Offer directions?"

"I think you're stretching with that." She watched her feet, hesitating before each step on the loose dirt and rocks.

"Okay, how about this? Why is a guy who tracks drug deals part of the time and spends the other part behind a desk doing paperwork out walking around in his suit in the middle of the afternoon?"

"I can see your point. And his hiking explanation is crap. No way could he handle that rough trail dressed like that, which means there's another way in here, the liar."

"No kidding. Now stop talking about the agent." When part of the trail tumbled and Cal's foot slid, she grabbed his arm to steady him.

"Okay there, flyboy?"

It was a strange sensation being on the receiving end of a rescue. New and a bit unsettling. Kind of knocked the cockiness right out of him for a second, which he assumed was her goal.

He cleared his throat in an effort to clear his head. "We should double-time it to the crash site because Josh might be right about one thing."

"What's that?"

Cal pointed up the canyon to the gray clouds rolling in. "A storm is on the way."

Josh swiped the beading sweat off his face with his forearm. The damn suit was a nuisance. He wished he could work in casual clothes like Ted did because, despite the wind, the sun beating down turned his navy jacket damn hot.

Surveying the rich landscape of rocks and trees, Josh decided he would rather be back in an air-conditioned room. But this crusade by Cal and Cassie made relaxation impossible. Thanks to their nagging interference, he had a huge problem.

He walked the short distance to the edge of the overgrown and mostly unknown dirt road access used by rangers to get in to this end of the park.

Ted sat in the Jeep with the window down listening to the radio. "Have fun out there?"

"Not really."

"Cassie is not going to stop looking into this." Ted reached out to turn the music down.

Josh balanced his hand on the window and ducked his head to see Ted. "I know."

"Can you tell what they're doing?"

"Getting in the way."

"Any chance you can convince them to find another hobby? Preferably one on Maui. Hell, on any island but this one."

"They're determined." The sweltering heat made Josh's shirt stick to his skin.

"We've got to figure out a way. If these two walk into the wrong place again—"

"I know." Josh wiped a hand through his hair. The entire scheme was getting too complicated. He had not counted on all of these outside interruptions.

Ted leaned back against the headrest. "I don't want to lose anyone else."

"Makes two of us. And I'm worried that they'll start asking the wrong people the right questions and blow everything."

"And end up like Dan?"

"That, too."

Chapter Twelve

It took another half hour for Cassie and Cal to reach their destination, as unimpressive as that destination turned out to be. Thirty minutes of sliding downhill, squabbling, and Cassie hated to admit it, ogling.

The one benefit of following behind Cal on this ridiculous romp through the dragging heat was the view. She could wipe her mind clean, forget everything else including the real reason for the terrible hike, and focus on his impressive butt.

"This must be it," he said.

Cassie's head shot up just as she smacked into Cal's expansive back. "Sorry."

"Lost in thought?"

From the knowing smile on his face she wondered if she had extolled his body's virtues out loud. "Something like that."

"The site is down there," Cal said. "You can see the yellow police tape outlining the general area. It's been knocked down in most places, likely by the wind, but the footprints start right about here."

Cassie's heart withered. She actually felt it deflate inside her. "Don't forget the scorched earth."

A deep pit, burned black, marred the landscape where

the helicopter had crashed to the ground. The resulting fire singed the few trees in the area and marked a crude circle around the hole and up the incline to where they stood.

"I was trying to be respectful," he said in a low, almost reverent, voice.

She appreciated the gesture, but gentle words could not soften the reality of the violent death that had occurred here. To her, the area constituted sacred ground.

She tried to separate her emotions and concentrate on the investigation. To ignore the waves of sadness and concentrate on cold facts. Having Cal turn all soft and mushy would not help that plan one bit. She needed his scowling seriousness right now.

"This is about as close as I got last time. How do we get the rest of the way?" she asked.

"Slide."

"Please be kidding."

He lifted one eyebrow. "Believe it or not, I am not known for my sense of humor."

Cal delivered the comment in such a deadpan tone that Cassie had to chuckle. When he started down the slope, she followed his lead. After all, this was the guy with all the training.

They angled their bodies, dragging their feet along the loose rocks and dried underbrush, slowing the rapid descent by touching their palms against the dry ground. Cal whistled, proving the damn man enjoyed every minute of the treacherous slide.

After a few minutes, they landed in the middle of the site and immediately went to work. Searching in silence, they covered the general area, picking up and discarding useless scraps of paper and material.

"This is hopeless." She crouched down, inspecting the ground and muttering more to the dirt than to Cal.

"That's not the woman I know."

His wording caught her attention. She glanced over at him a few feet away. "Do we know each other?"

"I know the basics."

"Which are?"

"You're smart, loyal."

She drew figures in the dirt to keep her finger busy. "You make me sound like a puppy."

He shrugged. "But a cute puppy."

Only Cal could deliver squishy lines like that and make them sound real. "Might want to watch out for my bite."

"You're also bossy and grumpy."

"So, you're done with the compliments?"

He dropped the rock he was holding. "You're human, Cassie. Imperfect and complex. Interesting and attractive in more than a physical way."

She held his heated gaze until looking at him became uncomfortable. Well, uncomfortable for her. His sexy smile suggested he was just fine with whatever kept zinging between them. That made one of them.

She tried to ride the emotions whipping through her, one minute experiencing growing feelings for Cal and the other being ashamed of having thoughts about anything other than Dan's death. He died here. In a horrifying ball of fire, right on this site. He deserved her full attention.

She gave herself a mental shake and dug back into work. The task wasn't easy. Almost all evidence of the crash had been removed. Finding anything new or relevant would be difficult at best.

After another fifteen minutes, after turning over every rock only to find more rocks, Cassie was on the verge of giving up. Her feet burned. Her hair was plastered to her head. She needed a warm shower and an even bigger bottle of wine. Cheap or expensive, it didn't matter.

"Here we go." Cal made the statement as he stood at the base of a tree looking up into the branches.

Cassie walked over and stared up, her movements mimicking his. She had no idea what they were supposed to be seeing. Darkening clouds hid the bright sunshine, and the subtle smell of burning wood lingered in the air.

Maybe it was some kind of ecology lesson. "Well, it's a very nice tree, or it was before most of it caught fire."

Cal slowly turned his head and glared down at her as if she had lost her mind. "You don't see it?"

Didn't she just say she did? "The tree?"

"I'm talking about the bag."

She squinted, trying to focus on what was left of the top of the tree. "There's a bag up there?"

"What did you think I was talking about?"

"No idea." Which was not unusual.

"If you see something, go get it." She pointed into the tree to prove her point.

"Yes, ma'am." He dropped his pack and wiped his hands on his pants.

From a standing position, he pulled his arms back and jumped up, catching the lowest branch dangling about nine feet off the ground. After a few seconds, he disappeared up and into what was left of the tree.

Cassie decided right then to find out whatever the Air Force fed its boys and buy some of it. Aerobics like that were impressive, especially in energy-zapping heat.

"Do you have it?" she asked even though she still didn't know what the "it" was.

He didn't answer, but a ripped canvas laptop case dropped at her feet.

"I guess that's a yes," she mumbled.

"Is this where I say 'I told you so'?" he yelled down from the burned-out top of the tree.

"Not if you want to live." She kneeled down to investigate just as Cal jumped to the ground next to her.

"Is it Dan's?"

"If it is, about half of it's missing." Part of the bag was torn, its edges ripped and frayed. If a computer had been in there at one time, it was gone now.

Cassie slipped her hand into a ripped side pocket and grabbed the tattered papers crumpled inside. "What the hell?"

"Looks like we found something."

Gray clouds continued to roll overhead and rumbles of thunder echoed in the distance. "Well, look fast. The weather is turning and we need to get moving."

Cal looked up and his scowl grew as dark as the sky. "Damn. We need to find shelter."

She thought about punching him. "Didn't I just say that?"

"I mean now, Cassie. We're about to get hit by one hell of a storm. We'll be drenched in a few minutes and these papers will be useless."

Her stomach flipped. "Can we make it back to the helicopter?"

"No way." He shoved all the papers into the bag and tucked it under his arm, leaving some to stick out and others to fall to the ground.

She grabbed the dropped papers and shoved them into her pocket. "What are we going to do?"

"Move."

Before she could protest, he took her hand and started tugging her behind him as he traveled back up the hill. So much for his attempts to be less bossy.

"Cal." She pulled back on her arm to throw him off balance.

"What are—"

"We need to go the other way."

"Why?"

She remembered the area from her last trip. Part of how she got control over her tears that time was to focus on the landscape and memorize every detail of the place where her brother died. "There's a small inlet about twenty feet down."

His resistance faded and the tug-of-war between them stopped. "Can we fit inside?"

"I didn't take that close of a look."

"That's not very comforting."

"Well, Mr. Difficult. Do you have another idea?"

He nodded as if warming to the idea. "It's worth a try."

She refused to let him off the hook that easily. "And then there's the part where we don't have a choice."

They turned and started down the canyon wall. This time instead of fighting, her hand slipped into his. Working together, they fell into a steady rhythm. The worn soles of her sneakers slipped across the rocks and rubble as she fought to keep her balance, but his hands held her steady.

Seeing became more difficult as black clouds filled the sky. She feared they were two seconds too late. "The storm is blowing in too fast."

"It's going to be tight." Pebbles rained down as he rushed them down the steep decline.

She stopped watching her feet and peered over his shoulder to gage the distance to potential safety. A vertical drop loomed in front of them. All she saw was Cal and miles of dirt and trees in front of him in a sixty-degree slope to the base of the canyon. This wasn't her worst nightmare, flying to the site claimed that award, but this was close.

"Did you see another place higher up? Maybe one that doesn't involve scooting down a mountain?" she asked.

He flashed her a bright smile. "You tired of being in charge already?"

"It's a thankless job, far as I can tell."

"Come on, it's too early to admit defeat."

She was not sure that was true. She was seconds away from waving the white flag. "You sure?"

"Move that impressive butt of yours. We only have a few minutes."

The childish comment should have pissed her off. Instead she felt a wave of giddy relief. Probably the same sensation all victims of tragic accidents feel right before the end.

"Impressive, huh?" Sounded like the feeling was mutual.

He leaned back and whispered over the howling wind. "Didn't hear you. What did you say?"

Good thing. "I said a little rain won't kill us."

"Sure you did."

His wink let her know they were talking about *exactly* the same thing.

Chapter Thirteen

Cassie and Cal hit the small inlet just as the skies opened and the rain pounded down. The deluge soaked their clothing in the two steps it took to get inside.

The dark, cool, ten-foot-square area provided a refuge from the harsh storm, but imprisoned him in a new kind of hell. Concentrating with Cassie standing next to him looking the way she did was hard enough. Staying in control after her clothing turned transparent proved impossible.

Did the damn things shrink? Sure seemed that way. That top of hers looked a lot tighter than before.

"That was close," she said as she waved her arms, sending drops of water flying in every direction.

"Close would mean we missed the rain. We failed on that score." Two more seconds and he would fail on an even more important score—keeping his hands off Dan's grieving baby sister.

Cal looked away and cursed the rain. He knew the weather would turn, but he had hoped they would conduct their investigation and hike to safety before the worst hit. His timing was off.

And now Cassie was all but naked.

"Have any idea on what we can talk about?" she asked as she slipped deeper into the cave and away from the splashes of rain that kept blowing into the cave.

"No."

"You could use a little work on your charm."

He was too busy thinking about car chases and any other non-Cassie subject that popped into his head. "I'll be fine once we're out of here."

"Now's your chance to regale me with tales of your exploits."

He could think of better ways to spend time. "I thought women didn't like to hear about stuff like that."

She rolled her eyes in the disgusted way only she could do. "I meant *work* exploits."

That was a relief. "Oh."

"We could try something more basic."

He watched her sit down on the cold dirt floor. "Like math."

"Like bio stuff. Your parents. Siblings. That sort of thing."

He recognized digging when a hole appeared right in front of him. That was the only explanation for the sudden interest in his real-life story, one that was not exactly a secret to anyone who had ever read a newspaper.

"Sounds boring," he said, knowing his past was actually the opposite.

"A man's background says a lot about him."

The lining of his stomach froze. She had managed to touch on the one subject guaranteed to shut him down. "I think everyone knows enough about that."

"What does that mean?"

He studied her face. The mix of curiosity played out as he watched. She didn't know. For whatever reason, Dan had not shared that part when he retold the rest of his stories.

"My family's history is pretty well known."

She laughed. "Are you sure you're not just thinking a bit more highly of yourself than you should?"

"It's been in the papers."

She stopped laughing. "Wait. You're serious?"

To anyone else, the simple questions would not bring back a flood of bad memories. For him it was more of a nightmare than any rescue or mission he'd ever been on.

"If it's too personal, we can talk about something else." Her words came out as a whisper. One tinged with a touch of pity.

With that, she touched on the very reason he hated this subject. People feeling sorry for him. Cal despised that. He decided he'd rather get the story out on his own terms than deal with a false wave of compassion.

He leaned back against the opening of the cave. "The story has been on television. There's a book."

"They're famous?"

"Not in a good way." He blew out a long breath as he contemplated how to tell the story by only hitting the low-lights. "There's even a movie about their relationship."

"An actual movie?"

She was looking at him. He could tell from the sound of her voice. Faced him head on, likely with sympathy in her eyes.

"It was a big-money divorce. A best-selling author and a scientist." He started the story without ever glancing in her direction. "The problem was the dead mistress."

He heard her move and glanced at her. With a nod of his head, he asked her not to come any closer. "My dad's."

"Cal, I—"

And now for the worst part. "Dad insisted Mom killed the other woman. Mom insisted Dad did. Any of this sound familiar?"

Her mouth fell open. "Of course it does."

Yeah, everyone knew the scandalous parts. His mom had a huge following. The papers went wild at the idea of a murder triangle dealing with someone so public. "Some of the information got blown out of proportion, but a woman is dead. There's no good news there."

So few people knew the truth. In general, Cal didn't think it was anyone's business. He certainly didn't want to be defined by his parents' bad choices. Having a generic last name and having a guardian who insisted that a false first name be used for him in the movie helped give cover.

"I'm sorry."

He waved his hand. "Long time ago. It's over."

"Hmmm." She followed the non-word with an all-too-knowing look.

"What?"

"Nothing."

Oh, there was something. He could feel it but he did not have to play into it. He let two full minutes pass with no noise but the sharp rain and wind outside.

Then he cracked.

"It's been twenty-five years, Cassie."

"But it still impacts your life."

"Well, sure. Stuff like that doesn't make sense to a kid." Hell, it didn't make sense to him as a grown-up, either.

"I mean that it affects how you deal with women."

Here we go. "Did you get a psychology degree that I don't know about?"

She propped her chin on top of her knees. "It doesn't take a genius to figure out the fact your mother is in jail—"

"Was. She got out on appeal."

"She did?" Cassie shook her head and raced on before he could talk. "Well, it doesn't matter. What happened played a role in how you see women."

"I like women just fine."

"Hmmm."

He wasn't touching that sound a second time. The first time took him on a journey into his love life. Yeah, no thanks. But now she knew his secret. There were others, but one of the big ones was out there.

She didn't seem repulsed. Also managed to keep the blame where it belonged—on his parents. He never accepted the idea of the catastrophe being his fault. His sister struggled with that. Not him. He put his energy elsewhere.

When quiet descended in the cave again, he turned to the noise outside. Ominous clouds raced up the valley as if someone had hit the FAST FORWARD button. He tried to imagine any poor bastard out on a boat in the middle of the ocean right now. Being in a cave was bad enough.

Cal knew from being stationed in Hawaii years earlier that when a storm settled on this part of Kauai, it hovered. In a matter of minutes, the sun disappeared and the wind kicked into full speed.

Their cover consisted of little more than a recess carved into the rocks. A slight overhang protected them from the worst of the rain. They would stay dry, but true comfort was not an option.

Then again, he had not experienced a moment of peace and calm since he met Cassie. The woman had his stomach tied in knots and his groin begging for relief. If the near monsoon didn't let up quickly, he might crawl up the canyon walls, digging out with his bare hands, to get away from the temptation presented here.

"Does watching the rain help?" she asked.

Help what? was the question. "It looks like we're stuck for a while."

"At least we're not outside."

Yeah, because being alone in a cave with her was a better solution.

He glanced over his shoulder. She sat hunched in the far corner, her upper body curled over her bent knees. In the fading light, he could see she was trembling. The sexy shorts and thin T-shirt that distracted him during their hike and kept her cool despite the sun's heat proved even less practical now.

He beat back the erotic images floating through his mind. Mental photographs emerged of skimpy wet clothing clinging to her trim frame, followed by visions of the same clothing strewn all over the cave floor. Cassie naked and backlit by the fierce storm.

Jesus, he was in trouble.

"You need to get out of those clothes." He had no idea when the words formed in his head or how they escaped his mouth.

They must have surprised her, too, since her head shot up and a sharp gaze pinned him where he stood. "I'm fine."

That made one of them. "This is serious, Cassie."

"No, it's not."

"We could be here for a long time."

"So?"

He knew many ways to talk a woman out of her clothes to get her into bed. Doing so for practical reasons clearly was not his strength. "You'll get sick."

"Figures you'd think about that now. After I'm drenched."

He tried the less controlling route. "How about you slip out of those before you get cold."

A smile crept across her lips. "Are you trying to sweet-talk me out of my clothes, flyboy?"

He had no idea what he was trying to do, except engage in a bit of self-torture. "I'm only trying to help."

"How?"

How? "Huh?"

She leaned back, opening up her body to his view and balancing her upper body on her hands. "How would you help?"

What the hell was happening? "You need to get dry and warm."

"You have any suggestions how I do that?"

Lots of them. They all involved her being naked and strapped to him. He could see the entire scene unfold in his head. Their positions changed, but the results stayed the same. He was making love to her, slipping deep inside her as the storm raged around them outside.

Cal closed his eyes, trying to block out the sexual fantasy spinning through his mind. Instead, the mental pictures seared right onto his brain, gnawing at him to abandon his control and take her.

Imagining her sexy body, all pink and ready, made him groan. To keep Cassie from seeing his growing erection, he turned his back and faced out into the storm. With his arms stretched above his head and his fingers digging into the cold rock, he watched the driving rain wash away layers of dirt around the canyon.

The evidence of how much he wanted her pressed against his zipper. His skin itched as if begging to get his clothes off.

He was in hell.

He tried to think of something witty to say, but his tongue jammed his throat closed. When words failed, he tried reciting the alphabet to gain his composure. He never got past the second letter, whatever the hell it was. He couldn't remember.

Chapter Fourteen

Cassie noticed the look on Cal's face right before he turned. Kind of a mixture of shock and desire. Then there was that green cast around his mouth. Cal was waging some kind of internal battle.

She had lost hers.

He might be the wrong man, but this was the right time. For all his faults and annoying behaviors, she wanted him. Knowing his background and how he rose above it appealed to her on a very basic level. Controlling behavior and all, he had her attention.

His strength. His loyalty to Dan. His willingness to fly across the country to help out without having any real information. On an emotional level, the guy was rock solid.

On a feminine level, his body and face made her throw away her anti-flyboy rules.

She chalked the desire up to the adrenaline-fueled haze of the past few days. She'd been so low and desperate after hearing the news about Dan. They lived an island hop apart and still saw each other rarely. The brother she admired and worshipped from her youth continued to fascinate her into adulthood. Now he was dead and all she could do for him was clear his name. She'd been shot at, had her insides shaken up in the helicopter ride from hell, and was now hiding out from what felt like a hurricane.

Not that she was being dramatic or anything. Whatever the reason was for her feelings, the result was the same. She. Wanted. Cal.

She could analyze it and turn it over a thousand times, but nothing would change. Even though she knew waiting would be smart, she wasn't in the mood to do the smart thing. Not this time.

"What about you?" he asked in a strangled voice.

"No movies in my family."

He shot her a smile over his shoulder. "How boring."

"I think I preferred it that way."

"True." This time he turned around. One arm stretched across the cave's opening, blocking out most of the view of the unleashing outside. "So, who is Cassie?"

"What you see is what you get."

"That's rarely how it works."

"It is with me. There's nothing very exciting to tell. I was the good kid. Dan took chances. I stayed at home and studied." She did everything everyone expected her to do. She set a perfect path and never strayed.

"Nothing inappropriate? Shoplifting, drinking, hell-raising?"

"No, no, and no."

"What about that pilot? What happened there?"

Her inclination was to lash out and ask him about all of his women. That would put an immediate halt to this line of conversation. But he had shared something painful. Seemed only fair she open up a bit, too.

"Han."

"What the hell is a han?"

"Han is his name. Hanford Rodman the third." She couldn't say it without sneering, so she didn't try.

"That name didn't give you a hint he was a dick before you went out with him?" Cal shook his head. "This is what I was talking about earlier."

"Please spare me a reprise of your theory on women."

"I'm not wrong."

"Besides, he didn't pick the name."

"His parents took one look at him in the hospital, hated him, and stuck him with it. They knew he was a dick from birth."

"I didn't say Han was a . . ." When Cal raised his eyebrows, she conceded. "Okay, he was."

"What a shock."

She could stop there. Just retreat to a safer topic. Instead, she pushed forward. For some reason she wanted to tell Cal about her life. "His name wasn't the worst part about him."

He snorted. "Hard to believe since that's pretty damn bad."

"He fooled around." There, she said it. She never even gave Dan the details about the end of her relationship.

"He cheated?"

She decided the rest of the story would work better if she stared at the dirt, so she tried that. "He had a complete inability to keep his zipper up and hands to himself."

Cal's mouth twisted in distaste. "Like I said, a complete dick."

"A guy's guy."

"Wrong. No matter what women think, a real man doesn't have to prove his masculinity by sleeping around."

The guy was rock solid. She had prejudged him as a typical flyboy. How wrong she was.

Now that she had lost everyone in her life—her parents, brother, and the man she thought would play the starring role in her future—she wondered if taking the safe route made sense. What had following the rules gotten her? She had outward stability, a job as a graphic artist that paid the bills, and . . . well, nothing else, really.

Just this once she wanted to take a walk on the naughty side. To do something she wanted without thinking about where her choices would take her or how they fit into her life plan. Being with Cal made sense. They were attracted to each other. He intrigued her. The sexual tension between them sizzled.

A steady roll of thunder echoed in the distance. The wind carried the scent of tropical flowers. They were alone and stuck in a dirt hole in the wall with wet clothes and not so much as a dry washcloth in sight. They were young and able and more than willing. There would never be a better time. There would never be a more electric setting.

Hell, even Kauai wanted them together. It was as if nature and need collided to provide her with the answer to what she should do next.

"How do you do that?" she asked.

"What?"

She stared up at him, seeing all of him for the first time. "Make me forget about all the horrible things happening in my life right now."

"You deserve to think of something else."

"What if all I'm thinking about is you?"

The irritating and immediate pull stretching between them interfered with their goal of finding Dan's killer. The stray thoughts pulled them off message and filled her head with nonsense when she needed to concentrate on the reason her brother died at the bottom of a canyon.

"Then I'd consider my work a success."

A wall of heat slammed into her, pushing out the chill. "We have nothing in common."

"True."

"We don't even like each other."

"You're growing on me."

The idea of being with him kept getting better. If they gave in, exorcised those demons, they could move ahead and focus on Dan's death. An unhealthy dose of adrenaline and the informal investigation into Dan's shocking death carried her through the weeks of loneliness and sadness.

Now she wanted to feel something. To savor a man's touch without worrying about whether he would leave or cheat. Being with Cal would give her that. They did not expect anything from each other. She could fall into the sensations without thinking. That was what she needed.

A crack of thunder drew his attention outside. The distraction worked on her side. She scrambled to her feet and started across the small area to where he stood so still.

He did not turn around to face her, did not act as if he even heard her, but his shoulders tensed as she approached. He was aware of her, even if he was trying hard not to show it.

She vowed to hold nothing back. "Cal?"

"Hmmm." His body was rigid.

"Is the storm dying down?"

"No."

She stopped behind him until only inches separated their bodies and pressed her chest against his back. The sound of his sharp intake of breath was the green light she needed. The urge to touch him, to tour her fingertips over every inch of his body, overwhelmed her. She did not fight it.

Her palms grazed his shoulder blades, outlining every muscle and hollow before traveling down his back. And she was not the only one enjoying the tactile tour. His breath rushed out as she slid her hands around his trim waist and hugged his heated body close to hers. His body heat soaked through his wet clothes to touch her skin.

Their bodies met from chest to thigh, every inch of him against every inch of her. Still, the contact was not enough. She brushed her lips against the soft hair at the base of his neck as a fevered need raced through her. A rush of pure desire took over until she grew dizzy.

This made sense. This was right. Despite the pain and loss, the well inside her no longer remained empty. Something in him flowed through her, filling her. Spoke to her feminine core in a way that restored some of that power she thought she had lost when everything was taken away from her.

He whispered her name.

The soft, husky sound vibrated against her cheek and traveled down to her toes, awakening all those cells she feared had shriveled and died.

But she felt very much alive. Inhaling, she drew in a mixed scent of exotic flowers crushed by the rain and musky male in front of her.

She dropped a line of kisses along the top of his shoulder. He rewarded the gentle torment by dropping his head on her shoulder and rubbed their cheeks together in a gesture so sweet, she lost her breath.

"Cassie," he whispered as if he were dreaming of her.

"Yes . . ."

The muscles pulling across his midsection jumped as she swept her hands lower over his sensitive skin. Her fingers traveled up and inside his damp shirt to caress him. Nothing but tight, hot skin.

"Be sure, because I won't fight this." His command echoed through the muggy afternoon.

"Yes."

His fingers threaded through hers, trapping them against his flat belly. "Damn."

Desire rumbled through her, shutting out the storm. "Come inside with me."

"We probably shouldn't."

That was no longer the right answer. "But we are."

Chapter Fifteen

Cal knew it would be hours and not days before he'd regret this move. Finding willing bed partners had never been a problem for him. He never paid much attention to his looks except to keep his body in shape, but he was not clueless to his appeal.

Some women even thrived on doing military men. They offered. If he was interested, he accepted. He was a guy after all.

But this was different. *She* was different. This would mean something. She was his friend's baby sister. Worse, she was his *former* friend's baby sister. The "former" part made all the difference.

Sleeping with a smart, sexy woman worked for him. The idea of being with Cassie had his lower half begging for mercy. She was beautiful and available and sending every signal a woman could send to let a man know he should make a move. He just wondered if she would do the same thing if she had all the information, knew the facts about him.

If they both knew the score, he would go under without thinking. Take his shirt off, strip off her shorts, and never look back. Separate his head from his dick and keep them that way.

"I can hear you thinking," she said with a chuckle against his shoulder.

"Hard to do anything with the upper part of my body when you're using those fingers of yours." He tightened his hold on her to keep her from backing away.

Talk about sending mixed signals. He won that award at the moment. He should have let go. Should have, at the very least, told her the truth. Let her make the decision to do this based on all the facts.

That is what a decent man would do. He knew in that second he was nowhere near the kind of man he thought he was because he had no intention of stopping. Instead, he guided her hands over his skin. Let her fingers learn every inch of his bare chest.

With each stroke, his resolve crumbled a little more. "Cassie—"

"You feel so good." Her whisper carried through the cave, drowning out the roar of the storm outside and the faint words of warning in his head.

One final time. "This is your last chance to turn away."

He said it and meant it. If she showed an ounce of interest after this, he would not hold back. Forget the intellectual arguments and the guilt that would eventually come, he was going to do it. She was a big girl. She could make up her mind and didn't need him to protect her. Not about this.

Her hands traveled south, landing on his belt buckle. "I want you."

There it was. The permission slip delivered with her fingers. "Thank God."

No more warnings. She was offering. He was taking.

With a slight bit of pressure, he guided his hands where he wanted them to go. Even lower. She took the hint. Her fingers toured the waistband of his snug jeans and lingered there. Without any additional moves from him, she traced the bulge growing just below, brushing her hand back and forth until he had to bite his lip to keep from chanting her name.

"Damn, baby." That was as much as he could force out.

Her hands wandered over every inch of him as if soaking in his heat and learning his shape. She lowered his zipper, and he spun around to meet her face to face.

He brushed his knuckles across her cheek, savoring the feel of soft skin. The gentle touch contrasted with the insistent press of his erection against her hip.

When he lowered his head, she did not pull back. Instead, she met him halfway, bringing her mouth to a kiss so hot and tantalizing that he wondered why he had skipped the step until now.

Cassie wanted to say something profound, but she didn't trust her voice to carry any sound. Rather than talk, she fell into the moment.

Pleasure screamed through her as he scooped her up high in those amazing arms. She'd never really been one to buy into the overly romantic notion of being swept off her feet. It sounded too much like being rescued. But she could not deny the soothing sense of security that came from being so close that she could smell and taste him. The heat of his body warmed hers as he walked toward the back of the dimly lit cave.

Then he took her mouth again. This kiss went beyond testing and tasting. This one claimed.

In that moment, despite her independent nature, she wanted to give over a piece of herself to see what he would do with it. To cede some small measure of control and let whatever was meant to happen just happen.

Before she could fall full and complete into the burning kiss, the dark ceiling spun over her head. He lowered her to the hard ground and covered her body with his. Frantic hands tore at her clothing, pushing and pulling until her T-shirt bunched under her chin and her bra slipped down, exposing her breasts to his eager tongue.

A shot of humid air hit her skin right before his hot mouth settled over her. As his tongue danced across her skin, his fingertips brought her other nipple to puckered attention. He sucked and licked until her back arched off the floor and her heels dug into the dirt.

She got so lost in the sensations, of having every thought except those of him blocked, she nearly forgot to touch him. What a waste. When her hands found his back again, she reveled in his taut muscles. In the way tension thrummed off of him as he balanced his body on elbows above her.

He pushed up on his knees, his mouth breaking contact with her body for the short time it took to rip off his shirt. When he came down again, his chest was bare and his pants were unbuckled.

But she only saw his body for a flash. She wanted to look until she grew tired of the sight of his perfectly fit body, if that was even possible, but his mouth covered hers. Any thought of appreciating or talking or anything else dissolved into a pile of nothing. All that mattered was their mouths as they touched and their hands as they explored.

She lifted her hips, silently begging him to remove the rest of her clothes. She wanted them off. All off until nothing separated them.

Instead, he began to move. His mouth traveled down her body and over her collarbone while her hands roamed over her breasts. After his lips touched every part of her shoulders and upper arms, he slipped to her breasts to join his fingers.

He kept kissing and caressing until her heart thudded loud enough for her to hear the blood rush in and out, then her eyes fell closed. Then he went even lower, pressing a line of wet kisses in a burning path to her stomach. Her skin tingled with a sensation she could not define.

Air rushed into her lungs and squeezed back out every time he touched his mouth to her waiting flesh. Rough fingertips skimmed up her shorts. His eyes locked on hers as his thumb brushed against her growing dampness. Through her conservative cotton underwear he rubbed back and forth until her legs fell open to give him greater access.

A whimper escaped her lips as he bent to kiss her through her shorts. She glanced down, seeing his broad shoulder balanced between her thighs. When his other hand joined the first, with fingers in turn pressing into her and rubbing over her most intimate spot, the breath she had been holding shot out of her with a moan.

"Take them off." She wanted to scream the order but only had the breath to mumble.

He settled his heated body between her raised legs and reached for her zipper, lowering it with agonizing slowness.

"Cal. Please."

He punished her by rubbing his cheek against the flesh of her thigh. "Not yet."

After an eternity, he spread the zipper wide. Reaching inside, he stripped the material, panties and all, down her legs in one sweep. And he didn't wait one more second. He pressed a hard kiss on her bare flesh. No panties. No hair. Just lips against skin.

She needed this. A man who knew what to do with a woman's body could wipe away all the doubts and bad memories. Cal was that man. Those fingers, that mouth. He knew his way around a woman.

"Every part of you is pretty." He whispered the compliment against her shaved mound.

She should have been embarrassed or at least a bit uncomfortable at having him see her like this after such a short time. Hell, she knew almost nothing about the guy. Certainly not a thing about what he had been doing since he lost touch with Dan.

But the rational thoughts refused to stick in her head. She would worry and blush later. Right now she wanted him to explore every inch or her . . . and then do it again.

"Some parts don't see a lot of sunshine," she said.

He traced his fingers over her until her legs opened even wider in reaction. "This should."

"I think there are laws against that."

"Now that's a shame."

He dipped his head and licked her, his tongue slipping deep inside. Something inside her lower body clamped down. She could feel the tension tightening and spiraling.

His body stiffened along with hers. His muscles clenched as if he were trying to hold back and make it last for her. Cassie appreciated the gesture, but she wanted him inside her. Now.

His hands pinned her legs open as he kissed and licked, making her more and more desperate to relieve whatever kept ramping up inside her. She broke down and begged him to enter her, but he continued to focus on her sensitized flesh until the sensation traveling through her rocked one final time.

Her body bucked as she gasped, fighting for air to beat back the orgasm ripping through her. Her legs stiffened. Her hips rose off the ground. It was another minute before the convulsions churning through her subsided.

When he slowly climbed back up her body, every nerve ending tingled. "Beautiful woman."

She answered when her breathing returned to normal. "Talented man."

She gave in to the urge to brush her hand over his cheek.

She wanted to know the feel of him. She had heard him shoot off one-liners and sexist remarks. She wanted to know the feel of him at this type of moment.

He chuckled. "You know what?"

"I can't actually think now."

He dipped his head and touched his lips to her mouth in a gentle kiss. "It's my turn."

She thought about apologizing but refused to feel sorry for what just happened, even if she was a tad selfish. Instead, she folded her arms around his neck and brought his face back down for another kiss.

When they broke apart, she dropped her head back against the hard cold floor to catch her breath. "I'm still here."

He didn't answer. Instead, with a need that bordered on urgent, his hands swept down her body to her hips.

"Wallet."

Not exactly the comment she expected. "What?"

"Condom."

Reality smacked her. Protection. She had not even considered that. For the first time in her life, she did not take care to guard her health.

"I didn't—"

"Doesn't matter." He kissed his way across her chin. "In the wallet."

Wasn't he the prepared one?

Rather than dwell on what the condom meant or why he thought he would need one when breaking into a house, she stayed in the moment. She vowed to hold off on all analyzing and dissecting until later. Nothing had changed on that.

Her fingers slipped into his back pocket. She must have been going too slowly because he reached out and grabbed the wallet. One minute it was in her hand; the next it was between his teeth while he dug out the packet with his forefinger.

Two seconds later he threw the wallet, letting it land in a puff of dirt and sand. "I can't wait."

"Don't."

With an arm wrapped around her waist, he rolled over and slid his body beneath hers. The move surprised her. She didn't even know there had been stones digging into her back until they weren't anymore.

"You get the comfortable position this time." He lifted his hips to slide down his pants. The underwear stayed on.

Which was good since she wanted to take care of that for him. "And people say chivalry is dead."

He tried to talk but pressed his head into the floor and closed his eyes instead.

The sudden quiet scared her. "Cal—"

"I'm not going to make it much longer."

"Poor baby."

"I'm willing to beg you."

No need. Instead of answering, she let her fingers give her response. She slipped them inside the waistband of his underwear and watched his eyes pop back open.

With bold strokes, she pumped her hand up and down. His warmth, that incredible hardness, filled her hand. Like every other part of his body, his erection exceeded her expectations. He was long and full. She had her share of partners, less than most but enough to know every single part of Cal was impressive.

His groan lasted for about eight syllables. "Yes, baby."

"Now I have your attention." She pushed up on her knees and tugged his briefs down.

"You had it since before we walked into this cave."

If she hadn't believed his words, she would have believed that piercing gaze. He was holding nothing back. So she paid him back in kind. She tore open the condom and rolled it down over him.

Gone was his patient touch. His hands settled on her hips. He lifted then lowered her on top of him. First the tip slipped inside her. As she adjusted, he squirmed. She could feel his butt clench as he held back from plunging inside.

So she took over.

With a deep inhale, she inched her way down on top of him. The touch of his body sent a second shock of tremors running through her. She ignored the sensation and kept pressing. Her speed must have been too slow since he wound his arms around her with his hands landing on her bare bottom. The pressure brought her body fully down on top of him in such a swift and powerful move that she gasped.

She shifted her hips, going up and down in a beat that matched the racing of her heart. A groan echoed in her ears as her body began to shudder. She strained to keep her eyes open, to focus on his beautiful face as he found satisfaction, but her body splintered and the tremors rocketed through her a second time.

The last thing she remembered was the sound of her name bouncing off the walls as he shouted.

Chapter Sixteen

He was a dead man.

Cal lay there in the dank cave, pants at his ankles and Cassie tucked under his arm. With her hand trapped beneath his back, he tried to figure out when he had become *that* guy. The one who took advantage of every situation to sleep with a woman no matter how risky the outcome.

He jumped on a plane and flew across the country to find Dan. Hearing from him after all these years had given him hope they could hash out the past and move on. Dan's death put an end to that goal. Now Cal had to find out what happened to the helicopter while he figured out who kept using Cassie for target practice.

All of that investigation required he ignore one simple thing—the blinding chemistry he shared with Cassie. The reality arose not out of some noble desire to protect his friend's sister. No, he needed to stay away from her because she didn't really know the truth about her brother. Worse, about him.

It was like having sex under false pretenses. The sharp reality took some of the fun out of the post-sex moment. Apparently even he had his limits, which was good to know.

The police had their theories about Dan and his failures in the cockpit that day almost a month ago. To Cassie,

Deputy Greene's opinion branded him as the enemy. She refused to believe he could be right or that Dan could have played a role in his own demise.

Cal knew another piece of information, one that tended to corroborate Ted's theory of the events. While Cal didn't believe the official accident story, he did have some insight into Dan's flying past that made the police talk more feasible. About a previous time when Dan's reckless behavior cost the Air Force a multimillion-dollar plane. Nearly cost two men their lives.

But that wasn't the worst. How did he explain to Cassie he was the one who put Dan on the path that eventually killed him? She would hate him and he couldn't really blame her. Somehow, still, the never-was and never-would-be thoughts filled him with an odd sense of loss.

Cassie pushed against his shoulders with her palm. "Cal?"

He looked down into her sleepy eyes. "You okay?"

"Squished."

"And women say men lack a sense of romance."

"You weigh a ton." She wiggled her fingers.

Since those fingers were lodged in the small of his back, he felt every movement right down his spine. "Shit. Sorry."

He lifted his midsection and butt off the ground so she could pull her arm out. He did not let go of the rest of her. Their bodies remained locked and their legs tangled together.

"Are you going to sleep?" he asked.

She balanced her chin on his chest and glanced at the entrance to the cave. "Looks like it's still unfit for humans out there."

"What gave you the hint, the trees whipping around or that sound?"

"Which?"

He couldn't believe she did not hear it. "It's like there's

metal out there and the water keeps hitting it a bucket at a time."

She smiled. "Welcome to Hawaii."

"I told you I lived here before."

She snorted. "On a military base."

"Did I say that?" He pulled back to get a better view of her body as she lay sprawled all over him. "And what's wrong with living on base?"

"First, I was guessing."

"Yeah. And?"

"Nothing. Paradise costs a lot. Keeps the riffraff out."

"I'm assuming you don't work for the tourist board, or whatever it's called."

One hand moved under her chin while the other traced a pattern back and forth over his chest, her fingernails lightly scraping as she went. "Sometimes."

Cal realized he had no idea what she did or what she was sacrificing to be on Kauai looking for answers. "Since we're naked and stuck in the middle of nowhere, why don't you tell me what that statement means?"

"I'm a graphic designer."

As if that answered the question. "Yeah, you'll need to explain that, too."

"I design and assemble brochures, advertising promotions, and online campaigns."

She was talking about something other than poor police work and her brother's death. If she planned to share something about herself, he planned to listen. "I understand all of those words separately. Together, not so much."

She gave his skin a little pinch.

"Stop that." He smoothed his hand over hers.

"In other words, I designed the ad that the Hawaii Visitors and Convention Bureau—what you call the tourist board thing—uses to lure guys like you to the islands to spend loads of cash."

"That I get." He folded one arm under his head and watched the storm batter the ground outside. "You work for this convention thing?"

"I work for myself, which is why I can afford to be here now." She closed her eyes and stretched, letting out a tiny moan of pleasure.

She lifted her slender arm across his chest before snuggling in even closer. The whole show lasted about five seconds, but the move would run through his mind for quite a while. It was so utterly feminine and so damn sexy.

And that sly little smile playing on her mouth made him wonder if she had an ulterior motive. One that involved breaking down all of his good intentions to keep his hands in the neutral zone.

"What is going on in that pretty head of yours?" he asked when he just couldn't take the suspense any longer.

One eye popped open to gaze at him. "You are a die-hard chauvinist."

"Well, your head sure ain't ugly."

"I'll take that as a compliment. And, for the record, next time, you're on the bottom the whole time because my shoulders are bruised."

Yeah, there wouldn't be a next time. Not if he could help it . . . and he wasn't all that sure he could. "Are you okay?"

She kissed his chest. "Great."

"Did you get hurt?" He started to sit up.

She pushed him back down. "I was kidding."

He ran his hand over two scratches on her shoulder as thunder clapped outside the cave. Cal feared the bang was an ominous sign of things to come. He focused his attention on the rumbling darkness outside instead of the warm woman in his arms.

"Hey." She pushed up on her elbow. "What did I say?"

He took a deep breath and stepped right off the cliff into utter stupidity. "We have to talk."

She laughed. "That sounds like . . ."

"Cassie—"

Amusement drained from her face. "Oh hell."

"It's just that—"

This time she sat straight up, right at his side, with her shirt still pushed up against her throat. "You're going to give me the talk?"

"The what?"

"Now? Are you kidding?"

"I just suggested we take a few minutes and—"

"It was your tone. You're about to give me the you're-nice-but-this-shouldn't-happen speech." She shoved against his side. "Deny it."

Yeah, well, hard to do that when she was dead on. "This was a one-time deal."

He almost added "it shouldn't have happened" but stopped the words in time. He'd have enough to choke on later without eating a few more sentences.

"I don't believe this." She didn't even have to say that. Her wide open mouth said it for her.

He was a complete idiot. An idiot with the worst timing in the world. He hadn't even had the sense to wait for their bodies to cool before ruining the moment.

He lifted his body up on his elbows. Being flat on his back with her hovering over him seemed like a damn bad idea at the moment. "Look, it's not that it wasn't great—"

"Wait." Cassie held up a hand.

The words kept coming. "Cassie, it's just that—"

"I said, stop talking." She tugged her shirt down until her bare breasts were covered again.

Cal felt the loss like a blow to the stomach. He wasn't the obedient type by any stretch, but the murderous look in Cassie's eyes suggested he should exercise his right to remain silent. Her jaw clenched so tight he wondered if the bones would snap.

Seconds ticked by in silence. Even the storm had the sense to die down.

Cassie scowled but did not move an inch. He figured she wanted to be close enough to land a solid punch on his midsection if the mood overtook her. God knew he deserved a good hit.

Without a word or a warning, she scrambled to her knees and searched around the ground for something. Dirt kicked up as she ran her hands along the ground. Stray strands of blond hair slipped the rest of the way out of her ponytail holder and down to her shoulders.

He knew enough about women to know he would lose a limb if he reached out to her now. Despite that piece of wisdom, he felt compelled to do something. When he spied her panties, he tried to hand them to her. She ripped them from his fingers.

Before he could apologize, explain—something—she stood up and slipped her underwear up those lean legs.

Cassie loomed above him with hands on hips. Since she appeared to be about ten seconds from stomping on his balls, he sat the whole way up and reached for his pants.

"Let me get this straight." Her voice carried an icy sternness that would have made a prim schoolmistress proud. "Within seconds of getting lucky, you felt the need to set the record straight and let me know this was a meaningless one-night stand."

He refused to speak. Any word he chose now would only get him killed. He was a dumb-ass. He did not have any desire to be a dead dumb-ass.

"I didn't realize you were that guy."

Cal hated to ask but did anyway. "Which?"

"The kind who runs the second the sex is over." She pushed stray hair out of her eyes. "I'm not looking for a proposal here, but would it kill you to just enjoy the moment?"

"You're not built for short-term fun."

"You don't know a thing about me."

That's where she was wrong. After a short time, he knew plenty, including the fact she was a long-term gal.

All he had wanted was a little distance between them while he tried to figure out how to fix the mistakes he'd made in the past—this one and others. He somehow managed to put a whole damn continent in their path.

He was wrestling with enough problems without adding her to the mix. He had a long-overdue debt to pay. He also had to face the very real possibility the police got the cause of death right.

They might end up on very different sides of the final finding. Her anger now would be welcome compared to her anger then. "Cassie, I didn't mean—"

"Save it." Again with the hand. She raised it as if it had some magical force to make him stop talking.

"We're not done here."

"Yeah, we are." She slipped on her sneakers and stepped closer to the cave opening. "The storm is breaking up."

"It's still raining."

"Don't care. I'm going."

"We need to settle this first." Cal had no idea how to accomplish that deed, but he knew leaving like this was the wrong move.

She stepped outside and called back over her slim shoulder. "It's settled."

The damn woman walked right out into the rain with him stranded on the floor behind her with his pants at his ankles. "Cassie!"

When she didn't poke her head back inside, he jumped to his feet. Upset and trekking across a slick and dangerous landscape in the setting sun made her vulnerable. She could slip and fall.

He shimmied into his damp pants, jumping from foot to foot to find his balance in a rush. He scooped up what few supplies they had carried with them and Dan's backpack, and headed outside.

Maybe the slight chill moving through the air would cool her off before he reached her. He hoped but doubted he would be that lucky.

Chapter Seventeen

Cassie cursed when her foot slipped on the rock embankment for the fifth time. Her previously damp clothes were now drenched. Her chilled skin worked like a sponge. Being unable to see as her hair flipped back and forth in front of her eyes did not make the near perpendicular climb any easier.

The environment took sides against her as well. In the battle of sneakers versus earth, the dirt and rocks won without challenge. The battering rain had stopped, but the aftermath caused the dirt to pour down the sides of the canyon, cutting deep grooves into the land. Water sprang from everywhere. Thanks to gravity, it ran down when she was trying to go up.

All of that paled in comparison to the fury kicking around inside her. The sole responsibility for that fell to Cal.

She cursed, trying to fit every profane word she had ever heard into one long, venom-filled sentence. Cassie could not think of enough nasty names to call Cal or to ease the tightness forming around her heart.

She had taken a risk, let her seductive side take over, and he shut her down. Alone in a cave, miles from anyone, and he gives her a lecture about just how worthless to him was their time together. She wasn't looking for even a for-months relationship, but come on, they barely separated before he started in on his macho bullshit.

He made her furious. No one else sparked this sort of raw animal rage in her. Just Cal.

She debated racing back down the hill and heaving him into the base of the canyon. The violence of the solution appealed to her. Flyboys. They all sucked. Han started the lesson; Cal finished it.

Well if he wanted distance, he would have distance. Miles and miles of it.

"Cassie!" Cal's shout carried over the last rumbles of the storm across the canyon.

For a second Cassie thought she heard a hint of desperation in his deep voice. Then he bellowed a second time. Yeah, that would get her attention. The idiot.

Leaves crunched behind her. The wind whipped her hair around until the ponytail holder hanging on to the ends flew away. Nature worked against her on every level, but her pace never slowed. Despite the wet ground and the mist filling the air, she marched on, sliding with every step.

Somehow he made progress because he was almost on top of her. "Cassie, stop."

"More orders. What a surprise."

"You're acting crazy." Cal's rough voice vibrated in her ear as if he stood only inches behind.

"Go to hell," she mumbled, refusing to have a conversation just yet.

"It's not safe out here."

"Like the cave was safer." She snorted at the thought.

They slipped, fell back, and pushed forward against the elements for another fifteen minutes. He kept trying to talk. She kept shutting him down. Apparently ignoring the guy drove him apeshit. Good to know.

Time stretched between them. She took a few false steps that sent her sliding. When he reached out to help, she shrugged him off. The pattern continued until he broke the silence with another brilliant observation. "This is insanity."

This time she spoke up. "You need to work on your apologizing skills."

"I was trying to explain."

"That you're an idiot?" She stumbled and grabbed on to a boulder to steady her footing. "No need. I get that."

"I was trying not to be a jerk."

"Well, you failed."

Those wide eyes. The flat mouth. He had the grace to look hunted.

Good.

"It's just that you're not being very mature about this," he said after three seconds of silence.

Still the man kept fighting. Cassie marveled at his cluelessness.

"Well, you know women." She pretended to think about it. "Oh wait. That's right. You don't know a damn thing about women."

"That's becoming obvious."

She tried to walk away but only succeeded in turning sideways and jeopardizing her tenuous balance on the rocks. That was when the murmur of voices caught her attention.

"Cal." Her whisper was little more than an exhale.

"Look, I know I handled this situation badly."

She glanced around, trying to figure out the sound's direction. The rise blocked her view, but she knew where she was. This had to be bad news.

"Cal." Her plea was louder the second time, but he ignored it.

So, she pinched him. Not playful post-sex fun this time. Nope. A full-fledged pinch meant to get his attention.

He rubbed his forearm. "What the hell is wrong with you now?"

She shook her head, both to get back on the subject and to keep him from yelling. "There's someone at the crash site."

This time he understood. His head whipped around as he stood on his tiptoes. "Can't see anyone."

"Listen." She pointed at an outcropping of rocks over to the side. They might be able to catch a view from up higher and behind shelter.

She didn't wait for him to agree with her silent plan of action. She grabbed his hand. They walked as fast as the elements would allow.

Her head pounded in time with the fall of her feet. After being shot at, she should have been terrified. For some reason, being connected to Cal's body warmth, surrounded by his earthy smell, made her feel safe.

They reached the crash area and she tried to peek over the rocks, but Cal's shoulders blocked her view. Thanks to his size and position, he could see, so she was more than happy to let him take the lead.

"Who is it?" she asked.

"There are two of them, man and a woman. They're poking around looking for something." His voice held a sharp edge.

"Here?"

"Do they look familiar?"

He ducked down so she could lean up and over him to take a look. She got one second of staring time before he pushed her head back down. His touch wasn't gentle.

She wasn't a fan of the shoving. "Don't ever do that again."

"Would you prefer to be seen?"

"Than being manhandled? Yeah, maybe."

He let out a long exhale in what she assumed was an effort to maintain control. "Is this really the best time to fight?"

Seemed good to her. "We can pick it up later."

"I'll look forward to that." He took another quick look at the twosome. "Well?"

"Never seen them before."

"Even at the funeral?"

"Not that I remember." Her memories of that day blurred together. She hadn't watched the crowd. She spent most of those hours beating back the urge to crawl into a ball and weep. Getting through the debilitating pain had been all she could muster.

Cassie risked another glance. The strangers scurried around, picking through the burned debris and overturned rocks. They searched with a purpose, as if they knew exactly which articles to cast aside and which to study. Whoever they were, they were there for a specific purpose. They were not lost hikers.

"We may as well introduce ourselves," Cal said.

She grabbed his arm to stop him. "Have you lost your mind?"

"What now?"

It was the *way* he said everything that ticked her off. "What, you propose we walk right up there and say 'hello'?"

"Works for me."

"Because you're insane."

"You continue to show a lack of faith in me."

"I wonder why." When he shot her an innocent smile, she tried appealing to his logic rather than the testosterone surging around him. "Cal, these two obviously aren't up to any good."

"True. That's why we need to meet them head on."

The fresh air was rotting his brain. "No, flyboy. That's why we wait and watch."

"Now, what's interesting about that?" He winked at her before pushing up to his feet. He started up to the crash site, body tall and walk steady.

Cassie hoped this was not an example of his covert abilities. If so, the military needed to rework its training programs.

Since following seemed like the only intelligent option, she did. She caught up to him right as he walked out into the open and talked in a voice low enough so only he could hear. "You're an idiot."

"I know you mean that as a compliment." He took her hand and squeezed her fingers.

When his thumb rubbed gentle circles over her knuckles, her pulse jumped. She supposed he was trying to comfort her. Since she was fresh out of good ideas, she went with instinct and held on instead of shrugging him off. They may as well play the role of lovers since they sort of were.

Cassie plastered a bright smile on her face and tried to concentrate on her role rather than the feel of Cal's rough hands. "Hello."

At the sound of their approach, the skulking dark-haired woman almost jumped into a tree.

"Smooth," Cal whispered under his breath.

"What are you doing here?" The woman sounded less than thrilled about having company.

And how was she dry? Cassie noticed that little fact with some annoyance. The drizzle would not have soaked her, but the storm that had just passed through the canyon should have.

Cal stepped up and flashed one of those killer smiles that cut through a woman's common sense like a laser beam. "Hiking and got stuck in the storm."

"I see that." Light danced in the other woman's dark eyes as her hungry gaze roamed over his body. She almost hummed with approval.

Cassie noticed how the woman graduated from searching to flirting in less than two seconds. Cassie hated her on sight.

"I'm Louisa." Her attention focused on Cal.

Cassie felt as desirable as a piece of wet shag carpet. She figured she looked like one, too. Cassie wrapped her free hand around Cal's forearm and pulled her body closer to his, not out of any sense of misplaced jealousy. More as a way to keep from shaking Louisa.

Cal took it all in and smiled. "I'm Cal. This is Cassie."

"Cal." Louisa's voice dripped with lust.

"Let the folks get on their way." A man walked into the conversation.

Louisa. A man and a woman. Both of them searching Dan's wreckage. It did not take long for Cassie to put the pieces together. This was the infamous Bobby Polk. Her brother's supposed partner.

No freaking way.

Cassie looked the man up and down, taking in his faded jeans and the faded advertisement on his shabby T-shirt. Slicked-back hair and cheesy smirk rounded out the picture. She wasn't sure what rat hole this Bobby character had crawled out of, but she wished he'd climb back in there . . . and take Louisa with him.

From the tension radiating off Cal, Cassie guessed he had put it all together as well. She sensed they came up with the same conclusion about Bobby. He was a loser.

"They're lost," Louisa said.

"We are not." No way was Cassie letting this woman think she had the intellectual high ground.

Cal hid his disgust a bit better. "Just hiking."

Bobby glanced down the canyon. "That's a tough walk."

"It was worth it." Cal squeezed her hand as he said it.

Bobby hitched his chin in their general direction. "You two exercise buffs or something?"

"Not really."

Bobby shrugged. "I give. Why here?"

"This is a special place for Cassie. Her brother died here. We came up to check it out. Just hadn't anticipated the thunderstorm blowing in and stranding us."

Cassie considered stepping on Cal's foot to make him shut up. The last thing she wanted was for Bobby to know anything about her life.

Too late. Bobby's eyes darted back and forth, making him look like the weasel he was. "You're Dan's baby sister?"

The fake shock in his voice was a nice touch. Cassie found it as believable as Louisa's feral smile.

Cassie choked down the urge to scream. "You know Dan?"

"Everyone around Kauai knew Dan. Besides, we had what you might call a business relationship."

"Business?" Cal slid his smooth question in with ease.

"Yeah, I'm Bobby Polk." The guy gave his name as if everyone knew who the hell he was.

"And?" Cassie asked, making the syllable sound as bland as possible.

"Dan and I entered into a business deal a while back."

Cassie tried to slip her hand out of Cal's grasp, but he wouldn't let go. Probably afraid she'd strangle this loser.

She went for ego bruising instead. "Funny, but Dan never mentioned you."

"I guess he wouldn't, would he?" Bobby coughed out a hollow laugh. "Dan wasn't the type to get his baby sister's permission before signing a contract."

Was every man on the island an idiot? "Excuse me?"

"He was a man's man."

Cal gave her hand a quick squeeze before she could fire off another question or call this Polk character a liar.

"What kind of business was that again?" Cal asked.

Bobby's empty smile slipped. For a second he looked more animal than human. "Import-export."

Cassie figured that was code for drug trafficking, which meant this guy had *nothing* to do with Dan.

"He's being modest. Bobby's a genius." Louisa eased around Bobby and planted her curvy body in front of Cal.

Bobby reciprocated by looping his arm around Louisa's shoulders. The gesture looked more intimidating than loving.

"You were explaining . . ." Cal said.

"I sell antiques. Dan helped with transporting the items."

Maybe it was the air of sleaziness that followed the couple around like a bad smell, but Cassie would bet her life savings that they worked the wrong side of the law. These two wouldn't know a priceless antique if one fell out of a plane and smacked them on their stupid heads.

"It's surprising Dan had time for those extra runs, what with his tourism business." Cassie hoped spreading doubt would crack their façade.

Louisa certainly didn't notice any part of the Dan conversation. Drool all but dripped from her surgically enhanced lips as she stared at Cal.

Hate was not a strong enough word to describe Cassie's feelings right then. Cal must have sensed something in the air because he bent down and placed a sweet kiss on her forehead. If he had started reciting Shakespeare backward she would have been less surprised. The simple deed was so genuine, so pure, that Cassie's heart actually fluttered. Who knew a heart could even do that?

For a brief instant, the real world fell away in a haze and only Cal existed. She thought about kissing him, about tracing that sweet dimple with her tongue.

Then Bobby chuckled and the spell was broken. "You two newlyweds or something?"

"Something like that." Cal answered before the question even left the other man's foul mouth.

Cal looked so serious, Cassie decided to play along and see what happened. She would seek a fake divorce later. "Exactly like that."

"How interesting." Louisa sounded anything but interested in that information.

Cassie's spirits soared. Suddenly she liked this game. If they were supposed to be engaged, she would enjoy it. She patted Cal's flat stomach with her palm. "Yes. Cal's indulging me. He thought coming down here was dangerous but agreed to let me have my way."

"Anything for you, honey." Cal squeezed her even closer. "And what are you two doing here again?"

"Nothing nearly as noble as you are," Bobby said.

Cassie didn't doubt that. This guy certainly didn't strike her as the honorable type.

"Dan had some expensive items that belonged to me on his last flight. They went down with him in the plane. Uninsured and, so far, unrecoverable. I was trying to see if anything managed to survive the flight."

"You weren't able to get out here before now?" Cal asked.

"Understandably, after I heard about Dan's accident I wasn't thinking about finances."

"Understandably," Cassie mumbled back.

Cal rubbed his thumb across the back of Cassie's neck. She couldn't figure out if it was another warning or meant to soothe her. Either way, it kept her from lunging at Bobby and wrapping her hands around his neck.

"The police couldn't help find your things?" Cal asked.

"Probably, but we didn't try. You see, Dan and I kept our partnership quiet. I figured the hassle in trying to explain the arrangement and tracking down all the receipts wasn't worth it."

"Dan liked the idea of a silent partner," Louisa added.

Cassie's insides turned icy. "Did you have something to do with the business?"

Louisa's back snapped straight as she shot a look of triumph. "The contacts are with me. My father and I have been in the antique business for years."

Bobby glared at Louisa. It was a wonder the woman didn't disintegrate into a pile of dust right there. "We should get going."

"Careful. The rocks and ground are unstable thanks to the rain." Cal's eyes locked on Bobby as if daring him to make a mistake.

Cassie wasn't sure what was happening, but the air carried a new charge it hadn't possessed a few minutes earlier. Bobby's gaze wandered to the backpack in Cal's hand. Dan's backpack.

"We better go before the storm heats up again," Cal said as he looped the pack over his arm, almost cradling it. "Enjoy the camping."

Cassie waited until they were out of the couple's earshot to drop Cal's hand. "What do you think?"

"I think we got to the pack before they could, and Bobby's pissed."

"You really think there's any chance Dan was in partnership with them?" She tensed, dreading the answer.

"Dan had his faults. Hanging with garbage like that would've been somewhat out of character."

A sentence so carefully constructed that there was only one conclusion. Her heart slammed to a halt. So did her feet. "You think Dan was doing something illegal. You believe the rumors."

"This isn't the time for this conversation."

She refused to be put off. The issue was too important to drop. "We've got time."

"We need to get to the helicopter. The last thing I want to do is keep my back to those two."

Her stomach dropped. "You think they're dangerous?"

"I think we can count on it."

Chapter Eighteen

The march back up to the helicopter proved more taxing than the slide down. Having Cassie walk ahead of him was pure torture. With each step, her shorts rode up her firm legs, giving him a peek at their impressive length and reminding Cal how good it felt to be inside her.

How the hell was he supposed to hike when a growing erection kept pressing against the inside of his pants?

"When did we get engaged? I just thought you should let me know since I'm to be the fiancée and all." The amusement in her voice was hard to miss.

"When I couldn't think of anything else to say."

"Aren't you a hopeless romantic?"

Yeah, if romantic meant horny bastard.

But at least she was talking to him again. The silent treatment ranked dead last on his list of favorite female tricks. Made him absolutely fucking crazy. Probably why she did it, why all women did it. As a group, females came up with the ultimate in male annoyance and pounced.

While he stewed in male indignation, rocks tumbled out from under Cassie. She lost her footing and fell forward, reaching for the nearest anything-but-him for balance.

He dropped the bag and caught her around the waist in

time to prevent her from slicing her head open on a rock. "I got you."

"I told you I needed boots."

"What we need is to stop climbing." In fact, he'd be happy to be anywhere other than right there. The canyon might appeal to some people. Since Dan died there, Cal did not see the supposed beauty of the place.

"And when is that going to happen? It feels as if we've been walking in circles for hours."

"We're going in a straight line." He glanced up and saw nothing but rocks slanted toward a cloudy gray sky. "Soon."

"That's not exactly comforting."

Comforting. Not a word he'd use to describe whatever it was they had together. Since catching her, he could not find the strength to remove his hand again. Her stomach rose and fell in rapid succession under his palm. Being this close, he could feel her breath brush across his cheek.

He wanted her to lean into him, but she kept her back straight and well away. Everything about her shouted for him to stay away.

For some reason that pissed him off. He knew distance was the right call. Still, his body refused to listen. His mind ran even a lap or two behind that. He knew what he *should* do and what he *wanted* to do were two very different things. For whatever reason, he went with the latter.

He buried his face in her hair and inhaled the scent of fresh rain. Before he could work through the pros and cons of this plan, his hands roamed from her stomach and up higher to rest just under her breasts. It took him a few seconds to realize that the husky moan he heard echoing through the barren emptiness around them came from him.

"What are you doing?" she asked.

"Something dumb."

"I thought we had to keep moving before it got too

late?" She ended the sentence with a sharp intake of breath when his right hand inched even higher.

"We do." That was reality. For a few seconds, he wanted to live in the fantasy.

"Is this your way of apologizing for how you acted in the cave?"

"No. This is." Cal did not wait another second. He turned her and pressed his mouth against hers.

She did not fight. She did not exactly jump into his waiting arms, either. The scene at the cave left her skeptical. He could feel the internal war waging inside her, almost see her body give in as her mind rebelled. He wanted sexual awareness to take over and blow out everything else.

When he gentled his touch, let his mouth brush over hers, deepening with each pass, she relaxed against him. Her touch at first lazy and calm turned electric. Need pulsed off her. A hot little tongue slipped between his lips. She suckled and licked at his mouth until his knees buckled.

The power of her kiss shook him. She morphed from cool to hot without a stop in between. They matched in their desires. Matched in their need to be in control and in charge. Certainly matched just fine when their clothes were off. Their goals and histories were the problems.

He lifted his head and stared down at her. He kept hoping the right words would fall into place. That somehow he could explain everything that happened earlier and warn her about the man he had become.

"Cassie—"

"If you apologize for that kiss, I'll kick you back to Florida." She dug her fingernails into his arms as she delivered the threat.

He laughed.

She didn't. "A swift shot right in the—"

No way was he letting that happen. "I'm not sorry about kissing you."

"There's a nice change," Cassie said.

She kept zinging him with words, but her tone stayed even. She sounded neither angry nor frustrated. If anything, that husky voice carried a note of amusement.

"Admittedly, those last few minutes in the cave were not my most impressive. After the . . . well, you know."

His comment hung out there in the quiet of the moment. The rain had stopped. The wind no longer threatened to blow them off the cliff. Other than the sharp breaths bouncing around his head, all of the noise of the last few hours had stopped.

She did not respond; just dropped her arms to her sides and stared.

"You're not waiting for me to disagree, are you?" she asked.

He appreciated her speaking up since he was a second away from saying something stupid to fill the void. "Of course not."

A not-so-friendly smile crossed her lips. "Good, because I'd hate to drop you to the bottom of this deep canyon on your head."

He followed her gaze about three thousand feet down to the base of the gorge. "I'll pass."

"Maybe you're getting smarter." She treated him to one firm nod. "Good. Let's get to the helicopter."

She turned around and started climbing again, but he saw it. A fine tremor moved through her from head to toe. Yeah, the kiss shook her. She was trying to pretend it hadn't, but it had.

"By the way, you don't get to cop a feel whenever the mood strikes you."

But then how would he strangle her. "I've been around long enough to know when a woman wants me."

"Really? Can you tell when one is about to push you down a cliff?"

Since he could, he changed the conversation. "Let's go."

They climbed the last few feet to the flatter area where the helicopter rested. Cal knew immediately that something was wrong. Footprints. Someone had circled the aircraft.

"Looks like we had company."

Cassie looked over his shoulder. "We still do."

He followed her gaze to see Josh standing right behind them, coming around the back of the helicopter. "This canyon is getting damn crowded."

"No kidding," she whispered in response.

"May as well go over and see what he has to say this time." Cal took a lunging step to bring his body up and over the rise and put him right in front of the DEA agent.

"There you are." Josh's greeting was not a happy one.

"Good to see you, too," Cassie said.

"I've been waiting."

"If I didn't know better, I'd say you've been following us." Cal knew that was exactly the situation.

From their new viewpoint, high above the canyon, Cal could watch the last of the water drain down the sides and wash into the valley below. Josh would have seen them coming. Probably watched the kiss as he waited.

"This your helicopter?" Josh hitched a thumb over his shoulder.

A few bags littered the ground and the doors were wide open. Cal knew the other man had rifled through the aircraft. The realization tested his already ragged control. "Well, I know it's not yours, so I'm not sure why you felt free to search it."

"Cal." Cassie said his name as a warning.

"You're on my turf, Wilson."

"This is a national park."

"I see an abandoned helicopter perched on an illegal landing site, you bet I take a look."

Cal noticed that this guy thought the entire island was his

playground. "Not to beat the same drum, but you're a DEA agent. Unless you're also a ranger on the side, I'm thinking this is out of your jurisdiction."

"I know what I do." Josh assumed the stereotypical agent stance: legs apart and hand on his hip right near the gun Cal assumed was hidden there.

"Do I look as if I'm smuggling drugs?" Cal asked.

Josh's eyes widened for a second before his face wiped blank again. "I think I need an explanation."

"We had some trouble with the wind, so we set it down here," Cal said.

"You're trying to tell me this doesn't have anything to do with hiking down to the crash site? The same restricted crash site no one should be visiting?"

Cassie placed a hand on Josh's forearm. "Cal did this for me. I needed to come back here to pay my respects."

Cal's blood pressure kicked up in response to the gentle touch. He practically had to beg for a kiss, yet Cassie did not hesitate to get all touchy with this other guy.

"I can't imagine how difficult this is for you, Ms. Montgomery." Josh shot a frown in Cal's direction. "But as your friend here knows, this type of stunt is dangerous. He should not have brought you here."

"I can speak for myself," Cal said.

"I appreciate your concern." Her smile beamed at Josh. If he noticed how grungy and in need of a shower she was, he didn't show it.

"You should know better." The edge moved back into Josh's voice when he turned his attention to Cal.

Cal's fists itched with the need to punch the smirk off the agent's smug face. If the lecture went on much longer, he just might give into the urge. "Guess not."

"What possessed you to fly in these conditions? To put Ms. Montgomery's life at risk?"

Josh's words suggested he wanted a beating. Cal was

more than willing to give him one. "You think you'd do a better job?"

Josh stepped in closer. "Hell, yes."

"Let's reholster those big guns, boys." Cassie stepped between them. "That's more than enough testosterone talk. I'm an adult."

"But you said someone shot at you," Josh said.

For once Cal thought the guy had a good point.

Cassie clearly disagreed because she waved him off. "That's irrelevant to this discussion."

"It is?" Josh looked at Cal for help.

"My point is this. If you two beat the snot out of each other, I won't have a way home. So, how about you get me out of here and compare gun calibers later."

A smile broke out on Josh's face. "The woman talks sense."

Cal smothered his grin under a fake cough. "Sometimes."

"We could try working together," Josh said.

Cal hadn't seen that one coming. "How so?"

"I want to know what's going on. If Dan's accident was something else, I want to know that, too."

Cassie wasn't smiling now. "I tried to follow the rules and work with you guys. Didn't work."

To prevent another fight about how the police bungled the investigation into Dan's crash, Cal stepped in. "Now's not a good time."

"Why?" Josh asked.

Cassie picked up on his silent message. "I need a shower. The thunderstorm rolled in before we could get back here."

Josh smiled wider than the canyon. "A shame getting caught out there like that."

Cal noticed the binoculars near Josh's feet. Looks like voyeur could be added to the list of Josh's abilities. Cal decided not to tell Cassie they likely had a witness to their cave sex.

"We managed to find shelter," Cassie said, oblivious to the fact Josh already knew that news. "And we weren't alone."

Cal liked the approach. No need for them to worry about Bobby and his sidekick if they could sic Josh on them.

Josh's smile vanished. "Who? Where?"

"At your restricted crash site." Cassie leaned against the aircraft. "Bobby something and a woman, can't remember her name."

"What were they doing?"

Josh asked the right questions, but Cal noticed the other man did not seem all that concerned with the answers. It was as if Josh knew what was happening and was there to watch it all. Cal wondered if he and Cassie were being followed. More important, if they were—why?

Cassie shrugged. "Looking around for something."

Josh turned to leave but then stopped. "Did you two find anything out there?"

Cal looked him right in the eye and lied his butt off. "Nothing there but rocks and dirt."

Chapter Nineteen

The second landing went better than the first. Bumpy but not vomit producing. A definite step up. Still, Cassie shot out of the aircraft as soon as it set back down at the small private airport. She saw no reason to stay in the flying soup can one minute longer than she had to. Lucky for her no other planes were landing or she would have been crushed.

She was so happy to have her feet hit firm land that she didn't even mind the choking smell of fuel and buzzing sound of helicopters over head.

Her stained clothing hung on her and her muscles burned from all of the unexpected exercise. It was hard to tell what looked more rumpled, her or her once white T-shirt. The bottoms of her feet thumped, and she was pretty sure she smelled.

"How'd it go?" Ed hustled out of the office and over to the helicopter.

Cassie stood and waited for a greeting of some sort, but Ed was too busy running his hand over the aircraft. If Ed were alone, he'd probably kiss the thing.

Cassie's crankiness got the better of her. "Yeah, we're fine; thanks for asking."

Cal came around from the other side of the plane to join them. He nodded to Ed and received one in return. "She had a rough day."

She was tired but not so much that she could not fight back. "I had the same day you did."

"I was talking about the helicopter."

He held the ragged duffel and two others in his hands and somehow managed to look fine. More than fine. Other than ruffled hair and dirt on his pants, the man did not show one sign of having hiked for miles and gotten stuck in a downpour.

Cassie wondered if he was human.

"Afraid I wrecked it?" Cal chuckled as he watched Ed inspect the plane from a distance of about three inches.

"She's my baby. Just protective." Ed wiped some dirt off the metal. "No offense meant."

"None taken." Cal dumped the bags on the tarmac.

Ed finally paid attention to something other than the aircraft. "You look like hell."

"Thanks for noticing," Cassie grumbled back.

"Find out anything interesting?"

Too many things and only some of those dealt with a murder. "Dan's bag."

Having it this close and not rummaging through it was killing her. She wanted to rip into it and inspect every stitch. Something in there had to explain what happened to Dan and why.

"What bag?" Ed asked.

Cal picked up the laptop bag by a ripped handle. "This."

Ed frowned. "That? Are you sure?"

Her spirits fell. "What now?"

"Well, Cassie darling, I've never seen that before." Ed bent down and poked at the items inside. "Why do you think it belongs to Dan?"

The question knocked her speechless. "It was in the tree at the crash site. The documents have his business letterhead on them."

"Who the hell else would it belong to?" The frustration in Cal's voice mirrored hers.

Ed shook his head. "I don't know."

"There is no other reason for this stuff to be sitting down on the ledge," Cal insisted.

Cassie's stomach dropped to her feet. Their one clue was turning out to be another dead end.

Cal reached for the sack and pulled out a document. "You think this is fake?"

Ed glanced at it, then whistled. "I agree it looks real."

The bag had to belong to Dan. Cassie could not tolerate another false lead. "Of course it's his," Cassie said, a bit too loudly.

The men stopped their conversation and stared at her. Ed's glance contained pity. Cal looked at her as if she had lost her mind.

Cal's eyebrows lifted. "You okay?"

No, no, no. Between the flying and her defenses being down, she exploded. "Maybe it's the exhaustion or the starvation. Or maybe the idea that someone planted false papers in a tree makes me freaking crazy."

Cal continued to stare. Ed no longer looked too sure of her mental state, either.

She touched a hand to her forehead wondering if they had a valid concern. "Forget it."

Cal skimmed his hand up and down her arm. "Look, let's not panic."

"Too late," she mumbled.

"We don't know if the bag is authentic. We'll have to look at Dan's other papers and figure it out." Cal sounded so reasonable.

She debated knocking him over. After hours in the rain he managed to radiate confidence. His graceful movement and slight swagger were both irritating and irresistible.

"Hello, folks." Ted Greene snuck up on them without warning. Stepped right around the front of the helicopter as if he dropped from the sky.

"You're far from the office." In an almost imperceptible move, Cal slid Dan's bag closer with the side of his foot.

Ted smiled. "You're just the man I was looking for."

Cassie's heart fell down to her sneakers at that ominous statement.

From the flat line of his mouth, Cal didn't appear impressed, either. "I'm a popular man today."

Ted took a quick glance down at the bags at Cal's feet. "What does that mean?"

"Ask your DEA friend."

"Okay." Ted hesitated for a second before moving on. "Well, I wanted you to know that I looked in on Dan's house."

Another violation in a series of violations. Fury ripped through Cassie at the thought. "Now? You finally decided to check out something I said? Where have you been?"

Cal's eyebrows eased together. "Uh, Cassie."

She didn't feel like being reasonable. She had tried that. Went in being nice and asking questions. All the good-girl routine had gotten her was a stone wall planted in her face. Her brother was dead, her emotions were a mess, and she just had sex in a cave with a virtual stranger who excited her more than any other man on the planet. A woman could only take so much.

She ignored Cal and centered all of her pent-up outrage on Ted. "I'm waiting for an explanation."

"You told me someone shot at you. I investigated the allegations. That's what I do." Ted tapped on his badge. "Police, remember?"

"And?" Cassie realized she was tapping her foot and

stopped. Being surrounded by this many blockheaded males put her on edge.

"I think what she's so nicely trying to ask is if you found anything," Cal said.

Ted nodded. "Bullet holes."

It was an "ah-hah" moment. Cassie thought about turning in a circle with her hands raised in triumph to the sky. She settled for rubbing it in. "So now you believe me?"

"Yes."

"About freaking time."

"It's hard not to since the place was a wreck and the window blown out. Unless you two did some serious partying, the house was a target of something bad. I have twenty-four-hour protection on it now."

"Any idea what's going on?" Ed asked.

"Still investigating. We're dusting for prints. Doing the usual. I suspect we won't find much."

Cassie snorted but Ted talked right over her. "In the meantime, I think you two should get out of town."

She stopped him before he got started on that theory. "No way."

Ed looped an arm over her shoulder. "It might not be a bad idea, Cassie darling. No one wants to see you hurt."

All the men in charge of the island had been telling her to leave for weeks. She ignored them before. She was ignoring them now. "There is no way I am leaving."

"You're in danger," Ted said.

"No one believed I got shot at until someone also aimed at Cal, too."

"You could sound more apologetic about that," Cal pointed out.

Funny how he got the who-should-apologize-to-whom

thing backward. "You're lucky I didn't finish the job myself."

Ed clapped his hands together. "We need to focus."

Cal leaned back against the helicopter, that is, until Ed's harsh scowl had him standing straight again. "Sorry for touching the equipment."

"Just stay off it," Ed said.

"Look, I'm not talking about leaving forever." Ted raised his voice, sounding more like the cop-in-charge than ever before. "Just a few days until we can sort this out."

As far as she was concerned, the police, the DEA, even the boy scouts had weeks to settle the case and blew it. "You're not getting rid of me."

"I think—"

Cal cut the officer off. "Cassie's right. We're staying."

The stern statement made Cassie downright suspicious. Having Cal agree to anything that fast spelled trouble for her.

"She shouldn't be alone around here, Cal," Ed said.

"Agreed, but she won't be alone."

"I almost hate to ask." Cassie mumbled the comment but they all turned to her, so she figured they heard it just fine.

"You'll be with me." Cal's bravado dripped with testosterone.

No way could she stay attached to Cal's side without stripping him naked. The man acted like a complete idiot, but he was a fine-looking idiot. And, like it or not, they had a connection. The attraction stretching between them . . . well, whatever it was, it wasn't going away. Being in close proximity would only magnify it.

She could tolerate that if it weren't for the look that came over Cal's face the second after he gave in to his lust in the cave. That same look reappeared on their hike back up the canyon. He had a pattern. He ceded some of his bedrock control, opened up to her, panicked, and ran. Not actually, but mentally.

For a guy who prided himself on protecting the women of the world, he sure knew how to blindside them with sexual nonsense. One minute he could not keep his hands off her. The next he could not get away fast enough.

She refused to deal with days and days of that behavior. "You didn't ask, but the answer is no."

"Just a second, Cassie darling. Let's hear Cal out."

"Yeah. How do you expect to pull this off?" Ted asked in a slow and tentative voice as if turning the idea over in his mind.

Cassie did not need to engage in that much analysis. "Does anyone care what I think?"

She knew the answer—no.

"Not really." Cal had the nerve to wink after he said that.

She knew she should be flattered on some level. At the very least, she should be understanding. After all, Cal saved lives for a living. Dan had been the same way. Turning off that part of his personality proved tough, even after he traded his high-stress life for a more casual one in Kauai.

She originally wrote off Ted as negligent and useless. Now she wasn't so sure. He kept popping up. Unlike Josh, Ted's concern appeared genuine. The same protective strains Dan had possessed seemed to run through Ted.

"We'll figure something else out," she said.

Cal actually laughed. "You'll do what you're told."

"Excuse me?"

Ted whistled. "You're a brave man to say something like that to a woman."

Cassie turned to the deputy. "Can I use your gun?"

Ted treated Cassie to a small smile. "Tempting, but I better say no."

"So what's the plan?" Ed didn't laugh, but he didn't listen to her protests, either.

Cal shrugged. "We'll use Dan's house."

Ted started shaking his head before Cal got the suggestion out. "Not an option. I cordoned off the cabin."

"Why?" she asked.

"It's a crime scene now. No one goes in or out without my approval."

"Give me the okay right now and it's settled." Cal made the statement into an order.

Ted did not buy the idea any more the second time. "No."

If she had her gun, she'd fire into Ed's precious helicopter to get their attention. "I'll decide where I go and with whom. I don't need a babysitter."

"A prison guard is more like it," Cal said.

"I can take you any day, flyboy."

"Oh please." He scoffed as if to emphasize how unlikely he believed that idea to be.

He made her crazy. "Want to try me right now?"

Ted coughed over a laugh. "I'd say no if I were you, Wilson."

Cal exhaled loud enough to drown out the sound coming from a group of men walking by on the way to a private plane. "Cassie, the bottom line is that we need to be around to investigate."

She could tell from the way Cal's jaw locked that he thought he was being reasonable. She thought he was acting like an ass.

"Hold up a sec." Ted's angry voice drowned out everything including a landing plane. "Let me make one thing clear. *We* are not investigating. I am."

"You forfeited that right when you ignored Cassie and her theories about her brother," Cal shot back.

She had one little problem with his phrasing but the basic idea was right. "They're facts, not theories."

All of the amusement faded from Ted's face. He took a threatening step toward Cal. "I will take you in right now if I have to."

"The boy is trying to help. He has a vested interest." Ed glanced in Cassie's direction. The other men followed his gaze, staring at her.

The sudden attention made her nervous. "Wait a minute. Why is Cal my responsibility?"

Ted broke the stalemate. "Find somewhere else to stay."

As far as Cassie was concerned, the man with the badge and the big weapon won the contest. "Okay."

"You gonna shoot me, Deputy?" Cal asked.

A tentative smile appeared on Ted's lips. "I'm thinking about it."

"Won't look good. A cop shooting an innocent Florida tourist and all."

"That's the only thing saving you."

And like that the mood lightened. Cassie chalked the entire incident up to some weird male-bonding ritual. Something masculine and hairy that she didn't understand. But none of this solved the immediate problem at hand.

"Now that we're all civilized again, where am I going to stay while the police are doing whatever it is they should have done weeks ago?"

"She doesn't let up," Ted said to Cal.

Cal snorted. "You don't have to tell me."

"You could go back to Oahu," Ed suggested.

Cal answered before she could say anything. "No."

Ted gave it a try. "Then you could try doing what everyone else in Hawaii does."

"Sleep on the beach?" Cal sounded serious.

Ted scowled at the thought. "Hell no. I meant check into a hotel."

Now that was a dangerous combination. Clean hotel room, wide bed, and Cal. They'd be twisting the sheets in no time.

She rushed to shut down that option. "Maybe Ed has extra room."

She was all but begging but Ed wasn't taking the hint. "Can't do, Cassie darling. You'd be better with Cal anyway. He looks big enough to protect you."

Being protected wasn't her concern. Keeping out of a prone position was.

"Good plan. We'll check in, get settled, and regroup," Cal said.

She thought about arguing but couldn't think of a better option at the moment.

"Fair enough," Ted said with a nod. "Anything I should know from you two while I'm looking around?"

"Like what?" Cal's blank look was impressive. Cassie thought the guy played innocent pretty well.

"Like whatever you found on your hike. Look, I'm not a simple, country officer. You two are hiding something. If you don't come clean, I can't help you."

"We got caught in bad weather," Cal said.

"Someone is causing trouble around this island and I want to know why. If you two get in my way or hide information I need, I'll bring you in on obstruction of justice charges. That's a promise."

This time Cal balanced a hand on the plane and ignored the way Ed's eyes popped in response. "Understood."

Ted's dark gaze traveled between Cal and Cassie. "Maybe

a hot meal will help. Come into my office in a few hours. Your memories should be healed by then."

Cal pressed his lips together. "Doubt it."

"Humor me." Ted stalked off.

Cassie waited until he was out of hearing range to take one final shot. "I thought we were."

Chapter Twenty

"I may well move in." Cassie twirled around in a circle in the center of the spacious hotel suite's family room.

Cal tried to smother his smile, but it kept creeping out. Watching Cassie prance around the expensive room, her eyes wide and her arms outstretched, mesmerized him. She was dirty and grimy. Her hair fell over her forehead, partially hiding her eyes. Her T-shirt, once sparkling white, now resembled more of a bland shade of gray.

He had never seen a more beautiful creature in his life.

This woman should be locked up for her own protection and for his peace of mind.

"I take it the room meets with your approval," he said.

She threw back the curtains and stared out at the manicured grounds and the midnight blue ocean outside the balcony. "It's amazing."

"I'd say." His voice barely registered as a whisper.

She shot him a startled glance over her shoulder. "Much better than staying at Dan's house. How are we paying for this?"

An interesting use of the word "we." "I got a military rate."

It was a lie but a small one. The way he figured it, she deserved to be spoiled for a day or two. He had the money and spending it on her seemed like a better investment than beer, though he planned to have a few of those later.

"This is one of those resorts I drive by and admire but never dream of staying in. Not in an oceanfront suite, anyway."

The room wasn't his style, either. Frivolous purchases had never been Cal's thing, and this room definitely qualified as frivolous. Bright yellow walls and big windows. Pillows everywhere. A butler available for the entire floor. A living room with a plasma-screen television. A bedroom with a huge-ass bed.

Other furniture adorned the suite, but all Cal noticed was that bed, seeing and thinking that he could make good use of it. It was so damn inviting that he almost tackled her and threw her in the middle of the bed the minute they walked through the door.

But forget all the dressing. He only needed a mattress. Firm or soft, it didn't matter so long as Cassie was there beside him. How he had gotten used to her being around in such a short time was a question he refused to dwell on. Not now, anyway. He tried to concentrate on mindless conversation instead.

"We're only renting all this magnificence for a few days. We have to give the dream back sooner or later," he said.

Her smile was so broad and genuine it filled the sunny room. "Seems fair."

He cleared his throat and carried his bag into the bedroom. He separated his few possessions into piles and tried to ignore the soft mattress right in front of him. "You should take a shower."

She followed him and hovered in the doorway. Brushing her hair away from her eyes, she smiled at him. The gesture, so sweet and feminine, had him gasping for air.

"Are you offering to help wash my back?" The deep

throaty sound coming out of her mouth sent a shock of adrenaline rushing to his groin.

"Huh?" He concentrated on the few clothing items in his hands as if folding were an Olympic sport.

"Were you asking a question or making a suggestion?"

Man, oh man. She was flirting with him. He could handle wrath, even figure out a way to deal with sadness. But this sensual side destroyed all of the barriers he tried to erect to keep her out.

"I thought you'd be more comfortable if you were, you know, clean." Now she had him blathering like an idiot.

"Then I'm on my own?"

The husky edge to her voice sapped his control. "I should unpack."

He didn't have any possessions left to put away. That's what happened when a guy traveled with three shirts, a pair of pants, and little else.

She walked to the opposite side of that inviting bed. Stood right across from him. Long fingers threaded through the tassels on the end of the decorative throw pillows. She twisted the unruly strands with small movements so seductive, so reminiscent of the gentle caress she used on his hard body, that he had to bite back a groan.

"Need any help?" she asked.

Only the kind that came from her mouth sliding over his erection and sucking on him until he exploded. "No, I'm good."

She winked at him. "I know."

Those sexy words sliced through him, melting away what was left of any resistance. He reached for her just as she scooted away and slid into the bathroom. One more step and he would have done a header into the pillows. As it was, he balanced until she left the viewing range, then fell to the bed.

He rolled over and lay there on his back, praying for a good reason to stop this madness. Without one, he was going to go after Cassie. Hell, even with one, he'd go after her.

A low, sexy humming emanated through the closed bathroom door. The tune was soft and vaguely familiar. The melody played in his mind as he imagined her peeling off those shabby clothes and revealing her high, firm breasts to his gaze.

For a second he contemplated clawing his way through the wooden door to get to her. Then the water rushed on, drowning out her riveting voice.

Cassie would be naked now. Ready to step into the bath and let the water cascade over her body. If she needed a washcloth, he'd be right there to help.

He tried to move, but his body refused to cooperate. He just sprawled across the mattress thinking that he should have gotten two rooms. A nice one for her. A bed of nails for him.

The door popped open and she stuck her head out. "Cal?"

Shit. "Ummm, yeah?"

When she didn't answer, he lifted his head. She peeked around the door with her hair piled up in one of those intricate fashions only women could accomplish. The style showed off her long, kissable neck and her creamy white shoulder blades. Cal never thought of a woman's neck and shoulders as irresistible until he met Cassie.

"Do you need anything out of here before I step into the bathtub?"

What a question. "Well . . ."

The words faded into nothingness when she stepped out from behind the door. Naked. Her bare skin glowed with a light sheen from the humidity created by the shower. Every curve was on view for his appreciation.

Admiring her was no hardship. His hungry gaze traveled

up long, lean legs, up to a slender waist, then settled on her ample breasts. With or without clothing, clean or dirty, a perfectly formed body.

Her pink tongue licked her full lips. "You were saying?"

Was he saying something? "I just—"

"Yeah?"

He leaned up on his elbows and took the plunge. "Mind if I join you in there?"

"I need to know what you're working on." Brad Nohea leaned back in his government-issue desk chair and stared at a work folder instead of giving Josh the eye contact he craved.

"A case with the police."

Brad lowered the file. "Be more specific."

"A drug case."

Brad squared his shoulders, making his too-tight short-sleeve dress shirt look even more absurd than usual. "Do you want to get fired?"

"Not really." Josh glanced around the room, wondering if this was all a man got after years of hard work.

Thirty years of service to the government and years at the DEA, and Brad sat in a small room, not much bigger than a cubicle, shuffling paperwork and supervising people who surpassed him in talent without even working at it.

Brad didn't go out in the field. He attended meetings, issued orders, covered up operations gone bad, and passed the blame. In Dan's case, Brad just plain hid from the truth. That was fine. That was Brad's choice. What Josh hated was Brad's insistence he hide as well.

"Did you call the NTSB about the Rutledge crash yet?" Josh slid the question in there as easy as if he were ordering a turkey sandwich for lunch.

Brad's face flushed with bright orange before turning an interesting shade of deep red. "For the last time—"

"We have information the investigators need."

"It was an accident. It doesn't involve us." Brad jumped from talking loud to actually yelling.

Josh figured this kind of stress was not good for a sixty-year-old man. All the more reason for Brad to come clean.

"Dan was working for us."

"We're done here." Brad stood up but didn't move.

"No, we're not."

"If you don't knock this shit off I'll have you sitting at a desk in the middle of Nowhere, Idaho, doing paperwork twenty-four hours a day."

Josh had heard this threat before. Heard a million just like this one. Usually, he had walked close enough to a line of propriety that he deserved the lecture. Not today.

He got up nice and slow. "Do you want me to quit?"

"There's the door." Brad pointed at it as if to emphasize his offer. "No one is stopping you."

"Keep in mind that if I leave here then I'll have zero incentive to keep your secrets. I could run right to the NTSB." Josh did some pointing of his own. "You might want to remember that."

Brad sank into the chair. "I don't know what you're talking about."

"Right." Josh got to the door before he could control his anger and speak again. "Keep telling yourself that."

Chapter Twenty-one

Cassie wondered when Cal would take the hint. A woman could only leave so many clues before she gave up, put on a robe, and went to the spa to get a facial.

That was exactly her plan back at the airport. But after walking into the posh hotel room and seeing Cal hover over that big bed, her good intentions and all sense of self-protection fell to the wayside. Since they had used a cave the first time, this would be a much more comfortable place to have sex.

The basic idea remained the same—them together now.

Looking at him now, she realized the clues were there ever since they crossed the hotel-room threshold. He had that stunned, just-hit-by-a-car look about him. Eyes wide and glazed, his hands alternated between flexing and clenching. The area just below his waistband bulged and strained against the material.

Except for the erection, he looked like a guy struggling with a case of severe terror. That explanation didn't make much sense from what she knew of Cal's history. Growing up, Dan regaled her with stories about the legendary Cal. Dan skipped the tales of the bedroom antics, but Cassie had overheard him telling other guys.

Knowing what she knew, the idea that Cal experienced

uncertainty when bedding a woman—any woman—struck her as laughable. If he turned her down or tried to reason with her in that condescending tone he favored, she would rip off his arm and beat him to death with it.

That was her new plan. Seduce and enjoy. She'd either have to refrain from looking at him afterward, or tie him to the bed and ask him to tell her what was happening in his head. She just wanted to break this pattern and enjoy the aftermath.

"Come inside," she said, purposely tempting him with both her nudity and her word choice.

She held out her hand. After a slight hesitation, he stood up and reached out until their fingers touched. A gentle shiver ran through her. No other man made her feel alive and uncertain at the same time.

He tugged her into his arms. Pulled her close and placed a sweet kiss on her bare shoulder. She snuggled her cheek against his and nuzzled until he lifted his head and kissed her full on the mouth. As with every other kiss, tiny explosions went off behind her eyes. Light or deep, his kisses sent a wave of dizziness moving through her.

"The water is getting cold." But his voice was oh so warm when he said it.

"I'm plenty hot."

"Good." With hands on her waist, Cal walked her backward into the steamy bathroom.

When he trailed a line of kisses along her collarbone, she dropped her head to the side to give him better access. Without any signal from her brain, her fingers weaved through his hair, loving every strand. Her other hand swept along his back, caressing every inch.

The kissing and touching ignited something sleeping deep inside. She had survived a bad breakup with a man who viewed fidelity as optional in a relationship. She grappled with the reality of her brother's death. So many hours had been spent trying to understand the men in her life and the dangerous choices they made.

Cassie wanted to stop all the thinking and dissecting and concentrate on feeling. There was only one way to do that.

She used her thumb to bring his chin up. "Hi."

A huge smile lit up his face right before he leaned in for a shattering kiss. Their lips slanted over each other, tender at first then with increasing force. His tongue flicked out, licking the seam between her lips, and her heart sank right to her stomach.

Without breaking his hold on her waist, he bent down and shut off the water, stopping the threatening overflow. "Get in."

She'd never bathed with a man before. The idea seemed so intimate, almost uncomfortable.

Until now.

With her clothes off, there was nothing to stop her from moving ahead. Rather than play coy or hide, she turned her body over to him. He may be hesitant about whatever lingered between them, but she wasn't.

He eased her into the tub. Water splashed over the sides and dripped onto the tile floor as she sat back against the cold porcelain. Eyes closed, she opened her body to his touch. For what felt like hours but really amounted to just minutes, sure fingers lingered on her breasts, coaxing her nipples into tight buds.

Then his hands were gone. He sat back on his hunches and started to strip out of his clothes.

She threw out her arm and stopped him. "Wait."

"For?"

"Go slower."

Uncertainty clouded his gaze. "Honey, slow is the one speed I don't think I can do for you."

The poor thing looked horrified. She guessed the bulge behind that zipper was driving his decisions. "I want you to ease out of your clothes."

"Uh, okay."

"Let me enjoy the moment."

"You want me to do a little dance?" His voice grew gruff.

There was an interesting thought. "If you want to perform a number, feel free. I just want to watch you undress."

She leaned back and put her feet up on the edge of the tub. She intended to enjoy this front-row seat.

He shrugged. "You're the boss."

"Yes, I am." She sighed as warm water covered her sore body up to her neck.

He stood on the small circular rug next to the tub. "Ready?"

"I doubt it."

He smiled as he lifted his arms above his head and stretched out like the prowling panther he was. Muscles bunched along his shoulders and rippled up his sleek arms. He grabbed the edge of his tight T-shirt and dragged it up his broad chest, revealing his hollow stomach, perfect V-shaped torso.

To encourage his impromptu striptease, Cassie kicked her leg out of the water, splashing his upper leg with tiny droplets. Resting her foot against his thigh, she curled her toes against his clenched muscle.

Cal reached down and smoothed his fingers over her damp skin, traveling up to her knee before she put an end to the touching tour.

"Now the pants."

He raised an eyebrow. "Really?"

"Do I look like I'm kidding?" She'd never been more serious in her life.

"No, ma'am."

He didn't play games, make her beg, or even make her sit

there for one more second. Instead, he reached into his back pocket and pulled out a condom.

"You always seem to have one of those handy." It was as if his pocket held a never-ending supply.

"Just took it out of my bag." His words slurred, thanks to the packet clenched between his teeth.

"I like a man who's ready for any opportunity."

He dropped the condom on the floor. "I bought a box when we stopped to get something to eat."

"Aren't you tricky?"

"Prepared." His fingers went right to his pants and fumbled with his belt and zipper.

Realizing at that second that being a silent bystander didn't appeal to her, she scrambled to her knees in front of him. "Let me."

Their eyes met in silent understanding as his hands dropped to his sides. Soapy, slick fingers explored the outline in his pants. Her thumbs rounded and explored until his body shook.

Wanting more, she leaned in and brushed a wet kiss over him to entice cooperation.

He rewarded her by bending his knees. "Damn, Cassie."

This honest wanting reaction was a confidence booster. Cassie had played a few bedroom games before now, but they tended to be at Han's request and for his enjoyment. This time the moment was for her. What she wanted and when. She loved the change.

Right now she wanted that zipper down. Cal had started the job, but she finished it with a slow steady pull that freed him to her hands. Sliding inside the rough material, she pulled him out for her touch.

His fingers clenched in her hair as she cradled and caressed him. "You're killing me."

That was the plan. Have him begging for mercy.

She threaded her fingers past the elastic band of his briefs and yanked them down his legs along with his pants, exposing all of him to her view. When she smoothed her palm along the length of his erection, his lower body bucked.

The rush of feminine power spun right to her head. He wanted her and she had the power to give him pleasure so intense it bordered on pain.

As much as she wanted to play, she needed him for more than that. She slowly pushed to her feet, using her hands and mouth to trace a path back up to his muscled stomach. By the time her tactile tour was done, her chest ached from the force of her labored breathing.

A smile broke across his sensual mouth. "You're my kind of woman."

She rubbed her wet breasts against him, feeling the slight tickle from the tufts of soft hair on his chest. The dampness in the air and the water from the bath made their bodies slick.

"Then shut up and take me." The whispered order bounced off the marble walls of the small room.

"Yes, ma'am."

Strong hands helped her out of the tub. As soon as her feet hit the mat, he dropped to his knees taking her with him. The move put him on the floor with her straddling him. His large hands wrapped around her body to pull her close. Once there, palms gently kneaded the flesh of her backside.

Need spiraled inside of her. They kissed and touched. Every inch of her bare skin rested against his. Then his back hit the floor.

He dragged her body down until she rested on her knees, suspended over him. His shaft jutted out, waiting for her. "You set the speed."

"You really ready for me?" Maintaining the teasing tone was tough as her insides fluttered and pounded.

He picked the condom up off the floor. "Here."

She grabbed the packet out of his hands and ripped it open. It took a few tries to get it unrolled. The tremors rumbling through her made holding anything steady impossible. As if sensing the churning firestorm inside her, he put his palms over hers and helped with the condom.

His hands moved to her hips and pressed down. When the very tip of him entered her, his head fell back against the hard floor. "God, yes."

It was not enough. She wanted the full length of him, every inch, deep inside. She braced her hands on either side of his head, balancing her weight above him and torturing them both with only the barest touch of their flesh. Then, with deadly slowness, she pressed herself down, absorbing his body in hers.

Sensations rocketed through her. Then she moved. She rode him, long and hard, until his breath rushed out and shivers wracked his body.

Soon his body stopped shaking and the tension took over. With stiff shoulders, he lifted his upper body off the floor to kiss her. After that, her speed increased. A rhythm deep inside her took control, sending her body up and down on his until her internal muscles pulled tight.

When she thought her body could not take another second of the barrage of sensations, she pushed down one more time. The move sent his body bucking. The friction of his body pulsing beneath hers made her hips flex without any signal from her brain.

The heat rolled through the room and off their entwined bodies. She rose up one last time and plunged back down as an orgasm tore through her exhausted body.

She screamed as she collapsed on top of him. Cal did not fare any better. He lay under her with his arms spread out to the side.

It took a few beats before she could speak again. "Forget the shower, I need a heart monitor."

A chuckle rumbled in his chest and beneath her ear. "I'm pretty sure mine stopped."

Cassie wondered if that statement was the closest thing to a compliment she would get from Cal. She balanced her upper body on her elbows and stared down at him.

"You gonna be up for another round, flyboy?"

The ceiling began to spin. He twisted their bodies until he was on top. "You're the boss."

"Now you're getting it."

"No, but I hope to after a few minutes of rest. I'm not twenty anymore, you know."

She laughed until his mouth covered hers. Then she lost the power to form words.

Chapter Twenty-two

Cal had been with enough women to understand his night with Cassie qualified as something different. His lack of control around her bordered on ridiculous.

In terms of stamina, his body performed well beyond any expectations. Throughout the night he made love to Cassie four times, waking her with his hands and his mouth, and losing himself in her over and over again. If Cassie suddenly grew fangs, he'd probably still find her alluring.

This was all Dan's fault.

The man could have warned him about his baby sister. Referring to her as typical didn't do her justice. Didn't let Cal get prepared either. He had no defenses against this woman.

"Hey." Cassie stood in the doorway between the bedroom and living area snuggled in a shapeless white terry cloth robe. Rosy pink skin, glowing fresh and clean from her shower, peeked out.

To be completely correct, this was her second shower of the morning. The first one ended up with Cassie perched against the tiled shower wall with a leg in the air, covered in nothing but him.

Who would have thought a black-and-white-checked room could inspire such passion?

He leaned back with his arms stretched along the top of the leather couch. "You look clean."

"Nice outfit." She nodded in the direction of his groin.

Cal glanced down at his striped boxers and gray T-shirt. He had slipped out of the room while Cassie was in the shower and bought the unappealing outfit at a small boutique in the lobby. Damn clothes cost a fortune.

"I prefer yours." Only because unwrapping that cloth wouldn't take more than a second. "Feel better?"

"Definitely." She nodded in the direction of the papers strewn across the coffee table. "What are you doing?"

"Separating the papers from the backpack."

Folding her legs beneath her, she sat down next to him. "Anything interesting?"

How did he tell Cassie that the torn papers in his hand put Dan in business with Bobby Polk? The documents on the official letterhead talked about Dan running antiques. The handwritten notes and what was left of the ledgers suggested something else. Looked like Dan received a percentage from the sale of the goods. Where those goods came from was the real question.

This was the same nightmare Cal experienced in the Air Force. He got stuck figuring out the truth. He had to set the record straight when Dan screwed up.

Pitching his voice low, Cal tried to soothe her for the shock to come. "Cassie, we need to talk about something."

Her face paled. "Don't do this again."

Not exactly the response he expected. Before he could question what was going on in that usually sharp mind of hers, she started yelling.

"What is wrong with you? Why do you keep doing this?" Her voice quivered.

He recognized her anger. The rest of her reaction had him stumped. Her anger could ignite in a nanosecond. Usually he did something to deserve it, but this time something lit her fuse before he had said anything.

"Want to explain what you're talking about?"

She tapped her fingers on the armrest. "This is the cave thing all over again."

What cave thing? "I have no idea what you're talking about."

Her mouth opened then snapped shut.

"Just give me a hint," he said.

"What did you want to talk about?"

"Among other things, the fact you've lost your mind."

She waved a hand in the air. "Before that."

"That we need to have a conversation about Dan."

"Oh." She made a clicking sound with her tongue. "Well, then, go ahead."

"That's it? All that outrage and now it's gone."

"Uh-huh."

He would never understand women. Especially Cassie.

She twisted the belt robe in her fingers. The tug opened the gap between the sides of the robe, exposing a bit more skin. "Did you find something in the papers?"

He glanced at the blank television screen in an effort to clear his mind and focus. "It's not about the papers right now. I'm talking about Dan and his time in the service."

She smiled. "Not you, too."

She kept throwing him off stride. "What do you mean?"

"Dan would talk for hours about the thrill of flying. Apparently the ladies were quite impressed with the talk."

"Except you."

"I'm not really up for a conversation about your conquests."

Cal decided to try another tact. "Did Dan ever tell you why he left the service?"

She shrugged her shoulders. "He said it was time to move

on. Spending all those years going into dangerous situations took something out of him."

Cal understood that reality. It just wasn't the reality of why Dan left the service. "It's tough work."

"Really, though, I think he regretted leaving the second after he did. He wasn't the therapy or meds type, but whatever plagued him manifested itself liked depression. He finally turned a corner when he opened the tourist business. Then . . ."

When her eyes filled, Cal reached out and squeezed her hand. "I know, baby."

"Sorry." She sniffed back the tears.

"You're allowed to mourn."

"I don't want to. Not now, but it just sneaks up on me without warning."

"You can't turn emotions on and off like that."

"You do."

Well, he was trying. "I miss him, Cassie."

She threaded her fingers through his. "I know."

He nodded because he didn't trust himself to say anything right then. She wasn't the only one who got hit with memories of Dan if she stopped long enough to let herself think about him.

"Anyway." She wiped her eyes. "I think he missed the service right until the end. He just learned to deal better with being retired."

Now he had to fix Dan's lies. "Are you sure?"

"About?"

"His removal wasn't voluntary, Cassie."

Her beautiful eyes narrowed. "Removal?"

"Dan had to leave. He broke the rules, got caught, and got escorted out of the service. There weren't any charges and he kept his pension along with an honorable discharge, but the facts pointed to something else."

She shot to her feet, leaving Cal's hand behind on the couch. "That's not true."

Her robe hung open. The belt remained wrapped around her hand but she didn't seem to notice that the rest of her was on display. All of her focus, all of her fury, centered on him.

"There's no mistake."

"Tell me."

A pain moved into his chest. He tried to breathe in but his lungs actually ached from the effort. "Cassie, you don't want all the details."

"You think I'm just going to take your freaking word for this?"

Would that be so much to ask? "I haven't earned that right yet?"

"No."

No thought. Just no. Part of him wanted her to agree, to at least leave open the possibility.

"Well, tell me your story." Her bare foot started tapping. "I can decide the rest from there."

There was no reason to back out now. He pushed and she made her position clear. She believed in Dan no matter what, even if that meant not believing in him. "Dan worked hard but liked to goof off."

"Sounds like all pilots to me."

"He stayed on the right side of the line, never endangered the team or a mission, until one day. He went up and made some bad decisions, and they ended his career."

Her skin tone matched the off-white robe. "Describe these decisions."

Cal hesitated about going on because there was no easy way to disillusion her. She held Dan up as some superhuman. Finding out he was human, and a flawed one at that, might destroy her.

"He was playing games while flying and had a near miss."

"An accident."

He delivered the final killing blow. "He was drunk, Cassie."

Her face pinched. From her eyes to her mouth, everything closed in.

"You should sit back down," he said.

Her fingers turned pure white where she choked off the blood supply with the belt. "Dan was not an alcoholic."

"Agreed."

"Well, then—"

"He drank too much. Way too much for a pilot and far too close to flying time. He broke those rules more often than I can tell you."

"Did you?"

"Never." Cal never claimed to be perfect, but that was not a sin that could be laid at his door. "He frequently got sloppy."

She shook her head hard enough to hurt herself. "I refuse to believe that."

"He was always looking for the next thrill. On this particular day, he thought he could handle the booze and perform a helicopter routine run. He was wrong. He hadn't dried out before he went up."

She pressed the heels of her hands to her eyes. Cal knew she was fighting between anger and tears. He wanted nothing more than to take her in his arms and comfort her. But her mindless case of hero worship was not doing either of them any good.

"Cassie, you need to listen to me." He reached for her hand.

She pulled out of range. "The person you're describing is not my brother. He never touched alcohol the whole time he was flying in Hawaii."

That was a relief. Cal hoped that meant Dan turned his

life around before the end. The idea of Dan being involved in something illegal, something that led to his death, made Cal sick.

"He was a good man." Her voice shook with fury.

"Yes. That and a great pilot and a loyal friend. He made mistakes and paid for them." Cal never understood what went so terribly wrong with Dan that day years ago. His best friend had strayed past class clown and walked right into danger territory.

It was bad enough Dan had to punch out and let a multi-million-dollar aircraft crash into the sea, but Dan's negligence nearly cost the lives of two other men, Cal included. Two weeks tied to a hospital bed did not cool his fury. He almost ripped Dan apart with his bare hands as soon as he was able to walk again.

Cal relieved Dan of command instead.

She wrapped her arms over her stomach and ran her hands up and down her arms. "You're talking about my brother and don't even care what you're saying."

"He was my friend."

"*Was*. And now I know why."

Her words sliced through him. He knew this moment would come. He tried to keep separate from her to prevent this scene. That failed. Problem was, there were worse moments ahead of them because only part of the story was out there.

Still, hearing her stark loss of faith damaged him. "I'm not shitting you, Cassie. This is real."

"I know Dan better than anyone. Even you. Especially you."

"Did you?"

"What is that supposed to mean?"

He refused to let her hide behind that lie. "I spent every day with him for years. You were his sister, not his best friend. Not the person he confided in."

"I suppose you think that was you."

"It was me."

Her whole body shook. "You have no idea what you're talking about."

He knew she was desperate to convince him. He stood up thinking to go to her, but she stepped back so fast she almost lost her balance.

He lifted his hands in surrender. "Okay. Just listen to me."

When she nodded, he forged ahead. "I was there. His stunt had consequences. I was one of them."

"You were in the plane?"

"Two surgeons put my leg together again and that was the easy part of my recuperation."

"We've been all over each other and I didn't see—"

He turned to the side revealing an angry scar that ran from just below the back of his knee to his ankle. "I don't exactly show it off."

She sat down hard on the chair opposite the leather couch.

"At first Dan denied the alcohol use. He had escaped without injury and showed up at the hospital, sober, and demonstrated the appropriate amount of concern."

"Now you're saying he didn't care that his plane crashed?" Her voice climbed an octave as she spoke.

Cal inhaled, letting the fresh intake of oxygen calm his rising anger. "I didn't mean it that way. Of course he cared. He also was concerned about saving his butt. Other people got hurt."

"You." It was a statement, not a question.

"Yeah."

"Is there more?" She tapped her fingers against the chair in what he assumed was supposed to be a show of disinterest. "Maybe you have some stories about my parents. Or maybe my grandmother. Why stop with Dan?"

Tears brimmed her eyes but did not fall.

Seeing her this upset punched him in the gut. "I'm not trying to hurt you."

"Well, you failed."

He slowly dropped to his knees in front of her, giving her plenty of time to get away from him. "You needed to know the truth."

"Why now? Why not before we had sex?"

He refused to touch that insinuation. They had enough to fight about and overcome without her manufacturing arguments. "As much as I don't like it, it is possible Dan was involved in this mess with Polk."

This time she shoved at his shoulders with eyes that mirrored her disgust. "What kind of friend are you?"

Good question. One Cal had asked over and over again since the incident that had nearly cost his life. At the time, he had debated turning Dan in. For Dan's safety and for the protection of those who worked with him, Cal had a duty to shut down Dan's ability to fly. At the very least, Dan needed help before he could go out again.

Out of fear of the deadly accident that could happen if Dan went unchecked, Cal issued an ultimatum. Dan had to come clean and get help. If not, he would face full charges for his actions.

After an internal battle that waged for days, Cal vowed to tell his superiors about the alcohol. About the fact Dan hid his use until it was too late to save the aircraft and spare the crew. If that was the only way to save Dan from himself, Cal would do it and face the consequences for his disloyalty.

Dan picked a third alternative. He went over Cal's head, worked out a deal, and walked out on the Air Force and their friendship forever. Until the recent contact, Cal hadn't heard from Dan. Cal had tried. Dan refused to reciprocate.

"Why are you saying all of this?" she asked in a voice full of hurt.

"Because it's the truth." He swallowed what remained of his good sense. "And because you deserve to know the truth about the man you are rushing to defend."

Chapter Twenty-three

Cassie wanted to scream and thump her fists against Cal's chest until he hurt as much as she did. "You know what I'm hearing?"

"Not really."

"Dan hit a hard time and you ran away from him."

Cal slouched back on his ankles. "That's not true."

"Did you decide Dan was no good? I mean, why else would you turn your back on him?"

"Dan didn't keep in touch with any of us after it happened. I tried. He wouldn't listen."

She didn't want to be near Cal right now, so she stood up and walked to the window. The stunning view appeared bland to her now. "This is unbelievable."

An absolute nightmare. The news refused to compute in her brain. The fun-loving Dan she knew could control his impulses. He did not fool around with safety. He would not have endangered Cal, a friend he held so dear.

But how much did she really know him? She fostered certain memories of him. There were whole parts she could not fill in. He left before she reached her teens and stayed away and in the air after. Still, she adored him. He was her big brother. Her hero.

She tried to calm the storm battering her insides. First

was Dan. Then the way Cal delivered the devastating information, so straightforward and clear, in a voice shaking with emotion. The way Cal called out in his sleep the night before. All that control loosened when he relaxed.

From the whispered words and frantic thrashing in bed, she knew he had survived some sort of ordeal. Now Cal wanted her to believe the source of that anguish came at Dan's hands. All of the details swirled in her mind. She tried to separate them out and make sense of them. The desperate need to hold on to the Dan she knew would not abate.

Through all of her confusion and the haze of pain that enveloped her, she looked down at Cal. Part of her wanted him to feel as lost as she did. To have him wallow in this awful middle ground where he didn't know what or who to believe. Then she noticed that he had not moved from his position on the floor.

With his head downcast he massaged the back of his neck. He had given her limited eye contact during the horrible conversation. Now he didn't look at her at all.

In a universe of confusion and uncertainty, it was clear that something else wasn't right. "What aren't you telling me?"

His head shot up. "Huh?"

"You're holding back something. What's missing?"

"Nothing."

For the first time since their brief relationship, Cassie sensed an outright lie. His gaze met hers, then slid away. There was more to this incident than Cal wanted to admit. She refused to believe any part of the story, but Cal believed it. For whatever reason, he was invested in the idea of Dan being the bad guy.

"People were wrong about Dan then and they're wrong now."

"Cassie, I only told you this because it could come out if we continue digging around."

"What do you mean?"

"Eventually someone will get the information. If there is an illegal operation going on and we prove that, a lot of people are going to be pointing a finger at Dan as an accomplice."

The story got worse and worse. "That's ridiculous."

"People could jump to conclusions. Decide that once a screw-up, always a screw-up."

The prospect of dragging Dan's solid reputation as a Hawaii businessman through the mud made her stomach flip inside out. Rumors started flying right after the accident. Questions about his competence. Crude smirks and side jokes whispered along with the public condolences. Now it would be worse. The rumors would crescendo into a deafening thunder.

"You think Ted will grab on to this to justify his accident finding."

Cal looked thoughtful. "Despite your theory on the police, my sense is that Greene knows his job. I also think he liked Dan."

"He had a strange way of showing it. I'm not sure I trust him."

She didn't know whom to trust at the moment. But she did know that whatever romantic notion she had about Cal was gone. They weren't on the same side. Dan trusted Cal enough to call him for help. She would listen and stay close, but the days of being naïve and borderline lovesick were over.

"So, what now?" she asked.

Some of the tension left Cal's face. "Well, boss, you have any suggestions?"

"When I do, you'll know it."

"Then let me suggest that we take a road trip."

She should have taken control of the conversation when

she had the chance. "I am absolutely not getting into another plane with you."

Right now being on land together held uncertainty, let alone sailing through the air in a grown-up version of a paper plane.

"We did okay last time." He managed to look innocent when he said it.

"Not going to happen. My feet stay on the ground."

"How about a car?"

"Where are we going?"

"To the building referenced in some of these papers."

"Aren't we supposed to check in with the police today?"

"We can do it later." Cal's stare was so intense it burned through her. The force of it made her want to squirm.

"Why do I think you're hiding something again?"

He smacked his lips together. "Did I mention that we have to drive straight up the only road leading to the top of the canyon?"

"I'm impressed there's even a road," she said dryly. "That'll be a nice change."

"Yeah, and some parts are even paved."

"The others?"

"Dirt. Rocks. Maybe a trench or two."

"Fabulous. I'm driving." She walked toward the bathroom.

"Cassie?"

She stopped at the sound of his voice but didn't turn back to him. Not this time.

"I'm sorry about Dan."

A rush of emotion clogged her dry throat. Cal could reduce her to a puddle of tears with only a few words.

"Oh, and Cassie? You sure I can't drive?"

"Why?"

"I drive like I fly."

Chapter Twenty-four

Cal glanced out the car window and down over the steep cliff just outside the car. "You do know that I could hop on one leg and still beat this car up the canyon."

"You're welcome to get out and jump around. Don't let me stop you." Cassie's slender hands never released their death grip on the wheel.

"I'm pretty sure my ninety-year-old grandmother could beat this pace." Cal prayed for a stiff wind to help push them up the mountain.

"Aren't we funny?"

"Bored might be closer to the truth." The scene outside the car resembled something out of an old movie. A slow-motion movie.

Cassie drove like a scared kid on the first day of Drivers' Ed. She hugged the shoulder even when one didn't exist. Her idea of a leisure drive lulled him into a coma. She drove at least twenty miles under the speed limit, which was quite a feat since the posted speed was only thirty. Several times he expected the car to lose traction and slide backward.

"You just drive faster than I do."

He wondered when she moved into the land of self-delusion. "There are trained bears that can drive faster than you."

"I meant that you drive too fast. You raced me all over the island."

"At no time was your life in danger from rioting drivers desperate to pass us." He reached over and tapped her knee. "Try hitting the gas pedal."

She slapped at his hand. "Don't touch me or the wheel while I'm driving. Ever."

"I have to do something to stay awake."

"Get out the map."

"I thought you were from here."

"Wrong island." She shot him a quick glance before returning her full focus to the road ahead. "Besides, do you know every road and part of Miami?"

"Panama City."

"Same thing."

"Not really." He pointed up to the left. "The building is after the next tourist lookout, behind trees and a huge fence."

"Or maybe we don't need a map."

"It's all up here." He tapped his temple.

"It's good to know something is."

"It wouldn't kill you to appreciate my survival and recon skills."

"Actually, this tendency you have to skulk about is fascinating."

"I don't skulk."

"Was that part of the military training or were you a petty thief in a former life?"

His head throbbed from a combination of this conversation and bad driving. "Is it too late to leave you at the hotel?"

"Tell me what you know about this building."

A great deal. While Cassie slept, he did a little research. Insomnia came in handy sometimes. "It's served many purposes over the years. First for the military, then for NASA. For a few years, the National Guard used it. Hell, even the U.S. Geological Service set up camp here for a bit."

She frowned at him before tugging the wheel too hard in a moment of panic. "Did you read an encyclopedia or something?"

"Please, try not to kill us." He glanced at the speedometer and saw that the car inched up on twenty. Six or seven months from now they'd get to their destination. "The building is supposed to be empty now. Its official status is United States government property not in use."

"What did Dan's papers say about the building exactly?"

"I only saw the address."

She hunched over the wheel even more. "That's it?"

"What, did you expect a big X with a note that this is where the bad things happened?"

"Well, yeah. Is that too much to ask?"

"Apparently."

She curled her fingers tighter around the steering wheel. "With all of those agencies using it, this place doesn't sound too abandoned."

He watched her fingers, mesmerized by their sleekness. With a jolt, he remembered what it felt like to have those eager hands curl around him. He leaned his forehead against the window and let the cool glass ease the heat on his lap.

"So, what's the plan?" she asked.

"What makes you think I have one?" He did, but he wanted her to admit she depended on him to come up with what happened next. It would be a small victory.

"You seem to have an affinity for breaking into other people's property with guns blazing." She put her turn signal on regardless of the fact there was not a turn for another mile. "I need mine back, by the way."

"It's daylight."

"And?"

"Burglary happens at night."

"Good to know you have boundaries."

"Let's just say I prefer not to broadcast the fact I'm sneaking into a place."

"Yeah, I was there the last time, remember? You entered the window and fell on your ass."

"You can sweet-talk all you want, but the gun stays with me." The idea of her holding a loaded weapon made his neck itch. Hell, he didn't even like her looking at one.

"It is mine, you know."

"The last thing I need is you shooting my leg off."

"I'd aim a bit higher." That big smile suggested she was a bit too excited by the prospect.

"I think you just proved my point." He nodded in the direction of the small clearing. "Pull over here."

"But there's no parking space over there."

"There's a shoulder."

Cassie glanced over at him and started laughing. "I guess it's good we made time for that trip to the hotel gift shop."

The woman definitely had a nasty side. "Yeah, thanks again for the snappy T-shirt."

"I really liked the way they put the little red heart between the words 'I' and 'Kauai.' It seemed *so* you."

"I look like an idiot tourist," he muttered.

"If it's any consolation, you fit in better now with the crowds than you did in that black commando outfit."

Of course, she looked adorable in her slim blue jeans and no-sleeve white polo shirt. Her skin glowed and her hair curled around her apple-shaped cheeks. She blended into their tropical surroundings.

He, on the other hand, looked like he should be wearing

black socks and slippers, with a camera tied around his neck. That would teach him to send Cassie on an errand when she was pissed. The way he figured it, he was lucky he wasn't wearing a pink jumpsuit.

Women . . .

Chapter Twenty-five

They walked across the grassy area until they ran into a ten-foot fence. The three-story steel-gray structure sat down a long driveway, the view partially covered by trees. A battered NASA sign hung from the gate protecting the entrance. Overgrown grass surrounding the place and boards covered the massive front doors.

"Nice digs," Cal said.

"The place is deserted." Cassie knew she stated the obvious, but the silence was killing her. "Of course, I'm not quite sure why NASA would have a facility up here anyway. As far as I know, the shuttle doesn't land in Hawaii."

"NASA uses sites all across the United States to track satellites and gather information, as well as for emergency landings."

Was there anything he didn't know? "Have you been memorizing the newspaper again?"

"It's all that expensive military training."

She picked up on his mumbling as he paced back and forth outside the gate. The dumb shirt and his serious expression didn't match. Despite the outfit, he managed the situation with an imposing control.

"Care to share your thoughts?" she asked.

"Hmmm."

An annoying noncommittal male grunt. Yeah, she just couldn't get enough of that noise. "Did you have something to offer that's actually a word?"

"Not yet."

Then she picked up on the focus of his staring. The shiny, new lock on the old gate. She stepped forward to investigate.

His arm shot out, catching her across the middle. "Watch out."

She traced her foot in the dirt. "I'm not really a wait-and-see kind of gal. Just tell me what I'm supposed to be seeing, flyboy."

"Look around you."

Rocks. Shrubs. "Uh, okay."

"There are tire tracks and footprints."

He definitely won the eyesight contest because she saw only dirt.

"There's been a lot of activity around here for a place where no one is supposed to be." He crouched down and balanced his elbows on his knees.

"Nosy tourists?"

"I doubt it. The tire tracks are on both sides of the gate."

Now that she concentrated, kind of squinted and crossed her eyes a bit, she saw the signs. The entire abandoned building scene looked contrived. "The paved driveway looks new."

Cal stood up and flicked her chin with a finger. "Good catch. Not bad for a gravy artist."

"Graphic."

"Whatever the term, you're quite an investigating partner."

Her heart rate jumped. "I believe *boss* is the word you're looking for."

"Come on." His smile was warm and inviting. He took off in a brisk walk, following the line of the fence around the outside of the building.

She raced after him. "More hiking? 'Cause, you know, a little desk work would be a welcome change."

He flashed that killer smile over his shoulder. "Getting soft?"

"You are so lucky I don't have a gun on me now."

They stumbled over rocks and skidded to a halt at the far side of the building. Good thing, because the back sloped down the sheer cliff leading to the ocean below. A few more steps and they would have been rolling downhill and ending in a splash.

She scanned the area. "Are those garage doors?"

"Three of them." Cal shook his head in disgust. "Looks like the bolted front door isn't the only way into this shack. Nothing like a back door to hide the comings and goings."

"Except if someone is watching by air."

"Care to explain that?"

"Dan would have seen what was happening here as he flew over." She held on to the idea. It supported her theory about Dan seeing the wrong thing at the wrong time.

She wanted to ask Cal his opinion but feared he would dash her hopes. Better to nurture the positive thought inside then let him squash it.

"Dan wasn't the only pilot to fly past this spot. We should see what Ed knows," Cal said.

"I notice you didn't suggest asking Ted or anyone associated with the police department to tag along."

Cal gently tugged on her elbow. "Funny thing, isn't it?"

"If I didn't know better, flyboy, I'd say you're starting to believe my side of this story."

"Let's just say that getting shot at the second I landed on Kauai made you more believable as an innocent victim."

What the hell kind of comment was that? "How charming."

"Yeah, well, I know how to make the ladies crazy."

"You do."

He smiled. "Interesting you admit that."

"Oh, that's not a compliment."

"You ever notice that these two are always exactly where they're not supposed to be?" Josh downed the remainder of his coffee and set the empty cup on Ted's dashboard.

"The car isn't a trash can." Ted's gaze never left the NASA building. Their lookout area sat a good hundred feet away down the hill, but his binoculars gave him a perfect view.

Josh snatched the plastic cup. "You want me to get out of the car and find a trash can. Better yet, I could walk right up and let them know we're following them."

"Yeah, and take your smartass attitude with you."

"It's all I have."

Ted's lips thinned into a grim line. "You never did tell me what happened in Nohea's office. The boss called you in for a chat. You came out fuming."

"He's an idiot bureaucrat."

"That's not news."

"I can't get his help on this."

"You mean investigating the crash?"

"Sort of."

Actually, not at all. Josh meant in getting Nohea to tell the NTSB the truth about Dan's involvement with the DEA. Forget about clearing the guy's name, though that was an issue. The bigger point was in catching the bastards who were running drugs and killing innocent citizens.

"Just end this operation. I don't like any part of this and don't like risking my office on your scheme."

Josh couldn't blame Ted for wanting to get this done. He only had half of the information and was taking a huge risk, both personally and professionally.

"You've made your position clear on how much patience you have left for this."

"We both have a lot at stake here. Cal is not going to let this go until he finds something." Ted's deep voice echoed through the car.

"He has the bag."

Ted shook his head. "That was a triumph, by the way. How did you let Cal grab it?"

"I planted it for Bobby to find. The guy's been all over the crash site. I put the word on the street about items being found and knew he would wander up there."

"You didn't count on Cassie and Cal getting there first."

"Apparently not." Josh took out his pen and tapped it against his teeth. The move helped him think.

"Not the best timing."

"Bobby knows. He and the girlfriend have been tailing Cal all over the island since seeing him with the bag. It's only a matter of time before they get to Cal."

"Sounds like everyone wants the damn bag." Ted started the car. "Also sounds like we've created a pretty dangerous situation for Cassie and Cal."

"For the plan to work, I need Bobby to have the bag."

Ted shifted into reverse and edged his car onto the road. "Then make it happen before someone else gets hurt."

"I haven't exactly been spending my days checking e-mail, you know."

"Doing your nails?"

"You might want to remember that you're not the only one in this car who carries a gun."

Ted smiled. "Just figure out the answer. I can only hold this together for so long. Cal doesn't trust me. Cassie even less so."

"Sounds like these two are smarter than we thought."

Chapter Twenty-six

Ed leaned back, balancing his considerable weight on the thin back legs of his metal desk chair. "I have no idea."

"I was hoping for something a little more helpful." Cal roamed around Ed's messy office, picking up papers and putting them back down without reading them.

For once, Cassie thought Cal was being pretty reasonable in his frustration. "Come on, Ed. You know what's going on around the island. People talk. Someone must have said something."

"All true, Cassie darling, but I'm as in the dark as you are about what's going on at the old NASA building. The government moved its operations out a few years back, something about needing more space. As far as I knew until I heard from you, the place was deserted."

"Dan never said anything about the building?" Cal flipped through the calendar on the wall, then let the pages fall back.

"No. And why don't you sit down?"

"Too restless," Cal said.

"So, another dead end." Cassie felt the disappointment like a kick to the stomach.

"Maybe not." Ed clicked his tongue against the roof of his mouth. "I did find something interesting."

Cal leaned on Ed's desk with a thigh perched on the edge. "You gonna make us beg?"

"Nothing too exciting, mind you, but something." Ed eased his chair back to stable ground and stood up.

He walked over to the four-shelf bookcase and slid some stacks of paper to the side. He reached to the back, pulling out a small box. After moving it around in his hands, Ed handed Cal the object.

"What is it?" Cassie moved in and hovered over Cal's shoulder.

Cal traced his fingertips over the box's lid with a reverent gentleness she found touching. Not so touching that she felt like waiting while he caressed the thing.

"Open it," she said.

"Patience is a virtue."

"So is speed."

He opened the small box and unfolded the paper inside with such slow and careful movements she thought her heart would explode. Leave it to Cal to pick this moment to be careful.

"Any closer and you'll be sitting on my lap," Cal said.

Amazing how it only took two seconds for the man to extinguish her good mood. "You wish."

Never mind the fact she had crowded so close to him that she was almost tucked up under his arm. There were two choices, shyly back away or come out fighting. False bravado won. "What I'd like is a little more action and a lot less talking."

Ed laughed full and loud, his body shaking from the force of it.

"She's not funny," Cal grumbled.

"No, but the two of you are interesting," Ed shot back, not missing a beat.

"We aim to please."

Being the butt of their joke did not appeal to Cassie. "Speak for yourself."

Cal kept turning the page over, rereading. Finally he dropped his hands. "Ed's right. The writing on this is nonsense."

Cassie leaned in closer until Cal's earthy, woodsy scent filled her head. Strong and dependable, sexy and charming. So many good things, except for his ability to turn his emotions on and off with a speed that knocked her breathless.

Cal exhaled as he read the information on the faded lined papers a second time. "There are ten lines of letters and numbers. No idea what any of it means."

"That's Dan's handwriting." She made the admission not knowing if the words helped or hurt Dan's case.

Cal glanced at Ed. "Why do you think this means something?"

"After the break-in we had here—"

Cal held up his hand. "Whoa. Wait a minute. Start at the beginning."

The information finally clicked in Cassie's brain. "What break-in?"

Ed plunked back down in his chair and folded his arms behind his head. "A few weeks before Dan's death we came in and someone had tossed the place. Dumped the drawers and rifled through the papers."

"No one ever told me any of this. Why am I only hearing about this now?" She had asked every question she could think of over the past four weeks and no one bothered to spill that information.

"Don't be upset, Cassie darling. This kind of stuff happens from time to time. Kids usually."

The logic didn't make sense. "Dan died right after. Don't you think the two could be related?"

"Back up a second." Cal took over the questioning. "Was anything missing?"

Ed shook his head. "Absolutely nothing. Ted chalked it up to a high school prank."

Her fury rose again. "Figures. Ted has a habit of viewing crimes against my family as delusions and exaggerations."

Cal frowned. "This probably isn't the best time to argue about the island's police department."

"Fine. If later is good for you, let me know." She looked at her watch to emphasize her sarcasm.

Cal stared at her for an extra beat, then turned back to Ed. "You were saying?"

"Dan had the paper in his wallet. After we cleaned everything up, he put it in that box. I didn't think anything of it until you started asking about Dan's business. Dan must have thought it was important enough to hide."

The secrecy hit her like a body blow. She thought she knew her brother so well. He fought off down times. Everyone did. Cassie chalked them up to island fever. Now she wondered.

He hid so much from her. Dealt with everything alone. The idea that he had grappled with depression and alcohol issues and never bothered to let her in sent a flash of sadness coursing through her. It didn't have to be that way. She didn't understand why he had made the choices he did when she was right there to help.

Cassie threw up her hands. "I guess we don't know where the box came from, either."

"I do." Cal's clipped words grabbed everyone's attention.

Well, of course he did. Cassie wondered how many more secrets she could tolerate on one day.

"Well?" Ed probed.

A sad smile played on Cal's lips as he turned the small box over in his hands. "A big-wig corporate recruiter once tried to lure a few of us away from the military, to get us to fly overpaid businessmen around the country. The guy handed out the boxes. As a joke, Dan and I put our own inscription on the bottom."

Cassie plucked the box out of the safety of his large hands and turned it over. "This is it?"

"What's it say?" Ed asked.

A rush of air caught in her throat, temporarily choking her. She struggled to force the words out. "So Others May Live."

"The PJ motto." Cal's voice shook slightly as he faced her, his gaze unflinching.

A sudden warmth flowed through her. "You were friends."

Cal stared at her with an intensity that made her gasp. "I loved him like a brother. Whatever else you think or hear, remember that."

Cassie had been running from her attraction to Cal from the minute she spied him climbing through her brother's window. Seeing the desperation in Cal's eyes now, watching him cradle the evidence of his loyalty to Dan in his hands, she tripped and fell right in love with him.

No fanfare. No fireworks. No long-term dating and getting-to-know-you phase. More like wrapping in a warm blanket on a cool winter evening.

She tucked away the knowledge of these newly realized feelings. Right now, loving him only clouded the issue.

Cal sobered and started issuing orders in true Cal fashion. "We need to work on the paper and figure out what the series of numbers and letters mean. Dan thought they were important enough to hide, so they must be."

Ed gave the box one more look. "Think it's code of some kind?"

Cal grabbed on to Ed's question with a ferocity that surprised her. "Absolutely. Dan wasn't the type to doodle. If he wrote something down and went to the trouble of keeping it safe, it's important."

"Unfortunately that doesn't help us solve this thing," Cassie said.

Cal nodded in Ed's direction. "Do any code cracking in your time?"

"I have some skills in that area."

This was too much. "Okay, enough with the spy stuff. You're an aircraft mechanic."

"True, Cassie darling, but I have other interests." Ed had the nerve to wink at her.

The machismo filling the room made her crazy. "I don't want to know about your interests."

"I second that," Cal said.

She inhaled nice and deep before diving into a new subject. "What are we doing next?"

"Easy. Ed's going to make a copy of the paper for me and keep the original. We're both going to work on the code and, in the meantime, you and I are going to pay a visit to Ted."

"For God's sake, why?" Cassie asked.

Cal handed the box back to Ed and watched him scurry into the other room as fast as possible for a two-hundred-thirty-pound male. Cassie figured he was following Cal's orders about making the copy.

"In the first place, Ted told us to come in." Cal stepped in front of her. Before she could balk, his hands found her arms and the distance between them closed.

"Like I care about that."

"Second, it's time to see what the police know about Dan's death, the break-in, and all the other crap happening on this island."

"No freaking way."

"You love that word."

"Which one?" She thumped on his chest. "Never mind that. Ted can't be trusted."

"Funny thing about trust. Sometimes the line gets blurry."

No question that loving Cal and liking him were two very different things. "It shouldn't."

"You're being naïve."

"You're being obtuse."

A grin lit up his face. "That sounds dirty."

And if she let this conversation go much further . . . well, they would be visiting a hotel room instead of Ted. "Time to go, flyboy."

Chapter Twenty-seven

An hour later, they walked into police headquarters as Ted glanced up from the file in front of him. "Nice shirt."

Cal had forgotten about his damn outfit. "Yeah, thanks for letting me borrow it from your closet."

"I bought it for him." Cassie stepped out from behind him in a mood bordering on playful.

Ted's eyebrow lifted. "So, you hate him now?"

Cal had thought the same thing when she took it out of the bag. "Seems that way, doesn't it?"

"A woman never tells," Cassie said.

Cal assumed the light conversation meant Cassie was ready to give Ted a chance. Either that or she planned to scream at the poor guy at the first chance. The scenario could go either way.

"I'm not one to question a woman's taste." Ted motioned for the officer standing nearby to take over at the front desk. "You two, come back to my office."

Ted started walking without seeing whether they followed. Cal had no intention of getting stuck out front a second time. He wanted to see what was happening in the police back office. Also planned to check the area for Josh. The guy supposedly worked for the DEA, but Cal had his doubts.

They walked through an open area with several desks. A few officers looked up as they passed. None looked familiar or all that interested in their presence.

Ted showed them into his glassed-in corner office and shut the door behind them. "Have a seat."

Since there were exactly two chairs in the room other than the one behind the desk, Cal took one.

"I was about to send out a car to haul you in." Ted sat down in his imposing leather chair and propped his feet up on his desk.

"That would have been a bit drastic, don't you think?" Cal asked.

"I think I need to do something to catch your attention and remind you the police run the investigations on Kauai."

"Oh, you have our interest. Don't worry about that." Cassie plopped down in the chair directly in front of Ted.

Tension vibrated through the room. The light talk hid something much deeper. Ted gave off an in-charge vibe, but something else bubbled there. A level of uncertainty that Cal couldn't pinpoint. But then, nothing had made sense since he landed in Hawaii.

What started as a desperate attempt to mend fences with Dan and pay off past debts turned into a confusing mess. He counted Cassie as the only positive thing to happen in days. Months, even.

"You two ready to tell me what's going on?" Ted continued to sprawl. His outward appearance stayed calm.

Cal sensed the man was poised to pounce. "We were hoping you'd tell us that."

Ted dropped his feet on the ground with a thud. "Me?"

"Without all the bullshit this time, if possible," she said.

Leave it to Cassie to cut through the chatter. She wanted action and made it clear she did not plan to leave without it.

Ted leaned forward, resting his elbows on his desk. "I'm not in the mood for riddles."

That made two of them. "I'm not telling any."

Ted nodded in Cassie's direction. "You have anything to add?"

"Cal's doing fine."

Cal had to swallow a laugh. When the chips were down, he could count on Cassie to follow his lead. She'd scream at him later if she wasn't satisfied with his performance, but public loyalty ranked high with her.

Ted's dark eyes narrowed. "Say what's on your mind, Cal."

"I found this."

Ted reached across the desk and took the copy of Dan's paper. Cal watched for signs of recognition. There weren't any. The reading took about two seconds.

"What is it?" Ted looked up with the same confused gaze Cal had seen on Cassie's face after she looked over the paper.

"We don't know," she said.

Ted looked back and forth between them. "What am I missing?"

Time to push the deputy around a bit. "Dan hid this note in his office after the break-in. You know, the one that occurred right before his death."

"Suspicious timing, don't you think?" Cassie asked, doing a little shoving of her own.

Ted's eyebrows lifted in confusion. "You think it's code for something? That it's related to Dan's death?"

Cal always admired an analytical mind. Ted had secrets, but he wasn't stupid. "Yeah. The break-in, the shootings, the crash. Something is going on here other than an accidental helicopter crash."

Ted rapped his knuckles against the desk. "Maybe."

No maybes about it. "We both know this is a small island for that many coincidences."

Ted stared at the desk for a few seconds before lifting his

head again. "You know this could point to Dan doing something illegal."

Cassie jumped up and wagged a finger at him. "Did you ever think maybe Dan *found* something?"

Cal tried to stop the Cassie train of doom. "Uh, Cassie—"

"That maybe Dan wasn't guilty of anything other than being in the wrong place at the wrong time?"

To his credit, Ted stayed calm under her assault. Cal wondered if the other man would give him lessons on how to handle her.

Then Ted surprised them both. "Yes."

Cassie shook her head as a downturned frown of confusion filled her face. "Yes, what?"

"Dan very well may have been in the wrong place. I agree with you. The possibility makes sense."

Cassie stood with her hands fisted at her side. From her stiff stance, it was clear she had expected more of a fight and could not quite turn off her rage.

Cal took pity on her. "Cassie, honey, sit down. If you threaten Ted, he'll have to throw you in jail."

"No way. Then she'd be here with me all day," Ted said.

Cal felt a tug of admiration for the other man. Didn't trust the guy, but did appreciate his humor.

"You're both hysterical." Cassie landed back on her chair with a thump.

For a second, Cal thought he saw Ted smile. If so it disappeared as quickly as it came.

"Any idea what these hieroglyphics mean?" Ted asked.

Cal took the plunge. "We think Dan saw something he wasn't supposed to see over at the old NASA building on the road up to Waimea Canyon."

Cassie scowled. "Aren't you chatty all of a sudden?"

He ignored her wrath. It wasn't as if this was the first time he'd experienced it. Nor would it be the last. "The list may have something to do with the building and its use to store items that shouldn't be there. We're working on it."

"Uh-huh." Ted tapped on the desk again. This time much louder than before. "And who is *we*?"

Cal silently berated himself for the slip.

"Us." Cassie wiggled her thumb between them.

Any amusement or pretend peace evaporated. Ted's tan face flushed red. "I warned you before that you need to leave the police work to the police professionals. Amateur sleuthing is only going to get you hurt."

Ted could not be more clear.

Cal chose to ignore him. "With all due respect, your office fucked up."

"Right." Ted leaned back. "How could I possibly be offended by that statement?"

"Cal's right. You brought this on yourself." Cassie waved her hand and knocked over a stack of files on the edge of Ted's desk. She caught them, but the move ruined her big speech.

Cal decided to take back over before she broke something. "Cassie could have been killed. Dan was. Do you see where I'm going with this?"

Ted's shoulders snapped straight. "I see that you're looking for an escort off Kauai."

"Even when you're confronted with the truth, you don't listen." Cassie practically screamed her outrage.

Cal expected reinforcements to burst through the door.

From the way Ted sat there, it was clear her tone did not impress him. "I hear you. I would guess that most of the population of Kauai heard you. Now, it's time for you two to listen to me. Hiding evidence or running around after false leads is not helping Dan."

"Maybe." Cal knew the word would tweak the guy, which was why he said it.

Ted's face grew even redder. "Turn over what you have to the professionals."

"We tried that already." Cassie settled back in her chair. The angrier Ted got, the calmer she became.

"Do you have more information for me?" Ted asked.

"You have what we have," Cal said.

Ted's black-eyed gaze pinned them both. "Now, why don't I believe you?"

"We came in with the paper as soon as we found it. Call it a good-faith gesture," Cal said.

"I call it covering your butt."

Cal smiled. The deputy definitely wasn't dumb.

Cassie crossed her legs. Let her foot wave in the air as she talked. "You wanted us to tell you about the shooting. Well, the second time someone tried to kill me. Not to be confused with the first attempt, which you thought was all my imagination."

Ted looked at Cal for assistance. "She always like this?"

Cal thought about lying but refrained. "Pretty much."

"I'm right here, you know," Cassie piped in.

"Believe me, we know." Laughter was evident in Ted's voice.

Chapter Twenty-eight

Cassie seethed. The whole scene played like something out of a bad movie. Dan was dead. Ted refused to look at the facts. Cal kept giving away the few kernels of information they did have.

And somehow Cal ended up in the driver's seat of the car with the keys in his hand.

He started the engine. "I'm going to do some recon at the NASA building tonight. I want to see what's so important inside there that requires a brand-new lock."

She underestimated Cal's ability to annoy her. "No, and how did you get the car keys back anyway?"

"I have the keys because your driving should be illegal." He glared at her out of the corner of his eye. "And what do you mean, *no*?"

"You are not racing around the island committing more crimes."

"I haven't committed that many."

"That's a matter of opinion."

"If you count them." He started to raise a finger as if he intended to do just that. "There's—"

"We are going back to the hotel. I'm going to sit at the bar and nurse a drink for an hour or two."

His complaining slammed to a halt. "That's a plan I can get behind."

"Good. It's settled then." She rested her head against the back of the seat and closed her eyes. Exhaustion pressed down on her, making her bones heavy.

"Right. You go to the hotel. I'll check the building."

She should have seen that coming. She forced one eyelid open. "You are not going anywhere without me."

"Then we both nurse a drink for a few hours until it gets dark, then head back up the canyon."

Figures he would pick that moment to come up with a reasonable compromise. She was so weary she could barely stand and he was making plans for a midnight covert mission.

"Think of the fun we'll have climbing that fence," he said.

Adrenaline raced through her fatigued body at the thought. Cassie decided right then she would need hours of psychological care when this nightmare was over. She was becoming as much of a thrill jockey as Cal.

"If you try to cheat me out of my drink, I'll shoot you." A woman had to take a stand somewhere.

"Fair enough."

Her eyes slipped shut again. "You might also want to change your clothes."

"But I look so good in this T-shirt."

The quiet car did not fool her. The car didn't move, and she could feel Cal looking at her.

"Cassie, we do need to talk."

That was never a good sign. He usually followed a statement like that with reminding her how little she meant to him. She could not handle that much truth right now. "We need to get back to the hotel and get that drink."

He finally started driving. The steady hum of the road beneath the car lulled her into a false sense of security. The song on the radio filled her mind, pushing out all of the doubts lodged in there.

Then he tried again. "We can't ignore this."

Yes they could. That was exactly her plan. "You're not giving *us* enough credit."

"We need to talk about what happened."

Cassie noticed he used the past tense. She squeezed her eyes tighter, trying to block out the maddening conversation. "Not now."

"You're running from a fight? That's new."

"Consider it a crawl. I'm too tired to run—"

The car lurched forward, cutting off her response. She heard the loud crack just as the tires squealed and the back end swerved to the side. The force of the blow sent her body flying forward and knocked her into the dashboard.

After the initial impact, everything moved in a slow-motion haze. She looked to her left and saw Cal's chest push into the steering wheel. The airbags didn't blow. The realization floated through her mind as a scream rumbled up her chest.

She tried to brace her weight on her forearms for fear of smashing into the window. The movement of the car rocked her body as if she weighed nothing. The seat belt stopped her forward momentum, but not until after she smacked her head into the window.

The spinning stopped, but the car kept moving. Cal's white-knuckle grip on the steering wheel did not let up. "Damn it, this guy's nuts."

"Is he drunk?"

"Doubt it."

The air raced out of her lungs, leaving her breathless and shaky. She watched terrified as Cal fought to control the car with straining forearms.

"What the hell?" Cal asked the question just as their attacker smacked into the rental car's rear bumper a second time. This hit sent them jolting forward until the harsh snap of the seat belts bounced them back in their seats.

In the haze, Cassie could see the dark car off to their left. From this angle, she could not see the driver or figure out the make or the type.

She did know the vehicle was preparing to ram them again. "Cal, watch out!"

"Hold on!"

She could barely hear Cal's shout over the sound of the blood rushing through her veins. A distant voice in her head told her to keep her head up and try to see the driver. She strained against her sore body. She made out a dark outfit just before Cal turned the wheel sharply, sending the rental car careening into the side of their attacker's vehicle.

Dirt and rocks kicked up as tires hit against the loose ground. Wheels screeched, drowning out Cassie's screams. The car listed to the side, the rotations taking it off the road. When the car spun to a stop, she bobbed in her seat before coming to a final landing. A fog of dust blocked her view but she thought their attacker had left the scene.

"I think we should . . ." The words died in her throat when she saw Cal slumped over the wheel. "Cal!"

He groaned. "I'm okay."

Cassie fumbled with her seat belt and released the lock. Blood was everywhere. On her hands. On his face. She slid across the seat and touched a shaky hand to Cal's cheek. "You're hurt."

"Don't care." His voice gained in strength the more he talked. "You okay?"

The look in his beautiful eyes was so soft and loving she wanted to melt right there. She soothed him with nonsense words. "I'm okay."

He reached out and grabbed her hand. "I'm getting out to take a look around."

He didn't look as if he could lift his head. "Just sit," Cassie ordered.

He shook his head, wincing as he did. "Don't move."

"You can't."

"Man, I'm getting too old for this." The grimace on his face said it all. Something inside hurt when he shoved the door open and staggered to his feet.

She was out of her seat and around to the driver's side of the car in two seconds. She had no idea where she found the strength or how her legs held her. "Get back in the car."

"I swear you're deaf. Baby, stay down until I know it's clear."

"You're injured. I'm in charge." She stared him down, daring him to contradict her.

He didn't, which she took as a sign of how much pain he was in. He had twice maneuvered the car to take the impact on his side. The man just never stopped protecting.

She touched his side and he hissed. "Cal?"

"My ribs ache a bit. No big deal. Trust me, I've had worse." He patted her hand.

"What can I do?"

"Promise me you're okay." He rubbed his thumb over her sore lip.

"I'm fine."

He stretched out, trying to hide his grimace, and touched his lips to hers. "That's all that matters."

With a careful touch, she buried her face in his chest and inhaled his unique scent. The fragrance of life. He weaved his fingers through her hair and kissed the silky strands.

"I was so scared," she whispered.

"You certainly hid it well. Damn you're tough under fire."

Yeah, so tough that her legs had turned into squishy wet noodles.

"That was too close." His voice was ragged. "We need to get out of here and get cleaned up."

She lifted her head. "I believe the proper procedure would be to call the police."

"Why start now?"

His wink took her by surprise. A chuckle rose from deep inside of her and bubbled out. She covered her mouth with her hand but the laughter kept coming.

Cal frowned at her. "Did you get hit in the head?"

"You know what I think?"

"I'm kind of afraid to ask."

"We should take taxis from now on."

Chapter Twenty-nine

Cal cupped his hands and let the water pool in his palms. When he lifted his head, the vision in the hotel bathroom mirror shocked him. Sunken eyes and an ashen color. A huge bruise on his shoulder and scratches on his face. Turning his hands over, he was surprised to see them tremble.

Damn aftermath.

He touched the bright white bandage wrapped around his ribs. His insides shook, not out of fear for his safety. For Cassie. She could have been killed and there was nothing he could do to stop it. On the deserted road, behind the wheel, all of his training and expertise had been damn near useless.

The mere idea of her being hurt made his blood run cold. The visual image of her beautiful body broken and bruised was enough to drive him to his knees. He did not know when she started to mean so much to him or why. The look of an angel but the stubbornness of a mule, yet he couldn't stay away.

He had to figure out a way to pack her bags and put her on a plane back to Oahu. It was time for her to go home where it was safer. Before he could change his mind, he wrapped a towel the size of a tablecloth around his waist and walked out into the bedroom. The sight that greeted him made his body tense up and his already battered muscles burn.

Cassie lay sprawled across the bed in an oversized robe. A loosely tied sash held the material together. Lean tanned legs peeked out from the opening, and she hummed a lazy tune and rocked her legs in time to the music drifting from the alarm clock.

The cuts on her face and purple blotches on the right side of her head caused fury to fill him once more. Despite his tough talk, they'd been to the emergency room to get checked over. Got some meds and took a few hours to sleep those off. Fought with the rental car company to get a new vehicle. Even talked with Ted and filed a report.

She deserved more.

"You should be at the hospital," he said to the quiet room.

"You're the one with bruised ribs, not me." She stretched her arms wide to the side. The gap in the robe slipped open even farther, revealing the mouth-watering tops of her breasts.

He stared at the ceiling and counted to ten to gain his composure. Jumping on top of her then sending her home would send a mixed message.

"Cassie, we should talk about what we're going to do next."

She lifted her head off the pile of pillows. "We're going to commit a felony. Maybe it's a misdemeanor, I don't know. It really doesn't matter because it's already decided."

"What are you talking about?"

"Breaking into the NASA building."

She had to be fucking kidding. The woman needed to rest, and a bodyguard. "I think you should go back home."

Her body stilled. "You better mean to Dan's house."

"I mean, Oahu."

"No."

No anger. No fighting. Just, no. She could throw him off balance easier than anyone else in the world.

"Cassie—"

"We're done talking about that subject, Cal." She turned over onto her stomach and shot him a heated look that spiraled straight to his groin.

The power shift in the room was apparent, and Cal knew he no longer held the top spot. To the extent it was his in the first place. But common sense demanded an attempt at reasoning. "We need to have a serious discussion."

"I said, no."

When she sat up on her knees, he could feel the water closing over his head. The opening of the robe invited him to take a long look as the beautiful creature crawled across the bed. The sight of naked, willing flesh made his knees buckle. She was the sexiest damn thing he had ever seen. And she was stalking him.

"You're hurt."

"I'm fine."

"But you have . . ." Words fell into nothingness as her robe slipped down bare shoulders.

"Yes?"

"Bruises."

She was on top of him now, rubbing her body against his. Gentle fingers released the knotted towel at his waist. "You look hot."

On fire was more like it.

"We should take some of these clothes off," she said between kisses.

"That will pretty much end the talking."

She traced his bruises with her mouth. "That's what I'm hoping."

A hot mouth inched lower, tracing every inch of skin with nibbling bites and a wicked tongue. Every injury got gentle attention. Her healing powers eased the ache in his muscles. When her head dipped one more time and she took him in her hot mouth, he forgot all about reasoning with her.

*   *   *

They ended up taking twenty-four hours to recuperate in the hotel room. The next night Cassie dragged her sore butt and injured body up a dark and deserted road to break into a building. Amazing how everything hurt more two days later.

The two wore black from head to toe. If the police stopped them, they'd be arrested for dressing like idiots.

"Tell me again why we parked so far away," she asked.

"Subterfuge."

"Overreact much?"

"Sneaking around would work better if you didn't keep shouting," he managed to whisper through clenched teeth.

Darkness fell over the area completely owing to the lack of streetlights. Hell, there weren't even any streets out here.

"I'm just saying you might be taking this covert operation thing too far." And a night or two to recuperate from their car accident didn't seem too much to ask.

Cassie had come along only because he threatened to leave her behind. She hated that.

Cal stopped without warning and turned around. The midnight blue sky obscured his face. "This isn't a game."

"Feels like one. This is the way you operate. This is about one more set of rules you're prepared to break."

His head fell to the side. "That's really how you see me?"

"You drive too fast, fly like a madman, and violate laws left and right. You live life on the edge."

"Sounds about right so far."

She wasn't sure how to respond when someone admitted to being a nut. "You're a typical thrill jockey. No risk is too great."

He looked up at the sky as if he were weighing her comments. "Was that how your last boyfriend acted?"

Now there was an unexpected turn in the conversation. "We're not talking about Han."

Cal dropped the small packet he was holding. "How can you say that name without laughing?"

"I don't know, Cal, which is short for Caleb." She cleared her throat. "I'm willing to talk about my past loves if you are."

"Don't have any."

"None?"

"Loves? None of those lurking about, no." While she stammered, he leaned in close until the tips of their noses touched. "Ready to get back to the actual topic?"

"What was it?"

"The way I figure it, my job on Kauai is to find out what happened to Dan and keep you from getting thrown in jail, which is a full-time job."

"Says the man with a propensity for trespassing."

"If you don't like how I do my work . . ."

"Yes?"

"Tough." He planted a hard kiss on her startled mouth. Before she could kiss him back, he started talking again. "Now, march that tight butt of yours up that hill before I throw you over my shoulder and carry you up there."

"Well, since you asked so nicely."

Her head reeled from the kiss. When he compounded his outrageous behavior by slapping her on the backside, she was too lost in a fog to even comment.

"Stay quiet."

"Stop bossing me around."

"That means no talking," he said.

"Thanks for the English lesson."

"I'm willing to help with any lesson you need, baby." Even in the dark Cassie could see him wiggle his eyebrows.

"Spare me."

He awarded her with a deep chuckle. "It was worth a shot."

She now knew these outrageous comments were meant to spin her up. She refused to play into his game. "I thought I was the boss."

"You can be in charge during our next burglary. Let's go."

They crouched down and approached the site at a jog from the south, stopping when they reached an outcropping of weeds and trees. She watched from behind while Cal scanned the location ahead for any movement. When it appeared the coast was clear, a prearranged hand signal indicated it was safe to move forward again.

The soft floral scent of the island wafted around them. They halted on the far wall of the building by the side facing the mysterious garages. Cal flipped open a small black roll and pulled out a miniature, sharp pair of wire clippers.

"Impressive," she said in hushed tones.

"I've been trying to tell you that."

Within minutes Cal peeled back a section of fence just large enough for the two to slide through. He squeezed his sizable frame through the small opening, then held out a hand to her. She grabbed on and followed him through.

He winked at her. "One lock conquered."

"If I didn't know better, I'd say you're enjoying this."

"It's fun unless I have to use the gun." He nodded in the direction of the building. "Ready?"

"I'm not here for the scenery, flyboy."

"You're my kind of woman."

His throwaway comment shot straight to her heart. "That's what all the boys say. Let's hit it."

All three garage doors proved impossible to open.

"What now?" she asked, figuring he had a backup plan.

"We walk in through the front." After checking the area, Cal went to work on prying the boards barring the door.

"You're not being very quiet."

Cassie was right but Cal could not figure out how to re-move nails without making a noise. The old wood creaked as he ripped it from the wall. Once he freed the lower portion of the door from obstruction, Cal poked his head through.

"For heaven's sake, be careful," Cassie choked out.

The little woman needed to lighten up. "It's clear."

He shimmied through the opening. He'd crawled through more tight spaces in the past few days on Kauai than in his entire life. Amazing how all of it traced back to Cassie.

"There is no light in here at all." She stumbled over some object but quickly regained her balance.

The oppressive darkness in the front room covered them like a blanket. Unable to find any lights in the room, Cal forged a slow path through the chairs and desks, careful not to trip or knock anything over. When he realized that wasn't working, he tried tracing a hand along the wall. If they couldn't see a door, they could still feel one.

"Feel anything?" she asked.

"Nothing I want to think about. Wait." His fingers scraped against a loose piece of metal. "A hinge."

"That means there's a door here somewhere."

He tested the door. "It's locked."

"Of course it is." Sarcasm rang out in the quiet darkness.

He dropped to his knees and used one of his prized tools to fiddle with the lock.

"You're pretty good with those things," she said from just inches behind him.

The barrier clicked open in a few seconds. Through a crack the next room came into view. A steady buzz from the fluorescent lights cut through the silent night. Racks gath-ered in the center of the football field–sized room, and the shelves overflowed with expensive-looking furnishings. Boxes and additional items littered the floor.

"I'll be damned," he whispered.

The opposite wall was solid except for two small doors. Cal assumed the garages were on the other side of those doors.

"Probably, but let me see." She pulled on his forearm until he stepped back. Then her eyes widened in shock. "This looks like a storage room for a high-end antiques shop."

"Something tells me NASA didn't leave those behind."

He conducted a visual tour of the room, looking for any signs of life. "My guess is that the rooms on either side of the warehouse walls are meant to throw people off. You know, fake rooms to give the appearance of a legitimate operation. The real action is in here."

"That makes sense, but what is this place?"

"I need to take a closer look. Stay here."

"Not on your life." She grabbed on to his arm with both hands and would not let go. "There are all kinds of beams and scaffolding above us. Someone could be hiding up there."

The woman had a point. "I'll be careful."

"Look, I'm all for heroics, but not for walking into certain death. Use your head, flyboy."

Tough talk could not hide the fear lingering behind those beautiful eyes. The pleading voice got through to him. She cared.

The realization filled him with an odd sense of comfort. For once in his life, the idea of having someone care didn't send him running for the door. He waited for the sensation, the need to bolt, to eventually overtake him. It didn't.

"I don't have a death wish," he said.

"Could have fooled me." Her mood flashed from concern to anger before he could blink.

"What's your plan, boss? We stand here and wait for the criminals to stop by and say hello?"

Cassie tucked a stray hair behind her ear. Since he liked

her hair mussed and sexy, he debated pulling it out again but decided against an action that would surely lead to broken fingers.

"We could tell the police," she said.

Telling him to grow another head would have been less surprising. "Since when do you trust the police?"

"When I don't have another choice. We've proven our point. Something illegal is going on. Now we need to turn this over to the professionals."

He went for the one button he didn't want to push. "And what if Dan was involved? What if we hand them the evidence that condemns Dan?"

Her shoulders shrank a little but her gaze did not waver. "According to you, Dan messed up before and got kicked out of the Air Force. His memory survived that. It can survive this."

The words died, leaving behind a charged silence.

"He didn't exactly get kicked out, Cassie."

She shot him a confused look. "But, I thought—"

A sharp clanging noise on the other side of the warehouse cut her off. He squatted and dragged her down beside him. Cal looked around the cavernous room, trying to find the source of the sound.

"See anything?" she asked in a low, clear voice.

"Shhh." A series of thuds preceded the sound of banging. "Someone's over there."

"We need to leave."

She was right, but . . . "We need to see who else is here."

She tugged on his sleeve. "Cal, this is too dangerous. Someone tried to kill us at least twice. We need help."

"If I knew who to trust, we could try that."

"We can't stay here." The tone was practically begging.

A deep male voice broke into their conversation. "The woman's right."

A hand snaked out and covered Cassie's mouth, smothering her stunned scream and pulling her out of the doorway. "Stay quiet."

The door closed with a click, plunging them back into the darkness of the front room. Cal cracked open the light stick in his pocket as he reached for his weapon. He stopped when he saw the identity of their unwanted company.

Josh stood with one hand over Cassie's mouth and a finger from the other crossed over his lips. Hard to miss the gun in that hand. "Not a sound."

A killing rage burned through Cal. Seeing Josh touch her, watching her face pale with terror, made him murderous. Josh could fire his weapon for all he cared. Cal doubted a bullet could stop him. "Let her go. Now."

"I need you both quiet." Gone was Josh's happy-go-lucky demeanor. The cadence of his rough voice ran fast.

Cal glanced at Cassie's face. Her eyes filled with uncertainty. "You are scaring the hell out of her."

Josh slowly lifted his hand. "Nobody do anything stupid."

Cal wasn't listening. He was beyond reason. His wrath detonated. Without any thought to the noise, he slammed Josh against the wall and knocked his head against the hard cement. Josh's gun clattered to the floor.

"Stop! Cal!"

"Listen to her," Josh hissed out.

Cassie grabbed Cal around the waist and whispered against his neck. "Cal, please. We don't know who else is here."

The pleading voice broke through the haze of anger encircling him. Josh owed her his life. Cal still wasn't convinced that the agent should get out of there without the help of a stretcher.

Instead of shoving the man back against the wall, Cal

reached down to pick up the discarded gun. "Start talking or I use this to blow out your tiny brain."

"You're not going to shoot me and we both know it."

That comment proved Josh had no idea how close to the edge Cal was. "Don't be so sure. I'm pretty sick of you appearing wherever we go."

Cassie turned to Josh. "What are you doing here?"

"Trying to save your butts. We need to get out of here."

Cal's temper still hadn't cooled. He stuck Josh's gun in the back waistband of his jeans so he wouldn't be tempted to use it. "We aren't moving one inch until you explain what's going on. This isn't routine surveillance. You're on some kind of off-the-books job."

"What gave me away?"

Cassie wasn't buying the charming act, either. Josh miscalculated on that one. "As far as I'm concerned, Cal should take a shot at you."

She was the only woman Cal knew who could face down a gun one minute and morph back into a sexy warrior the next.

Josh didn't even blink. "I followed you two to protect you."

"We heard you in the warehouse," Cassie explained.

"Not me."

The carefully crafted puzzle began falling apart in Cal's mind. "Wait a minute. We heard the sound coming from the other side of the wall. Josh was on you seconds later."

"And that means?" she asked.

Cal did not sugarcoat it. "There is someone else out there right now."

"Didn't I already say that?" she asked.

"Move over." Josh pushed them both to the side and opened the door a crack. "We need to get out of here."

Cal wanted to believe the agent's desperation was an act,

but he knew it wasn't. They were in danger. "Tell me who's out there."

"My guess? Bobby Polk." Josh held out his hand. "Give me my gun."

Cal did not argue. None of this was a coincidence. All of the pieces fit together somehow. He just couldn't figure it out.

"I don't see anyone," Cassie continued.

Josh and Cal looked at each other over Cassie's head. Josh took the lead in filling her in. "Just because you don't see them, doesn't mean they aren't there."

"What do we do?" Cassie asked.

Cal jumped in. "We leave the way we came, and we take Mr. DEA with us."

Josh nodded. "No arguments here."

Chapter Thirty

Cassie felt as useful as a potted plant listening as Josh and Cal lobbed insults at each other. All three had arrived at the hotel room a few minutes earlier and she had not heard a civil word since.

"Gentlemen, as enjoyable as this is, could we get down to business?"

Cal leaned back on the couch. "I'm waiting for him to say something worth listening to."

"I'm waiting for you two to tell me why you look as if you fell into the canyon." Josh surveyed their wounds as he talked.

"Car accident," Cal said.

"Ted told me."

"Of course he did," Cassie mumbled.

"You both okay?"

Cal smacked his lips together. "Like you give a shit."

"Maybe we should step outside and work off a bit of this excess energy," Josh suggested.

Cal moved his arm in a sweeping gesture toward the door. "After you, Suzy."

Cassie's temper exploded. "Enough! I'm tired of playing the role of room monitor."

"Yes, dear," Cal grumbled.

"Sorry," Josh grunted in agreement.

Time for reason to trump male stupidity. "You say you were at the warehouse to *protect* us."

"I'm thinking you don't trust me."

"Correct." She fell into the only empty chair in the room and massaged her pounding temples. The blinding pain behind her eyes undoubtedly came from the overdose of testosterone pumping through the small room. At least she hoped that was the cause.

"I followed you because you were about to stumble into the middle of an ongoing investigation. Months of planning shot to hell because you're nosy."

Cal folded his arms across his broad chest. "Describe the operation."

"No deal." Josh shook his head. "My only goal was to make sure you didn't inadvertently attract the attention of some very nasty folks. The information train stops there."

"Let me tell you what I think is going on." Cal traded lounging for straight-backed alertness. "Someone is running stolen goods through Kauai using that building. Those goods are either being used to finance drug transactions or the drugs are hidden inside."

Josh nodded. "Good story so far."

"Dan saw the operation on a fly-over and reported it to someone, maybe you. Now he's dead."

Josh whistled. "Nice addition."

Cassie noticed the agent didn't exactly deny the scenario. "We deserve an explanation."

"Cassie's right. We've been shot at and nearly run off the road—"

Josh sat up. "Tell me about that."

"Two days ago. Someone tried to make us part of the canyon wall. We escaped because Cal has the skills of a racecar driver and the brain of a two-year-old."

"Thanks." Cal's brow furrowed. "I think."

"Are you sure you're okay?" Josh reached out to touch her knee with obvious concern.

"Move your fingers before I break them off," Cal ordered.

She ignored the bellowing. "We're fine. The jury still is out on whether Cal sustained a brain injury, but we'll have to wait and see."

"You love my driving," Cal mumbled.

She was not about to get pulled off track after what had happened. Her nerves were at the snapping point and she needed answers. "The point is that someone wants to keep us from looking into Dan's death and I want to know why."

"There have been some rumors," Josh said.

Nuh-uh. "Be specific."

The bright light went out in Josh's blue eyes. Suddenly he hesitated. The change of mood put Cassie on alert. She steeled herself against the bad news she sensed was about to come.

Josh took her hand in his, a move that earned him a growl from Cal. "Look, I have a job to do here. You should go back home where it's safe."

Cassie refused to budge. "I'm not leaving."

Josh turned his scowl on Cal. "If it's true someone is trying to hurt you, then you have even more reason to get Cassie somewhere safe."

"Maybe if you would do your job, she'd be safe here and we wouldn't have to go somewhere else." Cal's voice softened as the deadly punch waited to land.

"Understand this, Mr. DEA agent. I am not going anywhere until I know what happened to Dan. If someone thinks Dan was doing something illegal, they can bring me the evidence. Got it?" Cassie stood firm.

Josh looked back and forth between Cal and Cassie. "Is

there anything I can do, short of arresting you two, to change your mind?"

"You could stop being an ass and tell us what's going on," Cal said.

Josh folded his hands behind his head. "You know everything there is to know."

"Then I guess we're done here."

"Are you telling me to go?" Josh asked with more than a little humor in his voice.

"It's late and Cassie and I have had a rough evening."

Cal had a plan. Cassie could sense it and played along. "A shower and a few hours of sleep will help."

Josh got up. Almost reached the door when he turned around. "If whatever Dan was involved in got him killed, these are dangerous people we're talking about. Don't take chances."

"If I wanted safe, I would have stayed in Florida."

Josh opened the door. "And when are you heading back there?"

Cal did not hesitate with his answer. "As soon as I can."

Chapter Thirty-one

Less than an hour later, Cal and Cassie pulled into the airport and headed for Dan's office to get the letter.

"Are you going to talk or are we done communicating for the day?" she asked.

Cal glanced over at Cassie. Her walk was brisk, her strides long. Seeing her struggle to keep up with his punishing pace, he slowed down. "Eventually."

Even in the middle of the night, after another series of terrorizing events, she managed to look cute. Tired and a bit sad around the eyes, but damn good. The parking lot lights highlighted the sunny streaks in her hair, as if begging him to run his fingers through the silken mass.

"Let's get that list and figure out what's going on," Cassie said.

Her tone put him on alert. "Okay."

"Then you can catch the first plane back to your precious Florida."

That explained it. His casual words to Josh had hurt her in some way. He never would have guessed he had that kind of power over her. "Cassie, it's not like that."

She ripped the door to Dan's office open with such force Cal marveled it didn't fly right off its hinges. "Doesn't matter."

Clearly it did. "You misunderstood me."

"I heard you loud and clear, Cal."

Cassie was not particularly good at hiding her emotions. Especially when she was pissed, which she tended to be around him. Often.

Yeah, he acted like a complete ass. Threw away a line for effect without thinking about the woman who had been sharing his bed. If Cassie's locked jaw were any indication, now was not the time to apologize. He wasn't sure that when the right time came he would recognize it.

He held the door to keep it from slamming back into her. "After you."

"Right." She slapped her hand against the light switch and bathed the utilitarian office in a harsh yellow light.

Someone or something had wrecked the place. Drawers stood open. Papers scattered around the floor. The few items of furniture in the room were either knocked over or broken in pieces.

He had walked into this picture before, just a few days ago in Dan's house. "What the hell happened?"

"Ohmigod no!" Cassie flew around Ed's desk and slid to her knees.

Cal's heart stopped beating. "Cassie?"

"Cal, help me." Her voice shook as hands tugged on the leg of his jeans, trying to drag him down beside her.

His gaze locked on what had her so upset. Ed laid sprawled face down and perfectly still.

Bile rushed up Cal's throat. "Jesus."

"Do something." She sprang up on her knees and grabbed fistfuls of his shirt.

Her desperation made him feel useless. The bleak sadness on her face tugged at his heart and sent an unexpected rush of emotion to his throat.

"Honey, I need you to calm down." He tried to block out her grief and focus on staying in control. "Call 9-1-1."

The haze of tears clouding her eyes cleared a bit as she visibly pulled herself back from the edge. Scrambling on her knees to the phone, receiver fumbling in her hands, Cassie made the call.

Cal went to work. His heartbeat hammered in his ears as he reached for Ed's wrist. Feeling a pulse sent a shot of happiness crashing through Cal. He had not realized how stiff he held his body until his shoulders collapsed in relief.

"He's alive." Cal exhaled for the first time since walking in the door.

She repeated his statement to the operator with a sudden giddiness. Cal wanted to celebrate, too, but the pool of blood and the nasty gash on Ed's forehead did not look good.

She hovered behind Cal's back, relaying Ed's status to the person on the other end of the telephone. Within three minutes, sirens echoed in the background. The high-pitched wail grew louder until the door crashed open and ambulance workers poured into the room, towing a cart and instruments behind them. Strangers shouted instructions and asked for information. Cal provided as many details as he could but he didn't have much of value to offer.

Cassie wrapped her fingers around his forearm and dug her nails into his skin. When she buried her tear-streaked face in his neck, he grabbed on to her and held tight, feeling her body tremble every few seconds in pure agony.

He wanted to spare her, to protect her from all of the violence spiraling around her. Despite attempts to block her view, Cassie refused to look away as the ambulance workers lifted Ed's limp body onto the stretcher. She watched over him like an avenging angel.

"What happened?" Ted rushed into the chaos and tried to direct the traffic.

From his disheveled appearance, it was clear the deputy chief had been shaken out of bed without warning. He wore his official police officer pants, but the white T-shirt he was tugging over his torso did not look as if it were standard issue. Neither were the baseball sneakers.

"Someone attacked Ed." Cal pulled Cassie closer, in part to prevent her from turning her wrath on Ted.

Ted shook his head in confusion. "Tell me the details."

"No idea. He was unconscious when we walked in."

"I need to go with him." Cassie struggled to break Cal's confining grasp.

He was having none of it. "Stay put and let the professionals do their job."

"Cal's right, Cassie. It's better to let the paramedics look Ed over." Ted patted Cassie's shoulder in a move awkward enough to be comical. "I'll check and see if they have a status."

Ted flashed his badge and shoved his way through the throngs of people milling around. The medical personnel working on Ed and the police officers setting up a perimeter immediately jumped to attention when they realized Ted was there.

"Is Ed going to be okay?" Her voice was so small and vulnerable Cal almost didn't hear her.

The temptation to lie to her, to give her whatever solace he could, overwhelmed him. But she had a right to know the truth. "I don't know, honey. Ted should be able to tell us something."

As if on queue, Ted stalked back to them. He tunneled a hand through his hair before lifting his eyes to meet Cassie's terrified gaze. "Ed's lost a lot of blood. That's not unusual with a head wound, but they aren't sure how long he's been here."

Her hand shot up to cover her mouth. "Oh my God."

"He's unconscious but breathing on his own. That's a good sign. The ambulance is going to run him in now."

Cassie bit her lower lip and nodded.

"Do you have any idea what happened? A robbery maybe?" Ted asked.

Cal debated telling the truth. "We came back to retrieve the copy of Dan's list."

Tension pulled Ted's facial features tight. "Is it here?"

"We never got a chance to check. We came in and . . ." Cassie's words trailed off when she focused on the bloodstain on the floor.

Desperate to give her comfort, Cal kissed her forehead. "It's going to be okay."

"Show me where Ed had it," Ted said.

Cal untangled his body from Cassie's and walked over to the shelves. The small box was upended on the floor. He crouched down and pointed at the memento. The empty memento. "It was in there."

"We'll need fingerprints." Ted kneeled down, careful not to disturb the crime scene. "Any chance the paper's here somewhere?"

Cal conducted a quick visual inspection of the room. Crumpled papers littered the ground. Separating one sheet from another was nearly impossible. "Can't tell."

Ted used a pen tip to shift the papers around. "I'd bet it's gone. There isn't enough money here to warrant a robbery, and no one would hurt Ed just for sport."

"Damn it." Cal repeated the word under his breath several times.

"I agree." Ted echoed his concern in an equally low tone.

An uneasy kinship sparked between them. For the first time, Cal knew Ted was not involved in the illegal activity going on in the area. "This is your town."

"That's right." Ted's voice sounded deep and harsh, as if he were chewing on gravel.

"Find anything?" Cassie poked her head between their towering bodies.

"The note's gone," Cal said.

"The copy is. I still have the original," Ted said.

Cal's inclination to bring Ted in on the note had been the right one. Without that, they would be even further behind now. "We should get to the hospital."

"Since I have the one with the big flashing light, we should take my car." Ted treated them to a slow grin.

"Better than letting Cal drive," Cassie mumbled under her breath.

"Why?" The confusion showed on Ted's face.

"He ignores every traffic law."

Ted shook his head. "Just what every policeman wants to hear."

Chapter Thirty-two

"I've gone over this a hundred times. The list is gibberish." Cal walked to the small window in the corner of
Ed's hospital room and stared out at the perfect blue sky.

A steady hum rumbled off the medical equipment. The
harsh smell of antiseptic slapped at Cassie, filling her head
until she felt dizzy.

"Let me see." Ted remained calm but his dark eyes
turned icy cold.

She felt safer with both of them there. Annoying or not,
their considerable size and bone-hard loyalty were hard to
beat. She refused to admit it out loud, but Ted seemed okay.

Cal's actions since finding Ed crumpled in a heap on the
floor made her love him even more. Once Cal found out Ed
didn't have any family or all that much money, he insisted
on paying for the extravagance of a private room, then ha-
rassed Ted to post a guard outside the door. Of course, con-
vincing Ted turned out to be a fairly easy proposition. The
only hardship came in persuading Ted that someone other
than he should do the job.

"We need to break the code." Ted turned the paper over
in his large hands. "Some of the matches are easy."

"Let me see." Cassie hopped off the corner of Ed's bed
and peeked over Ted's shoulder.

"For God's sake, Cassie. Give the man some room." Cal growled at her and glared at Ted.

"What's your problem?"

Ted glanced up and grinned. "I think I know."

"Don't test me," Cal shot back.

Ted chuckled but went back to reading.

Cassie was not in the mood for laughing. If Cal wanted a fight, she would happily oblige. Some screaming might ease the ache strangling her chest. Seeing Ed strapped down with tubes and tied to beeping machines made her blood run cold.

So much death and needless violence. She wanted to crawl back to her safe life and never deal with pain and sorrow again. Just existing, not getting involved and never being hurt.

But she knew that life could never be. Even though the Air Force and circumstances had taken Dan away years earlier, she felt his loss as sure as if a piece of her hand died that day in the crash. Like it or not, she was connected. And her newest tie was to Cal. Walking away from him and the challenge he posed for her filled her with a resounding emptiness.

And poor Ed. Except for the rise and fall of his chest, he remained still. He always seemed indestructible, larger than life. Just like Dan. But stretched out in the center of the bed with his hands folded over snowy white sheets, Ed looked frail and small.

"Wait a second." Ted skimmed the paper again.

"You see something?" Cal asked.

"They're names. You can make them out. Look." Ted announced his findings in a near shout.

Cal was at Ted's side in two long strides. Cassie ripped the piece of paper out of Ted's hands before the men could study it.

"I was reading that," Cal pointed out.

"She always this impulsive?" Ted asked.

"Hell, yeah." Cal reached over and grabbed the paper back. "Let's all look at it, shall we?"

"Here, I cracked part of the code." Ted pointed to his handwritten notes in the margin. "If you put these strings together, they spell out names."

"And these must be addresses." Cal wrote down his own doodles.

Cassie had no idea what either of them was talking about. All she saw were scribbles in pencil. "Anyone want to clue me in?"

"This is a list of last names and addresses." Ted had the nerve to talk slow as if she were dimwitted or something.

"Uh, yeah, I got that part. You don't have to start spelling the big words."

He had the grace to look apologetic.

"My guess is that these are the victims and this is a blueprint for the stolen items we found," Cal said.

The lightbulb flashed on in her brain. "I get it."

From the confused frown on Ted's face, she guessed his had just burned out. "Good, because you lost me."

"From the robberies," Cassie offered.

"Right." Cal continued to study the list. "Josh didn't tell you?"

Ted stared at both of them. "Let's slow down a bit."

"Better yet, we'll show you what we're talking about." Cal folded the paper and shoved it into his back pocket. "Let's go."

"Wait. Ed—" Her voice choked off.

Cal twined an arm around her shoulders and pulled her close. "He'll be fine, Cassie. Ted has him protected."

"Absolutely. He's safe," Ted agreed. "And you two have my full attention."

Twenty minutes later they stood in front of the massive door to the NASA building.

"I suppose the broken door is your doing?" Ted cornered Cal.

"Some of my finest work, actually."

Cassie shook her head. The urge to knock their empty male heads together was tempting her. "Can we go inside? This really isn't the place for chitchat."

Ted stood with his legs braced apart and his hands on his lean hips. "Do we climb through a window or use this door?"

"Cal tried the window thing a few days ago at Dan's house and it almost got him shot. Instead of reliving that moment, let's walk through the door like normal people." Cassie pushed her way past them. She tried to block out their voices but she could not help overhearing their irritating conversation.

Cal indicated for Ted to follow. "You heard the woman."

"You two have an interesting relationship," Ted mumbled under his breath.

Cal nodded. "You have no idea."

Cassie ignored them both and opened the door to the inner warehouse. She stopped dead, letting the men pile up behind her. "What happened in here?"

"What?" Ted asked.

She walked into the cavernous room, each step echoing off the walls of the now empty room. "The shelves are gone. The boxes. Someone cleaned the place out. And fast."

Ted squeezed by Cal and marched through the doorway. He turned in a circle, studying every inch of the huge room. "What am I missing?"

Cal followed Ted's trail around the room. "Everything, actually."

"The center of this room was filled with boxes of antiques, an obvious haul from somewhere. We're talking households worth of rather expensive-looking items," Cassie said.

The fluorescent lights gleamed off Cal's dark hair as he paced around the room. Cassie did not know how he could stay so calm. She couldn't even move her legs.

"When did you see all of this?" Ted's attention was centered on the floor.

"Last night."

Ted scanned the floor. Cassie guessed he was looking for footprints or some other sign that life had existed in that very spot only a few hours earlier.

Cal brushed his foot across the dusty floor. "Josh was in here. He probably saw it. Getting a load of that size out of here in such a short period of time would be a huge undertaking."

"You'd need a few people and trucks, or some other way to move the stuff," Ted said.

Cassie felt her blood pressure soar. "Are you saying we're making it up? Just another example of me being crazy, maybe?"

"No." Ted drew out his answer, making the word last for more than one syllable.

"Don't be so quick to discount the crazy part." Cal glared at her.

She scowled back. "It was a legitimate question. Until you came along, Ted didn't believe anything I said."

"Cassie." Cal packed a load of warning in her name.

"Not to state the obvious, but I'm here and I'm listening," Ted said.

He was. The heat rushed out of her. "So, what now?"

Ted took out his cell phone. "You go back and check on Ed. I'll send a couple of officers out here to fingerprint the place."

"What are you going to do?" Cal asked.

"Call Josh and see what he knows."

"That doesn't exactly sound promising," she pointed out before Cal could say something less flattering.

"Then I'll go back to the office and search out these names and addresses to see if they mean anything to anyone," Ted added.

She had no idea the police could do that. "How?"

Ted shrugged. "Check police records, that type of thing. The cities are missing but I can tell that most of the street names don't sound as if they're from any area in Hawaii."

"How in the world would you be able to know something like that?" Cal asked.

Ted and Cassie shared a knowing smile.

"You want to explain it?" Ted asked.

She knew Cal would never figure this one out on his own. "The Hawaiian alphabet is an abbreviated version of the traditional alphabet. The Hawaiian one doesn't use all of the consonants. For example, there isn't a *b*."

Cal's eyebrows pressed together. "You're telling me that no street name anywhere in the Hawaiian Islands has the letter *b* in it?"

Ted grinned.

Cal's mouth fell open. "Come on."

Ted clapped a hand on Cal's shoulder. "I can't promise you that all streets follow the Hawaiian alphabet, but most do. I'm just saying that many of the words on that list sound like mainland addresses, not Hawaii."

She couldn't resist taking a jab or two. "That's why you can't pronounce any of the street names."

"I thought you guys did that to make the tourists feel stupid."

Ted laughed. "That, too."

Chapter Thirty-three

"I hate this." Cassie sat on the side of Ed's bed and soothed her hand over his cheek.

The crack to the back of Ed's head left him with a lump and some swelling, countless stitches, and a rotating watch by the nurses. Cassie stared at Ed as if she could will him well. Her shoulders drooped and her body slumped with exhaustion, but energy still pounded off her.

A sick desperation clawed at Cal's insides. He wanted to help her, to ease her pain. He had no idea how to accomplish either. The warm, bright light that glowed in her eyes had all but been extinguished in this new wave of grief.

The hard tug of sorrow dragged at him, too. Seeing Ed, once so vibrant, struck down in such a vulnerable condition reminded Cal of the seriousness of their situation, of losing Dan. Cal grieved in his own way, by turning his concern into a lava-flow of anger.

He moved up behind her, resting strong hands on her slim shoulders. "He's going to be okay. His body suffered a significant shock, that's all."

"What kind of animal attacks a nice old man?" Her angry whisper tugged at his heart.

Cal knew Ed was not as feeble as Cassie liked to think. The older man had a gnarled, world-wise way about him.

He settled down to live out his days in the relative calm of the Hawaiian tropics, but his life started another way.

"Why Ed?" Uncertainty lurked in her wide eyes.

"Probably in the wrong place at the wrong time."

"You're thinking Josh had something to do with this."

Hearing the guy's name on her lips made his back teeth snap together. "I want to say yes just because I hate the guy, but I don't think so. He's a loose cannon, not a killer."

"But he's messed up in all of this."

Up to his eyeballs. "He's holding back the information we need."

"I wonder if Dan liked him."

The idea made the throbbing in Cal's head turn into a full-fledged hammering. In the end, Dan had hated him. Had cut Cal out and walked away from their friendship and his career.

With excruciating tenderness, she weaved her fingers through Ed's and rubbed the back of his hand with her fingertips. "I can't figure out if Josh is one of the good guys or not."

The words grated against Cal's nerves like fingernails on a chalkboard. "The guy is an idiot. Don't waste your time."

"Why don't you like him?"

Because she kept talking about him. "He's a liar."

"Shading the truth is part of his job, I guess."

Great, now she was making excuses for Josh. Cal reached the end of his patience. He could either yell at her or let it drop. Neither option appealed to him.

He paced instead. Long legs took him across the tiny room in three short strides. He needed a bigger room if he were going to rid his body of the nervous energy thrumming through him.

As if she were completely oblivious to his discomfort, Cassie kept defending Josh. "If he is on some kind of job, he probably can't talk about it or give us any clues."

She was one step away from having the guy sainted.

Cal prayed for a short case of deafness, the type that would selectively block out all discussion of Josh. Then he realized what she was doing. Nervous chatter. But understanding her actions and accepting them were two different things.

Unconstrained jealousy raced through Cal. He hated the sensation. Since it wasn't going away, he decided to feed it. But he could not stand listening to her drone on about Josh for one more minute. "Cassie."

"What?" He had her attention now. The same kind of attention passersby gave to a car accident.

"Stop talking about him."

She blinked several times. "Who?"

"Who have you been talking about for two hours? Josh."

"What's with the exaggeration?"

"I may kill him before the day is over, so don't get attached."

"Talking about anyone I know?" Ted stuck his head in the room.

Cassie smiled a greeting filled with genuine warmth. "Not you."

"Me then?" Josh stepped out from behind Ted's expansive shoulders and into the open doorway. He sauntered into the room and stood over Cassie's shoulder.

Cal was in hell. What was the world coming to if a man couldn't find peace in a hospital? All he wanted was to scoop Cassie off the hospital bed and carry her back to their hotel room and hold her until the unbearable pain left her face. The need to be alone with her pushed at him, wiping out all reason.

"You can take your agent-ass right back out of here." Cal knew Josh wouldn't listen, but it was worth a try.

Alarm registered on Cassie's face. "Cal, what are you doing? They can stay."

"I never said *Ted* had to leave," Cal pointed out.

Ted smothered a laugh with a fake cough, but his eyes were warm with amusement. Then his glance bounced off Ed's still form and sobered. "Is he doing any better?"

"Damn," Josh's shocked whisper said it all. "He looks worse than I expected."

The need to fight rumbled up inside Cal. "Really, what do guys who get their heads bashed in usually look like?"

"This is a hospital," Cassie said as if she were delivering some surprise announcement.

"Uh-huh. So?"

"Behave." Her voice sounded a bit more stern that time.

Josh took out Ed's chart and started reading. "Listen to your woman."

Cassie jumped in before Cal could comment. "I'm my own woman, thank you."

Cal knew she'd say something like that. Maybe if he let Josh talk for a few minutes, he could piss Cassie off. In the meantime . . . "This is as good a place as any for explanations. You got anything to say, Josh?"

"Yeah, you're jeopardizing my investigation. Back off or I'll back you off." Josh dropped the chart back on the metal bar. The clanking got everyone's attention.

Ted lifted both hands and stepped in between the men. "Let's put the turf war aside for a second. You can beat the hell out of him later."

"Good." Josh nodded in obvious satisfaction.

"He was talking to me," Cal said.

"Take it however you want." Ted nodded. "Josh, tell them."

Josh's smile faltered. "You know I can't."

Anger snuffed out the tenuous hold Cal had on his patience. He reached around his back in the general direction of his weapon. "Let me shoot him."

"There are rules. While I suck at following them, there are some in place for your protection," Josh said.

Ted didn't buy it. "If Washington had any idea how you operated, you'd be assigned to the kitchen clean-up crew."

Cassie cleared her throat. "This isn't the place for this conversation."

Last thing Cal needed was for her to rush in and save Josh's ass. "Ted's doing fine."

Her sad eyes took on a new fire. "You, not so much."

Ted sighed, his exasperation obvious. "Josh, start talking before I reconsider Cal's request and give him a weapon."

Josh let fly an impressive string of profanity. Cal felt a reluctant tug of admiration for this inventiveness.

"Damn it, Ted. If this backfires it's on your head."

"Agreed."

Josh turned back to Cal with his easygoing charm gone. "Your instincts are right."

"Flattery won't help." Cassie snorted. "Trust me."

"What you saw in the warehouse was stolen merchandise. Someone is running a fairly lucrative burglary ring where the homes of wealthy families are looted. Expensive items are taken and resold. The place is under surveillance. We have the whole move-out on tape."

Cal felt some sense of relief that they were talking about missing property and not something more serious. "This is all about stealing."

"Not quite." Ted glared.

Josh hesitated as if debating how much to tell. "And drugs. Some of the merchandise is used to transport drugs. Meth, to be exact. The adults transport the goods. A ring of kids then sells and supplies the ice."

Cassie let out a sound akin to a groan but more disgusted. "That's awful."

"Take a bunch of bored kids and an open supply of drugs and you get a disaster," Josh said.

Ted nodded in agreement. "It's a significant problem in Hawaii."

Cal decided to cut through the bullshit and get to the point. "What's with the list?"

Josh leaned against the wall under the window. "Dan had it and obviously hid it before he died. We've been trying to figure out how extensive the network is."

"I checked," Ted said. "The list includes houses here and houses in California. Some have been hit, some haven't."

Cal tried to work out the scenario in his head. "So, someone went to the trouble of checking out potential properties and preparing a list of victims?"

Cassie folded Ed's hand next to his side and stood up. "Sounds like it."

Not that any of this explained what was happening. Cal knew there was more information out there. Things Josh failed to share. "This is a joint DEA-police operation?"

"Sort of," Josh said.

"How did anyone put this together?" Cassie said, diffusing the situation. "I mean, I'm guessing that the police in Hawaii and the police in California don't regularly share information on domestic robberies."

Her quick mind attracted him to her from the beginning. That and her sexy little body.

Josh touched his hand against his shirt pocket. Whatever he was looking for wasn't there.

"Problem?" Cal asked.

"Lost my pen." Josh shifted his weight, looking as uncomfortable as Cal had ever seen him. "Unfortunately, the criminals moved past simple theft. They killed two people in two different houses, one here and one there. A maid who wasn't supposed to be home and a kid in bed sick with the flu."

Horror flashed in Cassie's eyes. "That's terrible."

Cal dealt with the blow differently. He seethed with the need to find the bastards and take them apart piece by piece.

Josh continued. "The murders still didn't bring all this together. A bigwig technology millionaire did. His house in California got hit, as well as his vacation home here."

"Talk about unlucky," Cassie mumbled.

"It was on purpose, and a dumb move. The man came to me. When I started looking into it, all of the arrows pointed to Bobby Polk and his girlfriend."

"Who else are you looking at as a suspect?" Cal asked.

Josh's gaze darted to Cassie then back again. "We're still investigating."

The way Cassie's mouth clamped shut suggested she was not going to accept that for a response. "Answer Cal's question."

Her voice vibrated with anger. Cal wanted to fight this battle for her. The vibes she sent out and the tension pulsing through the room showed she could play this one without him.

Respect. She demanded it. Earned it. Cal wondered again how he would ever walk away from this woman. He entertained spending a few more weeks with her. But he knew why he was in Kauai. Sooner or later he would have to tell her that he was the one who shredded Dan's military career and set him on the path that killed him. Then she would show him the door.

"You think Dan had something to do with all of this." She marched over to Josh and stood in front of him as if daring him to deny the charges.

"Damn." The expletive escaped Cal's lips before he could stop it.

She spun around with a storm brewing in those beautiful eyes. "You believe this? You think Dan was their courier?"

Cal didn't want to believe Dan had run that far afield. But what happened to a man when his dream got yanked away?

Cassie looked around the room. Her movements, disjointed and a bit frantic, ripped their way straight to Cal's heart. When she focused her full and unwavering attention on him, Cal felt his carefully balanced world tilt.

She pointed a finger at Cal's chest. "Dan trusted you enough to call for help."

The begging rang through his brain. In the span of a few minutes, unspoken doubts had driven her to her knees. Comfort words caught in his throat. He looked in desperation to Ted.

She backed away from all of them. "You're wrong."

Josh tried to lessen the blow. "Ms. Montgomery, I didn't say—"

A huge fist squeezed Cal's heart. "Honey—"

"Don't touch me." She pulled back before he could touch her.

The flinch speared through him like the slashing blade of a knife, so unexpected and immediate that he pressed a hand against his stomach to check for blood.

"I don't want any part of the lynch mob. I'm leaving." She grabbed for the door handle.

Her threat snapped Cal out of his stupor. "Stay right where you are."

"Get a clue, flyboy. I don't take orders from you."

Each word dug the wound deeper. "That much is obvious, but the criminals are still out there and it's clear someone helped cause Dan's helicopter crash. So, your little butt is not going anywhere until I know it's safe."

"May I make a suggestion?" Josh asked.

She didn't even look at the other man. "No."

"Then *I'll* try." Ted put a hand on the small of Cassie's

back. "Take a break. Go downstairs to the cafeteria for a few minutes."

"Are you nuts?" Cal tried to step in front of her.

"She can take the guard posted outside the door. We'll be here with Ed, so he'll be safe. Everyone needs to cool off."

Ted handled the situation in true police style. He spoke nice and calm with a low voice that soothed and convinced. He took a toxic situation and neutralized it.

Cal hated every minute of the strategy.

"Fine," she said.

The fact Cassie agreed so easily made Cal even more skeptical. "Not a chance. She stays with me."

Josh gestured toward the door. "For God's sake, give the woman five minutes alone."

"Thank you." She smiled at Josh, then pulled the door open. "I'll be downstairs."

The battle was lost. Cal knew when to give up, even if he refused to do so graciously. "You have ten minutes."

Her dull eyes showed only contempt. "I'll be back when I'm back."

Within ten minutes, she was downstairs at a table in the nearly empty cafeteria. Ten minutes later while the police guard fetched a cup of coffee, she slipped out the side exit.

Cal's betrayal ripped her stomach inside out and shredded her to the core. He believed the worst about Dan. All this time she had depended on Cal to defend her, to defend Dan's memory. At the first opportunity, he turned against them both. His words crushed her hope and left her heart bleeding from the open wound.

Away from the building, Cassie doubled over, bringing her forehead level with her knees. Tears pushed against the back of her eyes and her stomach cramped.

If this was love, she could do without it.

After a few minutes of feeling sorry for herself, she stood up, looked up, and saw nothing but perfect blue sky. Fluffy white clouds drifted by, carried by a soft cleansing wind. The air carried the smell of sea salt and plumeria.

The need to talk with Dan, to ask him all the questions stuck inside her brain, assailed her. Growing up she idolized her big brother. He was everything she wasn't—a daredevil, a sweet-talking charmer, a hero. Now Cal was trying to tarnish that memory.

It was time to move on and investigate without Cal. And she'd use his rental car to do it. She'd start with Dan's house. The police tape was up. There weren't any antiques or drugs there. She could tear the place apart.

Chapter Thirty-four

Josh waited until Cassie left the room to let out a soft whistle. "The pretty lady was pissed."

Cal did not need the newsflash. "Because of you."

"What did you expect me to say?"

"About Dan? How about nothing. Did you ever think about that?"

Ted leaned back against the window. "Thinking isn't always Josh's greatest strength."

Cal felt the need to do what he had failed to do during Dan's life—defend him. "You're wrong about Dan and his involvement in all of this. He had his problems in the past, but nothing like this. He would never get wrapped up in murder."

"I didn't say Dan was involved," Josh insisted.

Cal sensed the word trap. "You let Cassie think her brother was the mastermind, or at least an integral part of the plan."

"No, man. You did."

Cal looked to Ted for assistance. The deputy shook his head. "Sorry. Josh didn't make that leap. You and Cassie did that all without his help."

"I tried to step in and stop you, but you seemed determined to ruin Dan's reputation to Cassie. Interesting move, by the way." Josh sat down hard on the metal stool by the door. "I can only guess you like sleeping alone."

Cal felt the blood rush out of his head. He implicated Dan? He crushed her beliefs and hopes? "You're saying . . ."

Josh shook his head. "Dan wasn't involved. Not the way you think."

Ted balanced his hands against Ed's food tray. "That's a pretty definite statement. What haven't you told me?"

Cal watched the byplay between Josh and Ted with growing dread. For once, Josh didn't look smug. But that wasn't good enough for Cal. The man needed to crawl. Maybe Josh didn't say the words, but he led Cassie to the place where she felt betrayed.

Launching his body across the room, Cal knocked into Josh before he could see the attack coming or prepare. Cal slammed Josh's shoulders against the wall. Outrage drove him, feeding his adrenaline and giving him the advantage.

"What the hell are you doing?" Josh came out spitting. He fought back like a man gasping for his last breath.

Cal obliged. Planting an elbow on Josh's windpipe, Cal trapped Josh against the wall and quickly regained the upper hand. "Answer Ted. Tell me the entire story or I'll snap your neck."

The threat was not as empty as it should have been. A killing rage stole over Cal, wiping out all other emotions.

"Let him go, Cal." Ted said the correct legal words but there was no heat behind his order. He did not move to help, either.

"Not until I get a straight answer." Cal did let up on the pressure. Seemed that strangling the man before he could provide the information was not a smart move.

The bit of space allowed Josh a little leverage. He pushed against Cal, sending him back a few feet and putting enough distance between them to be able to fight back. "Try that again and I shoot you."

"Just tell me what I want to know."

Josh glanced at Ted. "Thanks for the help there."

"Well, I just figured out I put my job on the line without having all of the information from you." Ted stared at the ceiling as if wrestling to control his anger. "Is this what's going on with Nohea?"

Cal refused to get lost in verbal subterfuge again. "What is Nohea?"

"Brad Nohea. My boss at the DEA," Josh said. "Dan wasn't involved in the drug deals."

"You couldn't say that to Cassie and save me from the wrath I'm about to face?"

"I tried but you cut me off." Josh's raspy voice was the only sound in the room other than the beeping of the machines tied to Ed. "Dan figured out that Bobby Polk was using Dan's transfers and his plane to move drugs around the islands during what was supposed to be business-related runs. He contacted our office."

Everything fell into place for Cal. "And you were right there to use him. You had him risk his neck working for you, didn't you?"

Josh had set Dan up. Marked him for death.

Josh pushed back until his chair rolled against the wall, holding up his hands in mock surrender. "Before you go apeshit again, the answer is no. My boss enlisted Dan's help."

More fucking excuses. "Same thing."

"No." Ted stepped into Cal's line of vision. "You don't know Brad Nohea. Josh has been backstopping that idiot for years."

"And this time was no different." Josh lowered his voice. "I was already watching Polk. Dan started showing up at the drops. Knowing him, I doubted he was running drugs. After some snooping, I figured out Dan got roped into the deal by higher levels in my office and I approached him."

Another situation where Dan stepped into the middle of a mess and couldn't get out. Cal failed to rescue his friend not once, but twice. "You should have gotten him out. That was your job."

"Oh no. Don't lay that on me." Josh's anger now matched Cal's. "I tried to protect him, even warned him not to take the risk, but he wouldn't listen. Seemed to me Dan missed the excitement of his old career and was looking for the rush in all the wrong places."

There it was. Cal felt the last of his defenses crash in around him. It all circled back to him. He took away Dan's career. Dan found another one and it killed him. The line started with Cal's choices.

"Dan tried to gather intel and figure out where all of this originated because Polk doesn't seem smart enough to put this type of scam together."

"Once Dan died, why not come forward? At least tell Cassie the truth?" Cal asked.

Ted filled in that blank. "Because the operation is still running. Josh hasn't figured out if Polk is in charge or what Louisa's part is."

"And I needed evidence to tie Polk to Dan's crash."

Ted nodded. "That much I knew."

"The part you didn't know deals with Nohea. He's covered Dan's involvement in the Polk case. Rather than answer questions from the NTSB, he is pretending the crash is unrelated to Dan's undercover work with the DEA. He's buried the files and paperwork."

Cal thought he knew the answer but asked the question anyway. "Why the secrecy?"

"Something about how using private citizens would result in Nohea's termination and an investigation into the office."

All of this trouble just to cover someone's ass. Hell, Cal wanted to turn this Nohea guy inside out. "Tough shit."

"I agree." Josh took his pad out of his shirt pocket. "That's why I'm nosing around. I need to turn in Nohea. I'd prefer to do that in a way where everything is resolved so Nohea can't wiggle out of the charges."

"That's why you kept showing up wherever we were."

Josh flipped through a few pages and read some notes. "And why I shot into Dan's house to scare you out of it. Polk was on his way."

Cal spun around to face Ted. "Arrest him before I fucking kill him."

Ted exhaled. "Too much paperwork."

Cal edged closer, giving Josh no avenue to escape. "The other earlier shooting at Cassie?"

"Not me."

Cal loomed over the other man now. If Josh tried to stand up or wheel the chair anywhere, Cal would stop him. "You forced us off the road, you bastard. I almost lost control of the car."

Josh started shaking his head in denial before Cal finished his accusation. "Wrong. That wasn't me either. Not that and not Ed."

Ted shifted to stand next to Josh. "He's not lying about those."

"If I wanted to kill either one of you, I would have done it." Josh coughed. "I had a different job to do."

A red haze of madness clouded Cal's vision again. "A job that included endangering Cassie's life and costing Dan his."

Ted put a hand on Cal's arm. "For what it's worth, Josh is a good agent. He's trying to cut his way through the corruption and incompetency. And he's taken more drugs off the streets than I can tell you."

Josh stood up a little straighter. "You might not like my methods, but they work."

"Don't talk," Cal warned.

"Do you have any idea what I could do to you for threatening a federal officer?"

Ted glanced back at Ed then lowered his voice. "Interesting argument from the guy who's broken every rule and regulation, including shooting into a residence and endangering civilians."

"You're supposed to be on my side," Josh said.

Cal admired the guy even as he wanted to kill him. "I still want to kick your ass."

Josh smiled. "I get that a lot."

Cal wanted to hate Josh, but there was something about him. The fly-by-the-seat-of-his-pants attitude reminded him of Dan. Cassie saw it, too, had even commented on it.

Her face moved back into Cal's mind. And her ten minutes were up. "We need to find Cassie and explain this to her."

"Right." Ted whipped open the door and came face to face with a very nervous policeman. Sweat ran down the side of the guy's face.

Cal knew without a word that Cassie had slipped his grasp. "Where is she?"

The officer shook his head. "I don't know."

Chapter Thirty-five

Cassie dragged her weary body onto Dan's front porch and unlocked the door. Tearing through the yellow police tape, she walked inside the small cottage. Light streamed through the windows, highlighting the broken and damaged furniture scattered around the room.

Her gaze lingered on the photograph on the other side of the room, showing off Dan's sweet smile on a warm holiday morning. Somehow it had survived the rampage of burglars and police. When she closed her eyes she could smell the spicy scent of Dan's aftershave. Feel the loving squeeze of the bear hugs he liked to treat her to in greeting.

But he wasn't there. Never would be again.

The oppressive silence crowded in on her. Whenever she had come to Dan's house in the past, the residence had been brimming with people and pulsating with life. Dan loved his fun. Craved the feel of the open skies.

He was not a criminal. Thinking about the possibility made the energy flow out of her body and puddle on the floor. The last few weeks had taken a toll. Falling for Mr. Wrong certainly had not helped matters.

She had mourned Dan.

Loving Cal was killing her.

She walked to the small bedroom. This area had not been

spared. The tangled bedspread was in a ball in the corner of the room. Lamps lay where they had crashed to the floor. Clothing spilled out of the closet.

She sat on the floor and tried to block out Cal's memory. The image of his face, so strong and handsome, kept filling her mind. Eyes open or closed, it did not matter. He had wormed his way into her heart and his presence was as natural to her as breathing.

Her heart shredding, she turned her attention to the task at hand. Dan. She dragged the boxes out from the bottom of the closet and started rummaging through forgotten treasures. The job commanded all of her attention; then she heard the house creak.

Her hands froze. She strained to listen, trying to pick up any sound of movement. Nothing.

She swiveled around to face the bedroom entrance, rather than the back of the closet. Staring at the doorway, she looked for shadows. There was no evidence of life except for the sound of soft footsteps.

The intruder could be Cal, but she doubted it. Despite his faults, and those were many, she could not imagine him scaring her for sport. And God knew subtlety was not his style. Knowing Cal, he would just storm in issuing orders.

Bracing her back against the closet door, she glanced around the room, desperate to find anything that looked like a weapon. Her gaze landed on the broken lamp. The heavy base would give her a weapon of sorts.

She visually checked the room one more time, then crawled over to the lamp. Just as her hand reached out to grab it, a shadow fell across her path.

"Ms. Montgomery."

Her breathing skidded to a halt. "What are you doing here?"

A man's hiking shoe tramped down on the lamp. She was

eye level with a kneecap covered in faded blue jeans. Before she could scream out for help, a hand clamped her arm and whisked her to her feet.

"Remember me?"

Bobby Polk. He stood there with a cold smile.

She tried to buy time. "Of course. You were Dan's partner."

"You've been messing around in things that don't concern you."

"I don't know what you're talking about." But she did. She absolutely did.

Tears of pain rushed to her eyes when he squeezed her underarm in a vicelike grip. The tight hold stopped blood flow.

"Don't play dumb, Ms. Montgomery. I've been following you. I know you're not a stupid woman."

Her mind rebelled at the idea of him watching her for even ten seconds. "I don't—"

"Ever shut up? Yes, I know. I've heard you've caused quite a bit of trouble."

Fear rumbled in her chest. She was crazed with the need to break free. "What do you want from me?"

"We're going to have a little chat."

"Cal is here."

"No, sweetie, he's not. You see, I followed you from the hospital. I know you're all alone."

Cassie kicked out, aiming for any body part that would bring him down. Arms flailed and she lunged for the door. A firm arm snaked around her waist and drew her back.

"Keep fighting. That will only make me enjoy this more."

She clawed at his forearms, dragging her nails across his skin. He pushed away from her then whacked her across the mouth so hard the room spun.

She knew then that she was in trouble.

That was her last thought when he hit her the second time and blissful darkness closed in around her.

The young officer was all of twenty. His eyes were wide with fear. His terror-filled gaze centered first on Cal, then Ted, then skipped to his feet. "She's gone."

Cal shoved Ted aside and loomed over the shaking officer. "Where the hell is she?"

Ted stepped in. "Tell me what happened."

The guy's Adam's apple bobbed up and down as he swallowed. "I got her a coffee and she vanished. I checked everywhere."

"I made it clear she was not to be left alone for a second."

"But she—"

"You're not a damn waiter. You were to stick to her like glue." Ted yelled his point.

Cal's rage turned to ice-cold fear. Cassie was out there, right in the path of potential killers. If they had murdered Dan to get him out of the way, they wouldn't think twice of removing Cassie as well.

"Where did she go?" Cal's heart hammered in his chest.

The young man shook his head with such vigor, his body moved to the side. "I don't know."

Ted clubbed the other officer's shoulder with his fist, shoving him back out of the hospital room. "Get out of my sight."

"Let's think for a second," Josh suggested with the only calm voice in the room.

Cal struggled for control and lost. "What if someone took her?"

The question ate at Cal, burning a hole through his stomach lining.

"Dan's office." Josh's two-word statement hung in the air.

Ted and Cal looked at him.

"She either went to Dan's office or his house. She would try to find anything to refute the charges she thinks I made against him. The only other possibility is the hotel."

"How the hell would she get to any of those places?" Ted asked. "She's on foot."

"Is she?" Josh hitched his chin toward Cal. "How did you get here?"

"What?"

"Where are your car keys?"

Cal patted his pants. Nothing. A quick search of his memory gave him the answer. "She has them."

"Then she has transportation," Josh said.

Ted snapped out of his anger long enough to start issuing orders. "Right. We split up. Josh, you take the office. Cal and I will go to the house."

"What if she's not at either one?" Cal lost a bit of his soul to even utter the words.

"One step at a time." Ted clapped a hand on Cal's shoulder. "Let's go."

Chapter Thirty-six

Cassie slowly regained consciousness. Just opening her eyes hurt. The bright light of the room seared through her, making her gasp.

Bobby appeared in front of her. "Afternoon, sunshine."

She pulled back to put as much distance as possible between their faces. "What are you doing?"

"Nice room."

Despite the pain behind her eyes, she lifted her head and glanced around. The hotel living room. The touch of luxury she had enjoyed for days now had a nightmarish quality. Papers, pillows, and clothes littered the floor. The place had been ransacked.

She tried to sit up, but a spike of pain shot through her head. She lifted her hands and realized for the first time a braided rope banded her wrists together in front of her. All of the aches flared to life. Even her shoulder throbbed from where her weight rested against it on the couch.

She tried to swipe her hair off her forehead. Something kept weighing her down, causing even her nerve endings on her scalp to ache.

"Don't like the hat?" Bobby knocked something off her head.

A bloodied baseball cap rolled onto the floor in front of

her. Dan's Air Force cap. The low weight of cotton canvas should not have hurt, but the flood of relief was immediate once he removed it.

"I had to use it to hide the injury. Someone would have noticed that in the lobby."

She inhaled, trying to clear her head. To wipe out the fog and figure out what to do next. "How did we get here?"

"You tell the hotel staff your wife has had a bit too much celebrating and no one asks a question." He clapped. "Imagine that."

The crack reverberated through her head. "Damn hotel."

"Remember to complain when you check out."

She knew Bobby did not plan for her to leave the room in anything other than a body bag. "I'll get right on that."

She tried to remember the position of the phone in this room. Her mind would not focus long enough to catch the memory. Hell, even the bathroom had one. It was only logical there would be one in here.

He smiled. "I really liked the part where I got to dig through your pockets to find the room key. Nice ass."

Bile rushed up the back of her throat at the thought of his touching her. She vowed that would be the only feel that guy got from her.

"Figured out what's happening yet?" Bobby asked, still crouching in front of her. His mouth lingered close enough for her to smell the peppermint on his breath.

"No."

"See, we have a problem."

Yeah, him. "Just leave."

"I don't think so. I have a business to run. You and your boyfriend have been interfering with that."

Cal. She fought to keep his face out of her brain. If she let his image in, she'd lose control.

More than anything she wished she were back at the hospital fighting with him. She let her stubbornness and pain overcome her common sense, and now she was in this mess with this drug-dealing animal.

"I thought you were in business with my brother." It killed her to say that.

"I was."

"He didn't run drugs and stolen merchandise."

Bobby's smug smile fell into a thin line. "You've been talking with someone."

"It's a guess."

"I don't think so." He stood up, keeping close enough that his jeans clouded her vision. "Right now I have another problem."

"Like the fact the police are on to you?"

"You have no idea what the police are doing. I read that interview you gave with the paper. How you called Ted Greene an imbecile. They want you gone as much as I do."

Had she really said that? If so, she was grateful for it. Whatever she said then had Bobby thinking he was safe now.

He wagged a finger in front of her face. "You stole my property."

She shook her head and winced as a sheet of black blurred her vision. "I didn't."

"The bag."

"What—"

He grabbed her chin so hard she heard her teeth grind together. "Don't."

When he let go, she sucked in a huge gulp of air. "That belongs to Dan."

Bobby pulled her to a seated position. She didn't know if he was trying to be considerate or just positioning her better for whatever blow was to come. Either way, the move sent a wave of dizziness spilling through her.

"You looked inside, didn't you?"

Bobby spit when he talked. She tried to move away from him, but he held her in place.

"Answer me," he said in a shout.

"You could just leave the island." She twisted her wrists, trying to ease her hands out of their binding.

"You need to learn a lesson first."

She turned her head to the side and stared up at hate-filled eyes. "Are you're going to graduate from burglary to murder?"

"You think you'll be the first person I ever killed?"

The last shred of hope for getting out of this the easy way died. Bobby intended to take her out. In order to survive, she'd have to beat him.

But if she was going to die, she wanted answers first. "You killed Dan."

"Mother Nature did that."

She refused to believe the semi-denial. Looking at Bobby, she saw pure evil. The kind of guy who used kids to sell drugs and killed innocent people who happened to be home when he came to rob them. The guy deserved whatever Josh had planned for him. Whatever Cal would do to him once he found what was left of her.

"I don't believe you," she said.

Bobby leaned down with his face just inches from hers. "I don't give a rat's ass."

She vowed to go out fighting. Bobby had inadvertently given her the weapon by not tying up her legs. Her head throbbed but her lower body worked just fine.

Using all of her might, she kicked out and caught him in the stomach. His eyes widened right before he roared and fell backward with his arms folded over his middle.

"Bitch!" The profanity wheezed out of him as he hit the floor.

She didn't stop there. She kicked out, knocking his head against the floor. Then she screamed. She pounded and yelled and did everything she could to draw attention to her room. She only hoped some tourist decided to stay in instead of spending the beautiful day outside.

He started getting up. "Looks like I can't be nice."

Run. She had to run. She threw her feet on the floor and tried to sit up. The room spun, knocking her back to the couch. She would not die here. No. She would see Cal again. She would testify against Bobby. She would walk out of that room alive. To do all that, she had to get her legs to move.

Her hips would not hold her. Instead of standing, she fell to the floor right next to her attacker. On her knees with no use of her hands, she squirmed toward the door, dodging Bobby's outstretched hand and blocking out his howl of fury.

The door seemed to hover miles away. She blinked several times to focus. Just as her head began to clear, Bobby threw his body on top of hers, pushing her down and onto her stomach. They fought and crashed. She used her bound arms to block his blows to her face.

The fight lasted only a few seconds. The adrenaline punch could not outlast her injured and exhausted body. Without effort, he rolled her over to her back. Straddling her writhing body with his knees, he rose above her and shoved the discarded cap in her mouth.

He was in a killing rage. He bared his teeth and swore as he wrestled to subdue her. She turned her head, thinking a moving target would be harder to kill, hoping the thrashing around would get someone's attention on the floor below.

Cassie always thought her life would flash before her eyes before she died. Just like the movies promised, a series of flashes of every good moment in her life. But she saw only Cal's face. She would never have the opportunity to tell him how much she loved him.

Then Bobby drew back his fist and the world went blank.

* * *

"She's not here." Cal stated the obvious as he raced through the last empty room of Dan's house.

He was a man who lived his life on the edge, who had fought and killed for his country. This didn't even compare. This unknown ripped at him like having a part of his body torn away.

He bargained with his maker for Cassie's safe return. He would have promised anything to anyone in that moment. For a man who thought he never loved a woman, he was finding out the hard way that he did.

"Damn it." Ted stood in the middle of the disheveled bedroom and trailed his fingers through his dark hair. His usual calm façade was starting to slip.

Cal squatted down by the bedroom closet. "But she was."

Ted frowned. "How do you know that?"

"I can smell her."

"You're kidding."

Cal could feel her presence, too, but he decided to keep that fact to himself. Being a practical man, Ted wouldn't get it. Hell, a week ago Cal wouldn't have understood it, either.

"Look where you're standing. A struggle took place right there."

Ted glanced under his feet, then rubbed his index finger over a small dark pool. "Blood. Still wet."

The words crashed into Cal, nearly knocking him off his feet. "She didn't wander off. She's not out looking around for evidence. Someone has her."

Ted did not question him. "Bobby Polk."

The name drove a chill deep down in his stomach. "Yeah."

"He was probably waiting for her, looking for an opportunity."

"Why now?"

"Could be the list. Could be he's wrapping up loose ends."

"We have to find her." Cal heard the vulnerability ringing in his voice and didn't try to hide it.

"Time to call Josh. He attached a GPS monitor to Polk's car. With it, Josh can track Polk's movements all over the island. As long as Polk is in his car, we've got him."

For the first and only time, Cal appreciated Josh's way of operating. The tight fist squeezing his heart eased up a bit. "Is that legal?"

"Do you think Josh cares?"

Cal didn't care, either. "If he does one thing to bother me, I'm shooting him."

Ted nodded. "I'll give you my gun."

Chapter Thirty-seven

She could have been out for ten minutes or two days, Cassie wasn't sure. A warm breeze tickled her face and the familiar scent of plumeria comforted her battered body. She was outside. Bobby had dumped her body near the canyon.

With her eyes clamped shut, she listened. Slowly eyelids eased open to stare up at the clear blue sky. She knew she had to move. Staying here amounted to a death sentence. Bound hands didn't help, but she was strong. She could escape if she kept calm.

Black dots swam in front of her eyes when she tried to sit up. Vomit rushed up her throat but she choked it back down.

"Cinderella awakes." Bobby's sarcastic voice cut through her mental planning.

She glanced over and saw him sitting in the middle of the helicopter crash site. Her brain tried to catalog what was happening.

"Confused?" Bobby jumped off his rock chair and squatted down in front of her, spinning his switchblade in his hand. "Probably from the punch to your head. You started screaming and making all that noise. I had to get you out of there before security showed up."

"How?"

"Service elevator. Amazing what you can buy even in an exclusive resort." He pointed at her. "You might want to remember that next time you splurge on the suite. Not worth it."

Her cheek started to throb. Blinking hurt. So did moving, sitting, and breathing. Her body had been knocked around until her bruises had bruises. But she was alive and believed there was a chance to stay that way.

"I can see why Cal took such a liking to you. Lots of spunk." He ran the closed knife under her chin. "Bet you're great in the sack."

She blocked out these disgusting comments. She would not let him cheapen her relationship with Cal. Whether it was over or not, her time with Cal meant everything to her. The memories had sustained her since she woke up to Bobby's face. Cal's eyes, not Bobby's, would be the last she ever saw. She promised herself that much.

She struggled to sit up, ignoring the shots of pain that ripped through her head. "How did we get here?"

"You came the long way around last time. There's a rough path the rangers use, accessible by the right car, if you know where to look. It's not on any map, but it's there."

"And you knew about it."

He smiled, clearly impressed with his plan. "You in the mood to talk, are you?"

Polk leaned back against the rock with elbows balanced on knees. While he watched her, he threw the knife in the air and caught it. The game played on, tormenting her. It should have been so easy to reach out and steal the thing, but it wasn't.

"Tell me why you killed Dan."

"I didn't."

She turned her head to the side, unable to look at this guy one more second. "Sure."

"Since you're going to die anyway, I guess it doesn't hurt anything." The knife slapped against his palm as it landed again. "He helped transport the stolen goods. He didn't know about the drugs, but why should he? His tourist operation proved to be the perfect cover."

"Why are we here?"

"I thought you were supposed to be so smart." He swept his hand out in a grand gesture.

"Guess not."

"This is your final resting place. This is where you decide to end your life."

"This idiot is trying to drag her into the canyon?" Ted drove at top speed, his warning lights flashing, as he glanced in the rearview mirror at Josh.

"How poetic," Cal mumbled, distracted by the numbing dread spiraling through him.

"Meaning?"

Cal tapped his fingers against the passenger-side window. "Dan died there."

The unspoken sentiment was that Cassie might, too. Cal broke out into a cold sweat just thinking about it.

Josh handed over the mobile GPS tracker from his position in the backseat. "Polk's car is moving again."

Cal said a silent prayer that movement was good news and not something too awful to contemplate, like dumping Cassie's broken body.

As if Ted read his thoughts, he said, "That's a good sign. If he stops, we could lose him."

"But where is he going?" Cal looked on the device for roads. "The only way in there is by plane, boat, or hiking trail. The only road is filled with tourists."

Josh cleared his throat. "There's another way in."

"Of course there is," Cal muttered. "Remind me to kill you when we're done."

"The path is only accessible by trail vehicles and you'd need to know where it is. It's hidden. It's an emergency route for the Forest Service. The rangers use it, and don't talk about it. No one wants a bunch of cars driving in and out of here dropping off tourists." Ted said.

Josh took over. "It winds in through the side, on an abandoned trail that stops close to the clearing where Dan's helicopter went down."

"How convenient." Cal looked out the window but was too occupied with worry to notice his surroundings.

"You two walked right by it to get down in that cave," Josh said.

Cal's worry over Cassie battled with the temptation to throw Josh out the window. "You watched us?"

"Of course not." Josh ducked his head and focused on the GPS unit. "Just following all the leads in an ongoing investigation."

Ted gripped the wheel even tighter. "Any chance Cassie isn't with this nut?"

"He has her." Deep down, Cal knew Bobby had her at his vicious mercy. He refused to think about what was happening or what Polk had planned. If he did, he would crumble. Then he would tear the island apart rock by rock.

"Do we have a plan?" Ted asked.

"Other than to get her out safely?" Josh asked.

"That's good enough for me." Cal turned around to face Josh. "If it comes down between her life or yours, you lose."

Josh nodded. "Agreed."

Chapter Thirty-eight

"Suicide? No one is going to believe that. I'm not the type." Cassie sat on a rock with her hands tied, wracking her brain to figure a way out of the canyon and away from Bobby Polk.

Every part of her hurt, every last bone and blood vessel. But she wasn't about to let that stop her from fighting back.

"Every woman is the type." Bobby poked at the dirt about three feet away from her.

"That's very evolved of you."

"Shut up."

She tried to figure out if she could grab that stick away from Polk. With her hands tied, the odds weren't good.

"Or what? You'll kill me faster."

He laughed. "Too bad you have to die. It's a waste. If you had handled this differently maybe we could . . . well, doesn't matter now, does it?"

Her stomach heaved. The idea of Bobby touching her was too awful to contemplate. "I'd rather you kill me."

Cassie hated to antagonize the lunatic, but some thoughts were too horrid to contemplate. Spending one more minute alone with Bobby Polk qualified as a nightmare in her world.

"Soon." He flipped the knife one more time, caught it, and shoved it in his pocket. "After all, you're depressed."

"I'm not."

"Here you are grieving for your dead, destructive brother. No one believes your outrageous claims. The police think you've lost your mind. You've taken up with a strange guy." Bobby shook his head as he made a *tsk-tsking* sound. "You think you don't have any other choice."

"Your plan doesn't make any sense."

"You can't go on."

A helicopter flew up the canyon but turned before reaching them. She watched despite the pounding behind her eyes. Short of sending up a flare, she did not have a plan to capture a pilot's attention, so her mind raced trying to develop a viable one.

"It will never work, you know," she said.

"Sure it will. In one last dramatic gesture, you throw your body off the cliff where your brother died."

The enormity of his sickness hit her. "You're insane."

"No, you are." A mixture of desperation and madness moved in his eyes. "And I need you gone. You're a loose end, one that doesn't know when to shut up."

Bobby jumped to his feet. She considered the charred earth a sacred burial ground. Bobby's presence defiled it. And gave her the kick of adrenaline she needed to overcome the pain thrumming through her.

Bobby walked around the area. He talked tough, but being this high off the solid ground without a safety net was risky for anyone. She would bet his footing was not as sure as he wanted to pretend. Not when he thought she couldn't challenge him.

"You want one final smoke?" He glanced back at her over his shoulder.

"No." She didn't want anything that would interfere with her last chance. That and because she didn't smoke.

The opportunity came in the form of a lighter. Like with

the knife, he flicked the lighter into the air. She didn't wait for it to land. She sprang to her feet, ignoring every ache, and barreled toward him before he could prepare and gain his balance.

Speed gathered beneath her feet. She rammed into his side with her shoulder. The unexpected force knocked her sideways onto the rough terrain. The pain in her shoulder had her screaming, but the important thing was that her move worked. He went flying.

He fell to his knees in an uncontrolled roll. One more shove from her foot and he careened down the embankment, smashing into trees as shrieking screams filled the canyon.

His rage-filled yell came to a sudden stop, but Cassie wasn't taking any chances. She didn't wait to see him land. With her hands bound, her movements were awkward and her legs devoid of any strength, so she crawled. Her breath thundered in her ears as she got up, carefully placing each movement to prevent sliding down after Bobby.

She scrambled, knees then feet barely touching the ground as she glided over the rough terrain. When rustling sounded off to her left, it distracted her and she lost her footing, going down on her bruised shoulder.

New pain jolted through her. But she had to move. She wandered out of the clearing and into the brush where she had a chance of hiding. Stray branches scratched at her face, but she couldn't feel the cuts.

Louisa stepped right in front of her and stopped her tracks. "Nice work."

The sight was something out of a nightmare. Louisa's eyes were wild and crazed, and her clothes ripped and stained. The hand not holding the gun hung loosely at her side as if it were barely connected to the rest of her. Dirt covered every inch of her and blood pooled in the area above her right eye.

"What the hell happened to you?" Cassie asked, not sure she wanted to know.

"He tried to get rid of me first. Figured he could work the route without me. The dumb bastard couldn't even get this part right. Didn't shoot me or take my gun. Just pushed me."

Cassie gulped in as much air as she could take. Louisa looked ready to fall down but somehow managed to hold the weapon steady.

"You honestly didn't think that Bobby Polk was the brains behind this outfit, did you?"

"I admit it didn't seem likely."

Cassie searched her brain for a plan out. Taking down Bobby was one thing. Hurt or not, getting this woman out of the way would be tougher.

"Dan was bad enough. Never knew what side he was on." Louisa stepped closer. "But Bobby had to go."

"We agree on something then."

"I owe you for getting rid of the loser for me."

"Then let me go."

"I'm not that grateful."

Out of the corner of her eye, Cassie saw movement. For a second of blinding fear she thought Bobby had risen from the dead. Her only hope then would be for these two to kill each other and leave her alone.

Relief soared when Cal came into view. Part of her wanted to run to him. The other wanted to warn him to flee. His gaze locked on hers. Without a sound, they communicated. He wanted her to stay quiet. Maintaining contact was vital to her but she understood his message. Pretend he wasn't there.

"While I appreciate your help getting rid of the trash, we have a problem." Blood dripped down Louisa's sleeve and onto the dirt. "You have two choices. You can fall down the mountain on your own or I can help you."

"There's a third choice." Cal's gravel-deep voice cut through the relative quiet.

The scene unfolded in slow motion. Louisa pivoted to the side and grabbed Cassie around the neck. Cal whipped his gun into position as he yelled for Cassie to duck. The loud command shot through her nervous system and her limbs bent without conscious effort on her part, but Louisa held on tight.

Both women dropped to their knees still entangled. The landing sent a shot of agony right to Cassie's head.

"Put the gun down, Louisa." Cal aimed right at Louisa's head.

"Bobby was a mistake." Louisa increased her hold even as her words began to slur. "We had a good operation without him."

"Lower the weapon."

"We needed a patsy, and he was perfect. Stupid and mostly muscle. But he got lazy and greedy." Louisa voice took on a singsongy quality.

Cassie wondered if the other woman's wounds were taking their toll. Blood seeped into Louisa's shirt. Cassie felt her strength waning and figured Louisa must be suffering from the same.

Cal did not waver. "He's gone now, Louisa. Let Cassie go."

"You're the type I needed, strong and in control. It's not too late. My father's group is just as extensive and he doesn't depend on children to sell drugs."

The nightmare wouldn't end. Fear clogged in Cassie's throat. She could not let anything happen to Cal. She inched forward thinking to give Louisa a target if she needed one.

"Cassie, don't move." Cal roared his threat.

Louisa yanked her arm back, forcing Cassie's head up

and opening her throat to view. "Let's try it this way, big boy. I've got your girl. Drop your gun."

After a brief hesitation, Cal bent down and slid the gun to the ground. Hope fizzled out in Cassie's chest. She watched in horror as Louisa then aimed the gun at Cal. The crack of a gunshot bounced through the canyon.

"No!" Cassie slumped forward, searching Cal for signs of blood. She didn't realize the shot came from behind Cal until she saw Josh race into the small area, his gun raised in the air.

Cassie's lungs deflated as all air rushed out of her body. She thought she heard Cal yell her name. Noises became muffled, almost indistinguishable as a burning tore through her shoulder. Whatever held her up gave way. The sky swirled as her knees collapsed underneath her and her bones turned to jelly, sending her dropping to the ground. She hit the dirt, then rolled into a ball.

Voices ricocheted in her mind. Ted's face swam in front of her. Josh touched her arm, muttering nonsense words of apology before he jumped over her numb body and reached for Cal.

Then Cal was there. With her.

"Jesus, Cassie. Honey, talk to me." Cal's pale face bounced in front of her. She squeezed her eyes shut to make the moving stop.

"She's okay, Cal." Ted's firm voice pulled her attention away from Cal's frightened gaze.

"There was a shot." She spit the words out, using her last burst of energy to lift her fingers and trace the flat line of Cal's lips.

She loved him so much. And he was safe. The knowledge filled her chilled body with warmth.

"You're going to be fine." Comfort words spilled out of him as he cradled her in his strong arms and whispered to her in a deep, trembling voice.

Soft butterfly kisses soothed her forehead. Familiar hands caressed her face. She was too dizzy to concentrate as the corners of her vision darkened. She had to tell him something. To let him know before it was too late. But the blackness eclipsed her vision first.

Chapter Thirty-nine

Cal's heart ripped in two, leaving his insides shredded and empty. He ran in before Ted was out of the car or had the plan in place. It was a risk, but hearing Louisa's voice and seeing her lift that gun got Cal moving. No time to wait for everyone to take positions. He had to go fast or risk losing Cassie forever.

Then time raced forward only to stop at the point where a bloodstain spread on Cassie's shoulder. Seeing her body slip soundlessly to the ground pounded him into nothing.

Even hours later, the horrifying vision played over in his mind. Each time, a bleak despair ate at his gut. Now he sat in the chair at Cassie's side with elbows balanced on his knees and head bowed.

The hospital buzzed with activity. All around him people rushed in and out. The speaker squawked, calling for emergency personnel. Electronic equipment hummed and footsteps thundered down the linoleum hallways.

Hearing Cassie declare her love for him at the same moment her body slipped into a deep sleep had crushed him. Without Ted there to help, Cal doubted he would have had the strength to release her body to the ambulance crew.

The hours whirled by in a haze. Louisa was in protective

custody. Rescue crews were fishing Bobby's body out of the canyon even though it was far too late to save him.

Ted talked about hunting down Louisa's father. Josh wanted to round up the kids selling Bobby's drugs.

Josh. Cal had almost killed him. The bastard shot Cassie. He was the reason for the bloodstain. The bullet through Cassie's arm was shot in an effort to take down Louisa. Josh stood at the crash site and insisted it was the only way to rescue her.

Cal knocked him out with one punch to the jaw. He would have done more damage, but Ted pulled him off.

Ted slipped into the room now. "She doing okay?"

Cal nodded. "The painkillers knocked her out."

"That's probably a good thing."

"You don't have Josh with you, do you?"

Ted walked to the end of Cassie's bed. "No, he's being questioned."

"You're going to arrest him?" The idea appealed to Cal on some level.

"No." Ted paged through Cassie's chart. "He was in an officer-involved shooting. It's standard procedure."

"Couldn't happen to a nicer guy."

"What happens when he turns in his boss is a different story."

"Meaning?"

"Josh is convinced he's going to be the scapegoat for the DEA's mess."

Okay, right now Cal hated the guy. Still, he tried to do the right thing when the DEA failed. Cal appreciated that sort of dedication and integrity.

"Sleeping beauty awakes," Ted whispered with a smile.

"Cal?" Cassie's groggy voice was the most melodious sound he had ever heard.

He slipped to the front of his chair and leaned against the

bed mattress to be closer to her. "God, baby, how are you feeling?"

Her eyes fluttered open. "Confused."

Desperation gave way to need. He swallowed whatever words she planned to say with a gentle kiss.

The door eased shut as Ted slipped from the room. They were alone and suddenly, Cal had no idea what to say.

Her eyes grew wide with concern. "Were you hurt?"

Tenderness welled inside of him for this stunning woman who loved him. "You were the one who went down. Seeing that . . ."

His words choked off. He dropped his forehead against hers. He wanted to drink in her scent so he would never forget it.

"Louisa?"

"In custody." He kissed her eyelids, anything to stay connected to Cassie.

"Who shot me?"

The deep-seated anger boiled up again. "Josh."

"Why?"

"Let's just say he's lucky to be alive."

After a beat of silence, a single tear rolled down her cheek. "Dan was involved in all of this."

"No, baby." He kissed her again just to stop the tears. "Not like you think. He was duped and when he figured it out, he went to the DEA. He was working to bring Polk down."

Color rushed back into her cheeks. "Bobby said the crash was an accident."

"Ted thinks that's true, but he's going back over everything with the NTSB guys in case Bobby was lying to beat a potential murder rap."

She smiled. A breathtaking joy pulsed around her. "We should do that with the Air Force, too. You know, get them to reassess and maybe clear his name."

The happiness building inside of Cal shattered. "Cassie."

"No, Cal, listen to me." She grabbed his arm and pulled him closer. "Dan didn't do anything wrong. You can help me prove that."

Not now. Not when they were so close to putting all the awful events of the past few weeks behind them. "You need to concentrate on getting better first."

She tried to sit up, but he eased her back onto the pillows. "I need to clear his name. On everything. About everything."

There they were. The words guaranteed to damn him. "Let that go, Cassie."

She frowned. "What?"

His hand slipped from hers. "Dan wasn't part of a criminal ring. But he did deserve to be kicked out of the service."

"What are you saying?" Her harsh whisper bounced off the beige walls.

Ending it quickly was the best. No more games. She deserved the truth. "He crashed a multimillion-dollar aircraft and nearly killed us. Dan being Dan, he almost got away with it. He could talk his way out of anything. Charm anyone about anything."

"I don't understand."

"I couldn't let him do that. To himself. He was spinning out of control. I was the one who made him deal with it. Me, his friend. I forced him to make a choice and leave the service. I was going to turn him in."

"You?"

"I didn't give him any choice, Cassie."

Despite all the cuts and bruises, the wounded devastation had not appeared in her eyes until he started talking. He had done exactly what he promised he wouldn't—deliver the crushing blow before she even got out of the hospital.

This was the end. It was time to leave. He couldn't stand the idea of her kicking him out.

"I took away the only job he ever cared about and left

him with a life that led to his death." Cal heard his voice falter. "I'm so sorry."

"How could you—"

He cut her off, unable to listen to her disappointment. "I know. I have to live with it."

"Can you?"

"I'll leave."

"Cal—"

"But know this, I never meant to hurt you. I would have done anything to prevent that."

Chapter Forty

Cassie watched Cal's retreating back as he left her room. Her mood flipped in a matter of seconds from being thrilled to being lost. Dan was not guilty of burglary or worse, but he wasn't innocent, either.

In the end he tried to do something good and noble. He wasn't exactly the man she thought he was, but she had built him up, put him in a position no one could fulfill. Funny, charming, imperfect. Turned out Dan was all those things.

In holding him up as a hero, she had made Dan less than real. She did him a disservice. She could see that now and view him with a realistic eye. He was a good and decent man, her brother. He mattered and tried to make a difference. That was enough.

But with the realization about Dan came a very different understanding of her feelings for Cal. The depression seeping into her bones started when Cal walked out. He dropped his bombshell and split.

Getting weepy was one option. She could mourn the loss of their relationship and chalk the end up to one of the hazards in getting involved with a flyboy. Or she could fight.

She loved Cal. He was the best kind of man, not a particularly bright one at the moment, but in every other way perfect for her. Crying in a corner over Dan's youthful mistakes would not change that fact. So, she went with fury instead.

She lay strapped to a hospital bed, dealing with all of the horrible information that had been thrown at her over the past week, and he had left. He would be in his own hospital bed soon if he kept up this sort of stupidity. And she would be the one to put him there.

She slid out of bed, feeling every muscle tweak and scream in protest. With her butt hanging out the back of the humiliating hospital gown, she set her sights on Ed's room. Cal had better be in there or she would have to hit the streets in this ridiculous outfit.

She stopped at the door to listen to the male voices inside right before bursting in. The one voice she needed to hear boomed through the room. Now she had to decide whether or not to let him live.

" 'Bout time you woke up," Cal said to Ed.

"Where's Cassie darling?"

"She's fine."

She pushed open the door and limped inside. "No, she's not."

Ted took one look at her and whistled. "Oh boy."

Cassie noticed Ted wasn't so scared that he left the room. No, he settled back against the windowsill and waited. Well, if he wanted a show, he was going to get one.

"You," she said, pointing at Cal with one hand and holding her gown closed with the other, "are a moron."

"You tell him, Cassie." Ed's cheer temporarily distracted her.

Seeing him sitting up and smiling threw her off balance. "How are you feeling?"

"Getting better by the second." The older man's grin

grew bigger, filling his entire face. "We'll talk later. Go ahead. Give Cal hell."

"Why are you out of bed?" Cal's fury was evident in his voice.

Well, that made two of them.

"To kick your ass." She realized she could barely lift her foot, but she made her point. "That will have to wait until I can walk, but it's coming as soon as I recuperate."

"Jesus, you're stubborn." Cal reached out and took her arm. "We should go back to your room."

She accepted having somewhere to lean. "The last time we tried to talk alone you walked out on me."

"He's an idiot."

Cassie smiled at Ted in appreciation for his support.

Forget the embarrassment and insecurities. There would never be a better time to corner Cal.

"I told you I loved you. After I was shot. I said the words in my head, but they came out." She was sure of that now.

Cal's eyes searched hers. "You remember?"

"Do you think I say that sort of thing every freaking day?"

"You were in pain."

"No kidding."

"Delirious."

"And now I'm furious, in case you're wondering."

Cal's cheeks were hollowed out from tension. "I'm not holding you to anything you said."

No man could tick her off faster than Cal. "Don't treat me like a child."

His eyes grew soft, sad even. "Cassie, I told you the truth about Dan. About my role in his departure from the Air Force."

And that truth still hurt, but she understood why Cal did

what he did. That he wouldn't have done anything to intentionally harm Dan.

"You have every right to hate me," Cal said.

"You're an idiot."

A ruddy circle stained his cheeks. "I admit it's my fault, if that's what you mean."

"Not even close."

The look in Cal's eyes grew more bleak. "Dan's exit from the service, his choice to come here, ultimately his death. All me."

He was a sweet idiot, but still an idiot. "Did you crash Dan's helicopter?"

Cal was stunned enough to answer the rhetorical question. "No."

"For heaven's sake, Dan was a big boy. He made his choices and some of them might not have been great. He tried to redeem himself in the end by helping the DEA. That's who he was. That's how I'll remember him."

Cal held her stare. "He's dead."

She stepped forward over the pain and touched a hand to his cheek. "I understand you're scared."

"Uh-oh." Ted stood up straight.

"Now, Cassie darling. There's no need to namecall. The boy is suffering."

"The one thing I'm not is scared." Cal's voice was deadly soft.

"You grew up with a skewed view of family. You went on to live your life on the edge, thriving on the challenge and getting a high off the thrill."

Cal shrugged, but the tense lines around his mouth eased. "It's who I am."

"I'm offering you something else." She stepped right off the emotional cliff and into the abyss. In front of a witness and the police, she'd kill him if he didn't join her.

She slid her hand into his. "I'm offering you a job."

He frowned at her as if she'd lost her mind. "What?"

"With me."

"But I can't draw."

"You don't need to." Her other hand pressed against his flat stomach. "Come to Hawaii. Live with me. Run Dan's business."

Her words finally sank in. She was offering him a life. A real one. One he craved but didn't deserve or dare believe could be his.

Cal brushed the back of his hand under her chin, careful not to hurt her when she'd suffered so much. "I let Dan down."

"You came to Hawaii when he called. Your debt is paid. It's time to forgive yourself and move on."

"What is she talking about?" Ted whispered his question to Ed.

She answered. "Cal has some misguided belief that he owes Dan something. I'm releasing him of that burden."

"Why?" Cal asked because he didn't understand how she could forgive so easily. So completely.

"No man is going to stay with me out of pity."

Lurking behind those sweet amber eyes, behind the odd mixture of vulnerability and determination, Cal thought he saw a flicker of something else. Something that looked suspiciously like hope.

That's all it took for reality to punch him in the gut. She wanted to build a life with him. Despite everything, she forgave him. Loved him.

Instead of making him weak or uncomfortable, her love filled him with a power unlike any he'd ever known. He couldn't let her go. No matter how selfish the emotion, he loved her and refused to lose her.

Determined. Smart. Bossy and loyal. The perfect woman. His woman.

He tried to hide his smile and stay serious, but it pulled across his lips anyway. "Awfully sure of yourself, aren't you?"

"I'm sure of you." She slid her arms around his waist in a perfect fit and hugged him close. "Stay with me."

His world re-set. "I'm not an easy man."

"I don't need easy."

He held her gown for her. Gave him an excuse to keep her nice and close. "Good thing."

"I just need someone to love me."

The unspoken question hung in the room. Her eyes narrowed, as if she were willing him to say the right words in response.

But her fear wasn't necessary. When the time came, he knew the answer. "Done."

A smile lit up her face, bringing a rush of charming color to her cheeks. But in true Cassie form, she was not cutting him any breaks. "Done?"

"Yeah, that's what I said."

"Is that your idea of a romantic line?"

"Man, Cal, even I could do better than that," Ted said.

"Then, try this." Cradling her head in his hands, with his mouth hovering above hers, Cal gave her the same heartfelt pledge he had never given, or would give, another woman. "You are my life. When you say my debt to Dan is paid, you're wrong. He brought me to you, the love of my life. I don't know how a man repays that sort of gift."

Tears clouded her eyes. "Now that's romantic."

"If you'll have me, I'll spend the rest of my life trying to deserve you."

"Just try sending me away."

Cal dropped a kiss on her mouth, this one deeper and filled with promise. When he finally lifted his head, her smile beamed.

"That was nice," she whispered against his lips.

Cal let his heart and mind walk in step. For the first time, he believed that people who were committed could make it work. "Besides, someone has to stick around and teach you to drive."

Her laughter filled the small room. "Done."

Don't miss IMMORTAL DANGER,
the latest from Cynthia Eden,
out this month from Brava. . . .

His back teeth clenched as he glanced around the room. Doors led off in every direction. He already knew where all those doors would take him. To hell.

But he needed to find Maya, so he'd have to go—

"Don't screw with me, Armand!" A woman's voice, hard, ice cold. Maya.

He turned, found her leaning over the bar, her hand wrapped around the bartender's throat.

"I want to know who went after Sean, and I want to know *now*." He saw her fingernails stretch into claws, and he watched as those claws sank into the man's neck.

"I-I d-don't k-know." The guy looked like he might faint at any moment. Definitely human. Vamps were always so pale it looked like they might faint. But this guy, he'd looked pretty normal until Maya clawed him.

"Find out!" She threw him against a wall of drinks.

Adam stalked toward her, reached her side just as she spun around, claws up.

He stilled.

She glared at him. "What the hell do you want?" She snarled, and he could see the faint edge of her fangs gleaming behind her plump lips.

It was his first time to get a good look at her face. He'd

seen her from a distance before, judged her to be pretty, hadn't bothered to think much beyond that.

He blinked as he stared at her. Damn, the woman looked like some kind of fallen angel.

Her thick black hair framed her perfect, heart-shaped face. Her cheeks were high, glass sharp. Her nose was small, straight. Her eyes were wide and currently the black of a vampire in hunting mode. And her lips, well, she might have the face of an angel, but she had lips made for sin.

Adam felt his cock stir, *for a vampire.*

He shuddered in revulsion.

Oh, hell, no. The woman was so not his type.

Her scent surrounded him. Not the rancid, rotting stench of death he'd smelled around others of her kind. But a light, fragrant scent, almost like flowers.

What in the hell? How could she—

Maya growled and shoved him away from her, muttering something under her breath about idiots with death wishes.

Then she walked away from him.

For a moment, he just studied her. Maya wasn't exactly his idea of an uber-vamp. She was small, too damn small for his taste. The woman was barely five foot seven. Her body was slender, with almost boyish hips. Her legs were encased in an old, faded pair of jeans, and the black T-shirt she wore clung tightly to her frame.

He liked women with more meat on their bones. Liked a woman with curves. A woman with round, lush hips that he could hold while he thrust deep into her.

But, well, he wasn't interested in screwing Maya. Not with her too-thin body. Her too-pale skin. No, he didn't want to screw her.

He just planned to use her.

Adam took two quick strides forward, grabbed her arm and swung her back toward him.

The eyes that had relaxed to a bright blue shade instantly flashed black. Vamps' eyes always changed to black when they fought or when they fucked.

Sometimes folks made the mistake of confusing vamps with demons, because a demon's eyes, well, they could go black, too. Actually, Adam knew that a demon's eyes were *always* black, and for the demons, every damn part of their eyes went black. Even the sclera. With the vamps, just the iris changed.

Usually demons were smart enough to hide the true color of their eyes. But the vamps, they didn't seem to give a flying shit who saw the change. But if a human happened to see the eye shift, it was generally too late for the poor bastard, anyway, because by then, he was prey.

Gazing into Maya's relentless black eyes, Adam had a true inkling of just how those sad poor bastards must have felt.

A growl rumbled in her throat, then she snarled, "Slick, you're screwing with the wrong woman tonight."

No, she was the right woman. Whether he liked the fact or not.

So he clenched his teeth, swallowed his pride, and in the midst of hell, admitted, "I need your help."

And try DANGEROUS GAMES
by Charlotte Mede,
available now from Brava. . . .

The Thursday evening salons hosted by Mrs. Hampton had become one of the most coveted invitations in London society, each guest scrutinized by the hostess herself to ensure lively, engaging, and informed debate on the most compelling issues of the day. And while her townhouse in Mayfair was a modest affair, the company was always of the highest order, along with generous servings of food and drink to satisfy the most discerning guests.

Tonight, the room heaved with conversation, the latest rebellion in India taking center stage, while off to the wings, breathless discussion percolated about the arrival in London of the Koh-I-Noor, the world's largest diamond—destined to be presented to Queen Victoria and Prince Albert upon the opening of the Great Exhibition in under one month's time. Conceived by the Prince, the historic occasion would be held in Hyde Park in the spectacularly constructed Crystal Palace, designed to showcase England's and the world's advances in science and industry.

"Not at all, not at all, my dear Mrs. Hampton," Seabourne finally replied, clasping his hands behind his back and away from the tap of her ivory fan. "Your questions are diverting as always but never more so than the woman who poses them."

Lilly inclined her head towards him, raising her low voice slightly to compete with the surging exchanges going on around them. "Well thank you, sir. But you must hasten to answer my question as the buffet will be served quite soon."

John Sydons, the former publisher of the Guardian, guffawed, his muttonchops bristling. "And we shouldn't want that, Seabourne. I just saw a spectacular Nesselrode pudding float by along with a platter of oysters swimming in cream. So let's move along. Respond to the lady's query— has the situation settled somewhat this past month?"

Seabourne nodded portentously, the horizontal lines on his forehead deepening. "The political expansion of the British East India Company at the perceived expense of native princes and the Mughal court has aroused Hindu and Muslim animosity alike, a complex situation overall which I do not think will be resolved without a Parliamentary solution."

"A tinderbox is what it is," murmured Lilly.

"Indeed," seconded the man across from her, Lord Falmouth, Member of Parliament. Small and wiry, he barely filled out his impeccably tailored waistcoat and jacket. "It didn't help that our colonial government, in its boundless wisdom, furnished the Indian soldiers with cartridges coated with grease made from the fat of cows and of pigs. Ignorance and incompetence in one fell stroke. Amazing."

"The first sacred to Hindus and the second anathema to Muslims." Lilly splayed her fan in barely concealed annoyance. "We have an ineffectual and insensitive Governor and of course, an historic series of blunders, beginning with the Kabul massacre, that slaughter in the mountain passes of Afghanistan. I have heard it said that of the sixteen thousand who set out on retreat, only one man survived to arrive in Jalalabad."

"It was actually believed that the Afghans let him live so

he could tell the grisly story—such a severe blow and bitter humiliation to British pride." Lord Falmouth jutted out his rather weak chin. "Reports from the forty-fourth English Regiment are dismal. The troops kept on through the passes but without food, mangled and disoriented; they are reported to have knocked down their officers with the butts of their muskets. St. Martin is one of the few to have survived, if survive is the word one would choose to use."

"He's quite the loose cannon, or so one hears from the Foreign Office," added Seabourne. "Has publicly resigned his post, whatever it was, something to do with statecraft, certainly."

"You mean spycraft, surely," Lord Falmouth corrected.

"A shadowy figure one would assume and now one not to be trusted, given his precarious mental state," continued Seabourne. "The trauma and so on."

"My goodness. How clandestine and mysterious," said Lilly, frowning, only vaguely familiar with the St. Martin name. "One never knows what resentments these types of horrific experiences may nurture. I infer from your comments that loyalty is at question for these individuals who find themselves one moment at the service of their country and at the next entirely disengaged or worse . And what of his family? The St. Martin's do have a seat in the House of Lords, if I'm not mistaken."

"The parents passed away some years ago and his older brother died of smallpox soon after, if I recall correctly. However, St. Martin has never taken up his place in Parliament, having instead disappeared for years to the farthest reaches of the globe. In her majesty's service, one presumes. Although one can presume no longer with his resignation."

And be sure to catch
DEMON CAN'T HELP IT,
Kathy Love's newest book,
coming next month!

Jo breathed in slowly through her nose. What had she just agreed to? Seeing this man every day? She pulled in another slow, even breath, telling herself to shake off her reaction to this man's proximity.

Sure, he was attractive. And he had—a presence. But she wasn't some teenage girl who would fall to pieces under a cute boy's attention. Not that cute was a strong enough word for what Maksim was. He was—unnerving. To say the least.

But she wasn't interested in him. She decided that quite definitely over the past two days. Of course that decision was made when he wasn't in her presence.

But either way, she should have more control than this. Apparently should and could were two very different things. And she couldn't seem to stop her reaction to him. Her heart raced and her body tingled, both hot and cold in all the most inappropriate places.

"So every morning?" he said, his voice rumbling right next to her, firing up the heat inside her. "Does that work for you?"

She cleared her throat, struggling to calm her body.

"Yes—that's great," she managed to say, surprising even herself with the airiness of her tone. "I'll schedule you from eight a.m. to—" she glanced at the clock on the lower right-hand of the computer screen, "noon?"

That was a good amount of time, getting Cherise through the rowdy mornings and lunch, and giving him the go ahead to leave now. She needed him out of her space.

If her body wasn't going to go along with her mind, then avoidance was clearly her best strategy. And she had done well with that tactic—although she'd told herself that wasn't what she was doing.

"Noon is fine," he said, still not moving. Not even straightening away from the computer. And her.

"Good," she poised her fingers over the keys and began typing in his hours. "Then I think we are all settled. You can take off now if you like."

When he didn't move, she added, "You can go get some lunch. You must be hungry." She flashed him a quick smile without really looking at him.

This time he did stand, but he didn't move away. Instead he leaned against her desk, the old piece of furniture creak-ing at his tall, muscular weight.

"You must be hungry too. Would you like to join me?"

She blinked, for a moment not comprehending his words, her mind too focused on the muscles of his thighs so near her. The flex of more muscles in his shoulders and arms as he crossed them over his chest.

She forced herself to look back at the computer screen.

"I—I don't think so," she said. "I have a lot to do here."

"But surely you allow yourself even a half an hour for lunch break."

She continued typing, fairly certain whatever she was writing was gibberish. "I brought a lunch with me, actu-ally." Which was true. Not that she was hungry at the mo-ment. She was too—edgy.

"Come on," he said in a low voice that was enticing, coaxing. "Come celebrate your first regular volunteer."

She couldn't help looking at him. He was smiling, the curl of his lips, his white, even teeth, the sexily pleading glimmer in his pale green eyes.

God, he was so beautiful.

And dangerous.

Jo shook her head. "I really can't."

He studied her for a moment. "Can't or won't. What's a matter, Josephine? Do I make you nervous?"

Jo's breath left her for a moment at the accented rhythm of her full name crossing his lips. But the breath-stealing moment left as quickly as it came, followed by irritation. At him and at herself.

She wasn't attracted to this man—not beyond a basic physical attraction. And that could be controlled. It could.

"You don't make me nervous," she said firmly.

"Then why not join me for lunch?"

"Because," she said slowly, "I have a lot of work to do."

Maksim crossed his arms tighter, and lifted one of his eloquent eyebrows, which informed her that he didn't believe her for a moment.

"I don't think that's why you won't come. I think you are uncomfortable with me. Maybe because you are attracted to me." Again the eyebrow lifted—this time in questioning challenge.